Title Page

Bread Alone

Adventures in the Liaden ˥ˉ

Sharon

Publishe

Copyright Page

Bread Alone

Adventures in the Liaden Universe® Number 34

Pinbeam Books: pinbeambooks.com

#

#

"Degrees of Separation" first appeared in *Degrees of Separation: Adventures in the Liaden Universe® Number 27*, January 2018

"Fortune's Favors" first appeared in *Fortune's Favors: Adventures in the Liaden Universe® Number 28*, April 2019

"Block Party" first appeared on Baen.com, November 2017

"Our Lady of Benevolence" is original to this chapbook

#

Cover design by: https://selfpubbookcovers.com/RLSather

ISBN: 978-1-948465-20-5

Table of Contents

Acknowledgment and Dedication

The authors thank the following Fearless Tyop Hunters:
Kat Ayers-Mannix, Thomas Baetzler, Sam DiPasquale, Bruce Glassford, Kiri Guyaz,
Art Hodges, Christina Larson, mlplouff, Marni Rachmiel, Scott Raun, Kate Reynolds,
Eric Shivak, Linda Shoun, kris smelser, Anne Young

#

Dedicated to
everyone who strives to leave the world better than they found it

#

Man does not live by bread alone . . . – Matthew 4:4
With bread all sorrows are less. – Sancho Panza
Where there's no law, there's no bread. – Benjamin Franklin

1

About this Book

Bread Alone is a collection of four interconnected stories written about and around a place dubbed "the Bakery" by readers. Three stories, "Degrees of Separation," "Fortune's Favors," and "Block Party," are reprints—that means they've previously been published elsewhere.

There is also one new story, "Our Lady of Benevolence."

Also included are three "About..." essays, which tell you a little bit about how the stories came to be written.

Here, we're going to talk about how "Our Lady..." came to be written, and why this book exists.

As explained in "About Degrees of Separation," the very first Bakery story to be written— "Block Party"—came into being because Baen.com had commissioned a "holiday" story for their front page for December 2017. We fulfilled the commission, but that left us wanting to know more about the characters—all new to us. We then wrote "Degrees ..." to explain where they had come from.

A little while later, we were exploring another character new to us, a Luck called Mar Tyn eys'Ornstahl. Frequently, when we're attempting to understand, or "meet," a new character, we'll write a story about them. Pretty quickly, Mar Tyn was in bad trouble, and it was just—ahem—luck, that he stumbled into the Bakery.

In the course of "Fortune..." we "met" two other characters—Lady voz'Laathi, whose street name was Lady Benevolence—and Aazali, who was born a Healer in Low Port.

"Fortune's Favors" was written in 2019. Mar Tyn appeared in our novel *Trader's Leap,* in 2020, and we thought we were done with "the Bakery."

But, we were still wondering after Our Lady of Benevolence, and the little girl, sent away from her home to learn to be a Healer.

"Our Lady of Benevolence" is the story of those two characters.

You will note that the stories do not appear in the order in which they were written. We made the artistic decision to place the stories in internal chronological order–starting at the beginning and going straight through, to the end.

It's been an interesting exercise for us, and we hope an enjoyable read for you.

Will there be any more stories about "the Bakery"?

We'll all have to wait and see.

Sharon Lee and Steve Miller
Cat Farm and Confusion Factory, November 2021

About Degrees of Separation

This is a story about Paris, about love, and about bread.

#'

This story came about because we were commissioned to write *another* story in support of our 21st Liaden Universe® novel, *Neogenesis*, that story to be published to Baen.com on December 15, 2017. Because of the timing, our editor asked us to write a "seasonal" story.

This presented something of a problem, since . . . neither Liadens nor Surebleakans can possibly celebrate the US Thanksgiving, nor Christmas, Chanukah, Eid Al Adha, Kwanza, St. Lucia Day, or any of the other winter holidays celebrated on this, our non-fictional Terra.

Granted, Liadens celebrate Festival, but we suspected our editor didn't really mean for us to go there . . . and while Surebleakans *might* have a winter holiday, we felt it was a long shot, since their culture–before things went Horribly Wrong–was rooted in Standard Business Practice.

Then, we realized that Surebleak, having *been* founded as a Company Planet, would, very naturally, have a Company Picnic. And that's how "Block Party" came into being.

But! Having obliged us by arriving, the story brought with it another set of puzzles. The hero of the piece, for instance, appeared on Chairman Court in Surebleak, in the company of a gaggle of kids; they've been relocated to Surebleak by the mercs, after Liad's Low Port became a battleground following Korval's strike upon the homeworld.

The hero, Don Eyr, is waiting for the rest of his adult companions to rejoin him, including his lover, Serana Benoit. And

4

Steve and I got to saying to ourselves, All well and good, but really, *who are* these people? How did Don Eyr and Serana meet? How did they become the caretakers of so many children? And these other people–where did they come from?

And that? Is why *Degrees of Separation* was written.

We enjoyed discovering the answers to our questions; and we hope that you will enjoy reading them.

Oh, you want to know about Paris?

Well, it's like this . . .

Sometimes, when we're brainstorming a story, we'll use a shorthand idea or word to hold the place of an idea, word, geography, or person that we haven't fully worked out yet. This is, by the way, how *Plan B* became part of the Liaden Universe®–it was stuck in the manuscript to hold the place of the name of Korval's *real* emergency plan; we always intended to go back and fix it, except–

We forgot.

Something similar happened when we were talking over *Degrees.* Sharon, who was describing to Steve Everything She Knew about the story, said, carelessly–*and they send him to–oh, to Paris!*

. . . and the writing backbrain caught "Paris"–and ran with it.

And that is why there is now a Liaden Universe® story which is, in part, set in Paris.

Or, at least, *a* Paris.

We hope you enjoy the story.

Sharon Lee and Steve Miller
Cat Farm and Confusion Factory, January 2018

Degrees of Separation

One

Liad

In the port city of Solcintra, on a certain day in the third relumma of the year called *Phantione*, a boy was delivered to the delm of Clan Serat, who did not want him.

Serat had a son; Serat had a nadelm, twelve years and more the infant's elder. Furthermore, Serat maintained a regular household, and had no need of a second in the delm's line. Most especially *not* the child of a sister who had failed both Line and Clan.

Still, to refuse the boy–Don Eyr, as he had been named, exactly the name of the previous delm of Serat–would be to invite scandal, and Serat did not indulge in scandal. He was, therefore, given a place in the empty nursery, and thereafter forgotten by the delm his uncle, and unregarded by his cousin, who was away at school.

He was *not* forgotten by the household staff, nor by the clan's *qe'andra*. These persons were after all paid to tend the interests and the business of the individuals who together were Clan Serat. The delm having issued no instruction other than, "Take it away, and see it trained," in the case of his sister's child, Don Eyr received all the benefits and education which naturally accrued to a son of Serat.

Save the regard of kin.

The boy himself did not notice his lacks, for he was well-regarded, even loved, by staff.

His nurse was inclined to be gentle with an isolated child, and collaborated with the House's *qe'andra* in the matter of his education. He had a quick intelligence, did Don Eyr, an artist's eye, and a susceptible heart. Very like his mother, said Mr. dea'Bon, the *qe'andra*, who had served the House since the days of the current delm's father. She ought never have been sent to mind the outworld business; her talents had better been used at home, administering the clan. Well, well. Delm's Wisdom, of course; doubtless he had his reasons, for the best good of the clan.

The boy Don Eyr early showed an interest in baking, and the pastry cook took him into her kitchen to show him the way of cookies and tea tarts. When he mastered those, she taught him filled pastries, and cheese rolls.

The day he came to the notice of his cousin, the nadelm, he was removing a loaf from the oven in the back bakery, under the supervision of the kitchen cat, and Mrs. ban'Teli, the pastry cook. He had a wing of flour on one cheek, his hair was neatly, though unfashionably, cut; his hands quiet and certain. He wore a white apron adorned with various splashes, over white pants and a white shirt with the sleeves rolled, showing forearms already well-muscled.

"The nadelm, younger," his companion murmured, rising and bowing to his honor.

The lad lifted his eyes briefly from his task, and gave a civil nod.

"Cousin," he said, gravely–and set the pan he had just removed onto a cooling stone, before turning to the work-table, and picking up another pan, which he slid carefully into the maw of the oven.

The nadelm had only lately come from school, and was not so much accustomed to having his rank recognized. In his estimation, the lad had been perfectly civil, given that he had work in hand. Therefore, he waited patiently until the pan was settled, and the oven sealed.

"I wonder," he said, once these things were done and the boy turned back to face him. "I wonder if you might not have an hour to spend with me, Cousin. I feel that we should know each other better."

Don Eyr's gaze shifted toward the oven, doubtless thinking of the pan so recently deposited there. Mrs. ban'Teli stirred.

"I will stand for the loaf, young master, unless you think me unworthy."

A smile adorned the grave face, and the nadelm was able to make the judgment that Don Eyr was a pleasant looking child, in a modest sort of way.

"Yes, of course I think you unworthy!" he said with full good humor. "I suppose you will even turn out the first loaf when it is cool without my asking that you do so!"

"I might at that," the old woman said with a smile. She nodded to him, her voice taking on the brisk tones of an aunt, or a nurse.

"Take off your apron, wipe your face, and attend your cousin, child. I was baking bread before either of you were born."

The nadelm found himself a little put out by this familiarity from a servant. Don Eyr, however, merely said yes, pulled off his apron, wiped his face and stepped forward.

"Where shall we go, Cousin?"

#

In fact, they went into the garden, the nadelm not wishing to meet the delm just yet. He had spent much of his time away at various schools and fosterings. He did not know his father well, though he knew his delm somewhat better, and his young cousin, here—well, he knew the boy's mother had died on Ezhel'ti, where she had been sent by the previous delm to mind the clan's off-world affairs, with an eye toward increasing profit.

Instead, the clan's businesses had faltered, and finally collapsed, under her care, which his father the delm swore she had done a-purpose, in order to bring ruin to Serat. The question of why she might have subsequently committed suicide, if she had failed a-purpose, he waved away with wordless contempt. The woman had been disordered with envy; she had wanted nothing more than

Serat's Ring, and so the former delm had sent her away, as he had sent away his own brother, who had also aspired to Serat's Ring.

The nadelm, who was no fool, and who furthermore had learned how to do research and analyze information, had discovered that there had been an adjustment in the markets very soon after Telma fer'Gasta arrived to take up her duty. Ezhel'ti had been flooded with cheap goods when its sister planet unilaterally devalued its currency. Much history had been gathered from Serat's *qe'andra*, who had of course received reports every relumma, as well as the occasional personal letter.

The clan's businesses had been only a small portion of those destroyed by this rapid economic readjustment, and, from the records that she had forwarded to Mr. dea'Bon, it was plain that Telma fer'Gasta had very nearly preserved Serat's holdings. It had been a close-run thing, indeed, and for a time it seemed that she would hold the line. She had navigated the rip tide, she sold and consolidated wisely, she had–but in the end, she made an error; a small error, as their *qe'andra* had it, but it had been large enough, in those times, in that place. Certainly, she knew how news of this blow to the clan's fortunes would be received. It troubled the nadelm that she had chosen to kill herself; that action speaking to a . . . disturbing understanding of her delm and her brother.

She had placed her child in the care of her long-time lover, whose babe it likely was–and no shame, there, either, so the nadelm had discovered. The lover's clan was above reproach; their *melant'i* impeccable. Which is doubtless why they had sent the child to Serat.

All that to the side, the nadelm spent an informative and pleasant hour with his young cousin in the gardens, parted with him amicably at the staff's entrance to the kitchens, and went immediately to seek out his father and his delm.

Serat was in the informal parlor, reading the sporting news. He looked up sharply as the nadelm entered, and put the paper aside.

"Well, sirrah? And how have you busied yourself your first day at home in the fullness of your *melant'i*?"

The nadelm paused at the wine table, poured two glasses of the canary, and brought them with him to the window nook where his father sat.

He placed one glass on the small table by his father's hand, and kept the other with him as he settled into the chair opposite.

"I busied myself by meeting with our *qe'andra*, so that I might better know how Serat is fixed–which very duty you gave to me, Father, so *do not* stare daggers."

"Eh. And how are we fixed?" Serat asked, picking up his glass and sipping.

"Well enough, so Mr. dea'Bon tells me, though we are not perhaps expanding as well as we might do to maintain our own health."

"dea'Bon's been singing that song since the day I put on Serat's Ring," his father said sourly. "There is no harm in being conservative."

"Indeed, no," the nadelm agreed, "though there may well be harm in allowing ourselves to ossify."

"Pah."

"But that," the nadelm said, "is something for us to discuss at our business meeting tomorrow." He sipped his wine.

"After the *qe'andra*, I spent a very pleasant hour in the garden, becoming acquainted with my cousin, your nephew."

"So you wasted an hour which ought better to have been used in the service of the clan?"

"Not at all," the nadelm said, calmly.

It was too bad that he had found his father in one of his distempers, but, truly said, it was more and more difficult to find him elsewise. He sipped his wine, leaned to put the glass on the table, and settled again into the chair.

"The boy is one of Serat's assets, after all, Father, and you *did* charge me to learn how we are fixed." He paused; his father said nothing.

"So. I find that we are fortunate in our asset," he continued, taking care not to speak the lad's name, which would surely send his father into alt. "He is a bright lad, who has been well-taught, and who has thought about his lessons. His manners are very pretty, and his person pleases. His nature appears to be happy, and generous. Staff is devoted to him. He's young, of course, but after some finishing at a school, and a bit of society polish, I believe he will do the clan proud in the matter of alliance and–"

"Send him away!"

The nadelm blinked out of his rosy picture of the future to find his father bent stiffly forward, imperiling both glasses and table, his face rigid with anger.

"I beg your pardon?" he said, startled by this sudden change of temper. "Will you have him gone to school, sir?"

"Yes–to school, or to the devil! Staff devoted to him, is it? Scheming get! I know his game; haven't I seen it played before? Get the staff cozy in his hand, turn them against us. He thinks I don't suspect? No–send him away! He will not subvert our house with his schemes!"

The nadelm–stared. Then, he reached across the table, took up his wine glass and drank the contents in a single swallow.

"Father . . . you do comprehend that we are discussing a boy barely halfling? There is not the least bit of subterfuge. The staff love him because, frankly, sir, they have had the raising of him, and it pleases them to see him do well. If you would bring him closer to us–have the lad at the table for Prime, for the gods' love! He's too old to dine in the nursery, and he would be glad of the company. If he has fallen into error, you might teach him better."

"There's no teaching those born to deceit," Serat stated with the air of making a quote, though from which play, the nadelm could not have said. "Send him away, do you hear me? I want him out of this house by the end of the relumma."

"But, Father–"

Serat stood and glared down at him.

"You've done a valuable service to the house this day, worthy of a nadelm! You have found the plot before it came to fruition. We may act–we must act! See to it."

And with that, he turned and left the room, leaving the nadelm gaping in his wake.

* * *

"School?" Don Eyr said, frowning slightly at Mr. dea'Bon.

"Indeed, young sir. The clan would see you properly educated. The choice of institution has been left for you and I to determine between us. Now, I have here on the screen a file of catalogs, sorted by primary studies. Please sit here and examine them while I pursue my other work on behalf of the House. When Mr. pak'Epron brings us our tea, we shall talk about what you have discovered.

"Is this agreeable to you?"

School, thought Don Eyr, with a quickening of interest. Mrs. ban'Teli had spoken about schools–famous schools on far-away planets.

"Yes, sir," he said to Mr. dea'Bon. "Thank you."

"There is no need to thank me, young sir. It is my pleasure to serve you."

With that, the elder gentleman moved over to the big desk and the 'counts books. Don Eyr sat at the side table and considered the catalog file. Arranged by course of study. He extended a hand, and scrolled down the list, until he came to Culinary.

He opened that catalog and took a moment to consider, eyes half-closed, attention focused inward.

Mrs. ban'Teli had spoken of many schools, as he remembered—several of them with respect.

But she had spoken of *one* with reverence.

#

"I see," Mr. dea'Bon said, when he was presented with the list of one school which Don Eyr felt he would wish to attend.

"This is a very challenging choice," he continued, with a glance at the boy's bright face. "I wonder if you have considered all of these challenges."

"It is off-world," Don Eyr said, "so I will of course be obliged to live at school, and will not be able to help with the House's baking. But you know, Mrs. ban'Teli said to me just recently that she has been baking bread since before I was born, so I suspect she can train another boy very handily."

Mr. dea'Bon blinked, and inclined his head gravely.

"Just so. It is very nice in you, and proper, too, to think of the House first. However, I had been thinking that, in addition to going off-world to live at school, you will be required to acquire a new language—not merely Trade or even Terran—but the local planetary language. All of the classes are taught in that tongue."

"Yes," said Don Eyr, apparently not put off in the least by the prospect of not only learning a new language, but hearing nothing else from the time he rose until the time he sought his bed, every day for . . . years.

"My tutor says that I have a good ear for languages," the boy added, perhaps sensing Mr. dea'Bon's reservations. "He also says that I have been very quick learning Terran."

Mr. dea'Bon blinked again, thinking of Delm Serat, his inclinations, and stated opinions regarding off-worlders of any kind, and most especially Terrans.

"Your tutor has been teaching you Terran? " he asked, and did not add, "Does your uncle know?"

"Yes! Terran is spoken by a great many people living off-world, and, as my mother was sent off-world to mind the clan's interests, my tutor says the same may be required of me, so that it is only prudent to learn."

"I see. Well, then, you foresee no difficulties in learning yet another tongue. You realize, of course, that you will be alone, with neither clan nor kin to support you–" Not that he had such support in any wise, but one could scarcely name Mrs. ban'Teli in a discussion of this sort.

"Yes, I am aware. But there will be other students, after all, and the instructors, so I won't be *alone*."

"Quite," said Mr. dea'Bon once more, and played his last ace.

"Let us suppose that you will be accepted into this . . . ah– *École de Cuisine*. You will have one semester to prove yourself. If you fail to be the sort of student the institute expects, you will be sent back home."

He tapped the list of one.

"You have made no provision for a back-up," he said. "Your delm has made it clear that you *will be* going to school. Therefore, in respect of his wishes, you must chose at least two more schools to which you will apply."

The boy stilled; his smile faded–and returned.

"Yes, of course," he said. "A moment only, sir, of your goodness."

He leaned over the catalog, tapped two keys, and leaned back.

Mr. dea'Bon looked at the names of two more institutes of baking, and allowed that the rules of the game had been followed.

"That is well," he said. "Now, you will be required, also, to comport yourself as a Liaden gentleman, upholding the *melant'i* of Clan Serat. It will therefore be necessary for you to learn the Code and other necessary subjects, in addition to the coursework required by the school. Your tutor will work with you to build those study modules."

He paused; Don Eyr bowed.

"I understand," he said.

Mr. dea'Bon did not sigh.

"That is well, then. If you permit, I will ask my heir to assist you in filing your applications."

"That is very kind in you, sir," Don Eyr said. "My thanks."

Two

Lutetia

Captain Benoit of the Lutetia City Watch was bored. Society parties as a class tended to be stifling on several levels. Captain Benoit preferred the night beat in the city. Best was the university district, where she could feel the cool damp breeze from the river against her face as she walked. But, truly, any of the city beats–the outside city beats–were preferable to standing against the wall like a suit of armor, to insure that Councilor Gargon's guests didn't stab each other–literally–or steal the silver, or–the worst fault of all–injure the Councilor's feelings.

In point of fact, the City Watch was not supposed to stand watch over private functions. Councilor Gargon, however, was the patron of House Benoit, and therefore commanded such small personal services.

Fortunately, Councilor Gargon, unlike other Patrons Captain Benoit could name, possessed some modicum of restraint. House Benoit was most generally called when the Councilor was hosting a party, or giving one of her grand dinners. For the workaday world, she was satisfied with her Council-assigned bodyguards.

Tonight, the party was in the service of winning votes for the Council's scheme to route a monorail through the Old City. The Old City was protected by hundreds of years of legislation–no modern road could be built through it. That had lately become a problem because the New City had expanded, sweeping 'round the Old like a river 'round a rock. One might, of course, walk through the twisting, narrow streets of the Old City, or bicycle–but scarcely anyone did so. In main, citizens used jitneys, or rode the trains, or drove their own vehicles. They were in a hurry; it took too long to go through the

Old City–and the journey around the walls was becoming almost as long, what with the knots traffic routinely tied itself into.

Councilor Gargon was, as she so often was, on the conservative side of the issue. The radicals would drive a battle-wagon into the Old City, punching a straight line through its heart, which would become a wide highway, a short route from one side of the New City to the other.

The monorail . . . found little favor among busy citizens of the New City. The monorail was seen as a ploy, an effort to forestall progress, perhaps of use to tourists, or the indolent students, but who among the working citizens of the City had time to queue up at a monorail stop, and crawl over the ruins?

Thus, the party, and the trading and calling in of favors. Captain Benoit, who loved the Old City, tried to recruit herself with patience, but–truly, she would rather be out on her usual beat.

If you can't be where you'd rather, be happy where you are. That had been one of *Grand-père* Filepe's advisories. He had long been retired from the Watch by the time Captain Benoit had taken up her training arms, a ready source of wisdom, humor, and, often enough, irony, for the youngers of the household. He was not, of course, her genetic grandfather, nor any blood relation at all. House Benoit, like all the City Watch Houses, recruited their 'prentices from among the orphans of the city, of which there were, unfortunately, many.

House Benoit was one of eight; and second eldest of the Watch Houses. Common citizens were not, of course, trained in arms, or in combat. The arts of war were for the members of the Watch alone. All who came to Benoit took the House's name, and training, and bore the burden of the House's honor.

There.

The caterers were bringing the desserts out to the long tables, laying down plates of *chouquettes, macarons, petit fours, éclairs*. Captain Benoit sighed. She was especially fond of sweets, and tonight's party was being catered by the *École de Cuisine*, which was justly famous for its pastries, cakes, and small delights.

Ah, here came one of the younger students, bearing a *dacquoise*, and after her another student, carrying a platter of fruit bread sliced so thin one could see through each one . . .

The guests were converging upon the tables—and who could blame them? The younger student and the dark-haired youth who appeared to be the manager of catering, stood ready to assist. Others bustled about a second table, bringing out fresh pots of coffee, pitchers of cream, and little bowls of blue sugar that sparkled like fresh snow.

The younger student seemed somewhat nervous. The manager touched her arm, and she looked to him with a smile, her shoulders relaxing. Captain Benoit frowned, and brought her attention to those approaching the table.

Ah, merde, she cursed inwardly. Vertoi was here. She had not previously seen the Councilor among the guests; she must have come late. Vertoi was trouble, wherever she went; especially, she was trouble for those who had no standing, and therefore could neither resist her, nor demand justice from the Council. Vertoi being a Councilor, the common court had no call upon her; and she imposed no restraints upon herself.

Vertoi had an eye for beauty, and the younger student, now that Captain Benoit had taken a closer look, was very fine, indeed.

The catering manager took up an empty plate that moments before had held a mountain of *petit fours*, and handed it to his fair young assistant. She nodded, and left the table for the kitchen, just as Vertoi came up in the queue, her shoulders stiff and her face stormy.

Captain Benoit tensed. Vertoi was not above personally reprimanding an inferior, physically and in public, and she suddenly feared for the young manager's health.

He, however, seemed not to notice her displeasure, but leaned forward, his eyes on her face, his hands moving above the tempting sweets, discussing now the fruit bread; now the *éclairs* . . .

Vertoi turned away, leaving the manager in mid-discussion, holding an empty dessert plate. He put it behind the table, and turned to greet the next guest, his face pleasant and attentive.

She had seen him before, Captain Benoit realized. Seen him at the Institute loading bays, when dawn was scarcely a red-edged blade along the top of the walls, supervising the loading of trays onto a delivery van. In the afternoon, she had seen him, too, filling the beggars' bowls at the university district's main gates. She had noted him particularly; compact and neatly made, his movements crisp and clean. A pretty little one; and something out of the common way among the citizens of Lutetia, who tended to be tall, brown, red-haired and rangy.

As if he had felt the weight of her regard, the manager raised his head and caught her gaze. His eyes were dark brown, like his hair. He gave her a nod, as if perhaps he recognized her, too. She returned the salute, then a drift of dessert-seekers came between them.

* * *

He had sent Sylvie back to the Institute in the first van, with the empty plates and prep bowls. She, and the other three who went with her, would have a long few hours of clean-up in the catering kitchen, but he rather felt that she would willingly clean all night and into tomorrow, so long as she was not required to bear the attentions of Councilor Vertoi.

Don Eyr sighed. She becoming a problem, this councilor–not merely a problem for Sylvie, who, so far as he knew, lavished all of her devotion upon a certain promising young prep cook. No, Councilor Vertoi was beginning to pose a problem for the Institute and for the affairs of the Institute. Pursuing Sylvie while she was on-duty was a serious breach of what he had learned as a boy to call *melant'i*–and which he had learned here was an insult to the dignity of the Institute, its students, and, above, to the directors. He would of course report the incident to his adviser, as part of this evening's–well. *This morning's* debriefing. He was quite looking forward to that approaching hour, sitting cozy in Chauncey's parlor, tea in hand, and a plate of small cheese tarts set by.

Don Eyr did the final walk-through of the small prep area, finding it clean and tidy. He sighed, took off his white jacket, and folded it over one arm. Catering was not his preference. If he were ruled only by his preferences, he would be always in the kitchen, baking breads, and pastries, cakes . . . He felt his mouth twitch into a wry smile. Perhaps it was best, after all, that the directors insisted that all students learn catering, and production baking, and the other commercial aspects of their art–all of which would be useful, when he opened his own *boulangerie* . .

Satisfied with the condition of the prep room, he signed the job off on the screen by the door, releasing copies of the invoice to Councilor Gargon's financial agent, and to the Institute's billing office. A note would also be sent to his file, and to Chauncey's screen, so that gentleman would know when to start brewing the tea.

Don Eyr put his hand against the plate, the door to the delivery alley opened, and he stepped out into the cool, damp, and fragrant night.

The door closed behind him. Before him, the van, Keander likely already asleep in the back. Don Eyr shook his head. Keander could–and did–sleep anywhere, which might be annoying, if he did not wake willing and cheerful, eager to perform any task required of him.

He reached the van, hand extended to the door–and spun, ducking.

The move perhaps saved his life; the cudgel hit the van's door instead of his head, denting and tearing the polymer.

Don Eyr spun, saw his attacker as a looming, dark shadow between himself and the light, and launched himself low and to the right, half-remembered training rising, as he kicked the man's knee.

A grunt, a curse.

The man staggered, but he did not go down, and Don Eyr spun again, kicking the metal ashcan by the gate.

It rang loudly, though it was a vain cast. Keander could sleep through any din, though the softest whisper of his name would rouse him.

"Dodge all you like, little rat," came the man's voice, as the cudgel rose again. "Councilor Vertoi sends her regards, and a reminder to stay out of her business."

He swung again, and Don Eyr drove forward, catching the man 'round both knees and spilling him backward onto the alley.

The ash can produced another clatter as the cudgel, released from surprised fingers, struck it as Don Eyr rolled away.

"I will kill you," the man snarled, and Don Eyr, on his knees by the service door, saw him roll clumsily, heaving himself to his knees, even as a second shadow moved in, and with one efficient move kicked those knees out from under him, and delivered a sharp blow to the back of the head.

Straightening, this one moved to the pool of light, revealing herself as the Watch Captain he had most lately seen at the councilor's party, tall and fit, with her close-cropped red hair and her light eyes.

"Are you well, *masyr*? Do you require my assistance?"

"I am well, thank you, Watch Captain," he said, hearing how breathy and uneven his voice was. "I believe I will stand."

He did so, and stood looking up at her, while she looked down at him.

"Your arrival was timely," he said.

"Yes," she agreed, and shook her head.

"That was *most* ill-advised, *masyr*. This man has been trained to fight and to inflict damage. To attempt to meet him on his own terms ..."

"What else might I have done?" he answered, perhaps too sharply. "Stand and have my head broken?"

She was silent for a long moment, then sighed, and spread her fingers before her.

"The point is yours, but now I must ask–who taught you to fight? Is this now a part of the Institute curriculum?"

He laughed.

"Certainly not! A course of self-defense was taught me, before I came here. It was years ago, my tutoring of the most basic, and–as you observe–I scarcely recalled what little I had learned."

"No, no, having taken the decision to defend yourself–you did well. A man of peace, surprised at your lawful business, and, I make no doubt, exhausted from your labors this evening. Our friend, here, he had expected an easy strike, and now he will wake in the Watch House, with a headache, a fine to pay–and an account of himself to be made to his mistress that will, I expect, be very painful for him."

She stepped back, clearing his way to the van.

"Please, be about your business, *masyr*, and I will be about mine."

"Yes," he said.

He turned, after he had opened the door.

"Thank you, Watch Captain."

She straightened from where she had been placing binders on the fallen attacker.

"My duty, *masyr*. Good-night to you, now. Go in peace."

"Good-night," he said, and climbed into the cab, and drove away.

* * *

Policemen and criminals were not so very much different. So said *Grand-père* Filepe. Certainly, they tended to know the same people, to drink in the same places, to roam the same streets at very nearly the same hours.

So it was that Serana Benoit was at a table in a shady corner of a particular cafe on a small street near the river, eating her midday meal, when she heard a word, spoken in a voice she recognized.

The first word was followed by several more, forming a sentence most interesting. Serana closed her eyes, the better to hear the rest of it. The proposition was made, and, after a short pause, accepted, for the usual fee. Serana opened her eyes, and turned to signal her waiter for more wine, her glance moving incuriously over the occupants of the table to her right.

Yes, she had recognized Fritz Girard's voice; his companion was . . . Louis Leblanc. That was . . . disturbing. Unlike the hired bullies attached to the wealthy, who were used to express their masters' displeasure by way of a broken arm or a sprained head, Louis Leblanc performed exterminations. Showy, public exterminations, meant to remove a nuisance, and also to inspire potential future nuisances to rethink their life-plans.

The waiter arrived with a fresh glass, and Serana turned back to her lunch, ears straining. There came the expected haggling over price—perfunctory, really—before the two rose and left the cafe in different directions.

Serana finished her lunch, paid her bill, and returned to her beat, troubled by what she had heard.

* * *

"That's the last," Don Eyr told Silvesti.

The delivery driver nodded, made the rack fast to the grid inside his truck, and jumped down to the alley floor. He was taller than Don Eyr, as who was not? His mustache was grey, though his hair was still stubbornly red. There were lines in his face, and scars on his knuckles. He worked for the distributor, and before the day broke over the city walls, all of the breads, pastries, and other fresh-baked things from the Institute's kitchens would be on offer in restaurants across the city.

"A light load this morning, my son," Silvesti commented.

"Yes; one of our bakers did not arrive for her shift. Had she allowed us to know, we would have found someone else. As it was, we were half done before her absence was noted."

He handed over the clipboard.

"Here is the distribution list. When we understood what had happened, we contacted the restaurants. Three were willing to forgo pastries today for extra tomorrow, so that the rest may have their normal share—though no extras, today."

"Understood." Silvesti took the clipboard, running a knowing blue eye down the list, before glancing up.

"You've made extra work for yourselves tomorrow," he observed, "and a baker down."

"No, we'll call in some of the promising juniors, and let them see what the production kitchen is like."

"Scare them into another trade," Silvesti said wisely.

"Perhaps. But, then, you see what a similar experience did for me."

The delivery driver laughed, and tucked the clipboard away into a capacious pocket.

"Some never learn the right lesson, eh? Until next week, my son."

Don Eyr watched the van drive out of the loading yard, filling his lungs with air damp from the river. This was when the city was quietest; very nearly still. Occasionally, there came sound of a car moving over damp crete, some streets distant; or a ship's bell, far off in the middle of the river. It was not, perhaps, his favorite time of the day–there being some joy to be found in beginning the day's baking, and also the hour in which he taught the seminar . . .

Still, this early morning time was pleasant, signaling, as it did, an end to labor for a few hours, and a chance to–

A boot heel scraped against the alley's crete floor, and he turned, expecting to see Ameline, come out with her coffee and her smoke stick, as she often did, to sit on the edge of the loading dock to relax after her labors among the cakes.

But it was not Ameline, nor any other of the Institute.

"Watch Captain Benoit," he said, taking a certain pleasure in her tall, lean figure. She was not in uniform this evening, but dressed in leggings and a dark jacket open over a striped shirt.

"Tonight, only Serana Benoit," she said gently. "I hope that I did not startle you, *masyr*?"

"I had expected one of my colleagues," he answered. "My name is Don Eyr fer'Gasta. I think that our introductions the other evening were incomplete."

"Indeed, there was much about that encounter which was shabbily done," she said, walking toward him, her hands in the pockets of her jacket.

"I am here . . ." she paused, looking down at him, her face lean, and her eyes in shadow, all the light from the dock lamps tangled in her cropped red hair.

She sighed, and shook her head.

"You understand that it is *Serana Benoit*, who offers this," she said.

Melant'i. That he grasped very well. He inclined his head.

"I understand. But what is it that you offer?"

Another sigh, as if the entire business went against all the order of the universe. Her hands came out of her pockets, palms up and empty.

"I will teach you. We will build upon these long-ago basic lessons you received. A few tricks only, you understand, but they may be made to suffice. You have become a target, *masyr*, and you had best see to your own defense."

"A target?" he repeated, looking up at her.

"Oh, yes. One does not thwart Councilor Vertoi in any of her desires. And one *certainly* does not embarrass her enforcer."

"Councilor Vertoi is not permitted to disrupt my team while we are working," he said calmly.

Serana Benoit laughed, short and sharp.

"Yes, yes, little one; you have expressed this sentiment with perfect clarity.

Fritz Gerard, Councilor Vertoi, myself–none of us missed your meaning. Councilor Vertoi has done you the honor of believing you to be a serious man, and she has hired Louis LeBlanc to wait upon you."

Something was clearly expected of him, but Don Eyr could only turn his palms up in turn and repeat, "Louis LeBlanc?"

"Ah, I forget. You live sheltered here. Louis LeBlanc is a very bad man. He has been hired to hurt you, from which we learn that Madame the Councilor considers that you have damaged her reputation and so may show you no mercy."

Chauncey had a pet; a green-and-red bird that had learned to say certain amusing phrases. Don Eyr felt a certain kinship with the bird now, able only to repeat her own words back to her.

"No mercy? He is to strike me lightly on the head?"

Serana Benoit looked grim.

"Were you of Madame's own station, or in the employ of one of such station, Louis would have been instructed to kill you. That is mercy at Madame's level. She has, regrettably, seen that you are a catering manager, a mere minion who must be taught his proper place."

She took a breath, and added, softly.

"Louis . . . Understand me, I have seen Louis' work, and speak from the evidence of my own eyes! Louis will break all of your bones, not quickly; abuse tendons, and tear muscles. Perhaps, yes, he will strike you in the head, but I think not, for Madame will want you to *know* why you have become a cripple, and a beggar."

He stared at her, seeing truth in her face, hearing it in her voice. There were, perhaps, a number of things he might have said to her, then, but what he did say was . . .

"Come into the kitchen. There is tea—and bread and butter."

* * *

He was an apt student, Don Eyr, a joy to instruct; supple and unexpectedly strong. When she mentioned this, he had laughed, which was pleasing of itself, and said that flour came in thirty-two kilogram sacks.

She could wish that several Benoit apprentices were so willing, adept, and of such a happy nature. And as much as she enjoyed teaching him, she enjoyed even more their time after practice, when they would adjourn to the little room behind the kitchen, for a simple snack of tea and bread, and talk of whatever occurred to them.

Very quickly, she was Serana, and he was Don Eyr. She told him such bits of gossip as she heard in the course of her duties, and he told her such *on-dits* as had filtered into the Institute's classrooms and kitchens. She told him somewhat of life in House Benoit, and was pleased that he enjoyed even *Grand-père's* saltier observations.

For himself, he was the lesser child of his family, which he considered luck, indeed, as it had allowed him to pursue his talent for baking.

Yes, she enjoyed his company. Very much. Perhaps she watched him with too much appreciation; perhaps she regarded him too warmly. But she did not act on these things–he was a student, after all, clearly some years her junior, and she was his teacher.

It would not have done, and she did not need *Grand-père* to tell her so.

As for the training–apt as he was, he would never defeat Louis. The best he might do would be to surprise and disable him long enough to run to some place of safety. Whereupon the hunt would begin again. Louis might become fond of the child, if he gave good enough sport, and one shuddered to think what *that* might come to, when he was, as he must be, at the last–caught.

Still, they trained, and two weeks along there came the news that Louis LeBlanc had been taken up by Calvin of House Fontaine, caught in the very act of threatening a citizen. Serana knew Calvin; had known him very well, indeed, when they had both been foot soldiers for their Houses. It had been some time since she had sought him out, but she had done so after that news had hit the street.

"The Common Judge gave him four weeks, non-negotiable," Calvin said, drinking the glass of wine she'd bought him. "In four weeks, plus one day, he will be on the streets again."

"Is there any likelihood of a pattern-of-behavior charge?" asked Serana.

Calvin shrugged.

"The father had said some such at first, but he's quiet now."

"Bought off?" Serana guessed, sipping her own wine.

"Or frightened off." Another shrug and quizzical glance.

"Why do you care? Even if Louis is permanently removed, another will rise to fill the void." He raised his glass, as if in salute. "There must always be a Louis; to keep the Councilors from going to war."

"It may be that a replacement Louis will enjoy his work less," Serana said, and shrugged. "One might hope."

"This is on behalf of the new lover?"

"New student," she corrected.

"So? Does Benoit agree to this?"

"No need for Benoit to agree to what I do on my off-hours," Serana said, which was

not . . . precisely true. "Besides, he came from off-world, half-trained and a danger to himself and our fellow citizens. I make the streets safer by teaching him."

"A baker, I hear," said Calvin.

"You have big ears, my friend."

Calvin laughed and drank off the last of his wine.

#

"When," she asked Don Eyr as they sat together over their quiet tea. "When will you graduate?"

"Graduate?" He looked amused. "I graduated two years ago. I have completed my coursework, and taken the certification tests for master baker, pastry chef, and *commis* chef. At the moment, the Institute employs me to teach an introductory workshop to breads, and an upper level seminar in pastry. Two days, I work in the test kitchens; one day I supervise the distribution baking; and, as you know, I manage one of the catering teams."

Serana blinked, realized that she had been staring, and raised her tea cup.

Don Eyr began to butter a piece of bread.

"Soon, I will need to make other arrangements," he said. "Chauncey has been trying to entice me to stay and become faculty–to teach, you know."

"You do not wish to be a teacher?" Serana managed.

He put the butter knife aside and glanced up at her.

"In many ways, teaching is enjoyable, especially when one has an apt pupil. But, no. I want to *bake*, to feed people, and bring joy to their day. I have determined to open my own *boulangerie*."

His own bakeshop, bless the child; and she had thought him too young to understand her.

"A shop here–in the City?"

He laughed, dark eyes dancing.

"No one opens a *boulangerie* in Lutetia! What would be the point, when the Institute supplies all of the restaurants and coffee houses, and could easily supply a third again more?"

"You will leave us, then?" she persisted, which both relieved her, and filled her with a profound sadness.

He gave her a grave look.

"I think that I must, and I have a plan, you see. When I wrote to . . . my family's accountant, to inform him of my certifications, and graduation, he wrote back with information regarding certain accounts and properties which are mine, alone.

"My mother left me a property–a house and some land–on Ezhel'ti. Those funds have, in part, been supporting me here, with the remainder being placed into an account which Mr. dea'Bon has held in trust for me. The house and the account came to me upon graduation. I have been researching Ezhel'ti, and it seems a very promising world, with two large metropolitan areas, and a scattering of smaller towns. It remains to be seen if a city or a town will suit me best, but my intention is to emigrate and open a *boulangerie*."

He gave her a small smile.

"Mr. dea'Bon is retired from my clan's business, and finds himself wishing for a little project to keep him entertained. He has offered to advise me, which is kind. Certainly, I shall have need of him."

"Indeed," she said, and put her tea cup on the tray. "It may be wise, to leave as soon as your planning allows," she said, her lips feeling stiff. "The rumor inside the Watch is that Louis LeBlanc will be off the streets for four weeks, no longer. Since it is possible for you to remove yourself from danger . . ."

"I must stay until the end of the term," he told her. "I have signed a contract."

"How long?" she asked.

"Eight weeks. But after–"

"Yes, after. I advise, make your arrangements now."

"I will," he said, as she rose.

"You are leaving?"

"I have the early Watch tomorrow," she lied. "Good-night, Don Eyr."

"Good-night," he said, and rose in his turn to open the bay door and see her out.

* * *

The peaceful round of weeks flowed by, each day bringing its rewards. Don Eyr had dispatched letters, received some replies, and written more letters. He and Serana had kept to their schedule of sparring and suddenly, it was the day of Louis LeBlanc's release from mandatory confinement.

He would not have said that the date weighed over-heavy on his mind, though naturally he had noted it. And truly, he did not begin to worry until he left for their usual meeting.

He arrived in the practice room before her, which was not *so* unusual. He occupied himself with warm-ups, and moved on to first-level exercises.

When he finished the set and she still had not come–*then* he began to worry. It was ridiculous, of course, to worry after Serana, who was a Watch Captain and fully able to take care of herself–and any other two dozen persons who happened to be nearby. But he worried, nonetheless. He reminded himself that she had missed their meeting on two previous occasions, and had turned up, perfectly well, if appallingly tired, at the Institute, later, wanting her tea and buttered bread–and, more than that, someone to talk to about commonplaces, and simple things. It pleased him that she came to him for comfort on those nights when her duty was a burden. But, he could not help but recall that her duty might see her maimed, or killed, much as she might laugh off that aspect of the matter.

"You will worry yourself into a shadow, little one, if you worry about me. I have more lives than a cat—*Grand-père* has said it, so you know it is true! I may be late, but always I will come back to you, eh? My word on it."

Yes, but today—today an especial danger had been released back onto the streets, and he might be assumed to be angry about his recent confinement, and seeking to wreak havoc upon those whom he judged to be most responsible.

Surely, being the sort of man he was, LeBlanc would consider Serana's friend Calvin at fault, but Serana had told him that the Commander of the Watch had decided to hold Calvin at headquarters for the first day of Louis LeBlanc's renewed liberty, and also to set a guard around the Common Judge who had sentenced him.

These were, so Serana said, temporary measures, to give LeBlanc time to work off his ill-humor, and reconnect with his usual sources.

Work, said Serana, with a certain amount of irony, seemed to exert a steadying influence over Louis LeBlanc.

Don Eyr finished his workout early, without Serana to spar with, and returned to the tea room, where he took special care with this evening's snack; her favored blend of tea; and thin slices of the crusty chewy bread she had declared—rather surprising herself, so he thought, with amusement—the best she had ever eaten, beside which all other so-called breads were revealed as impostors. He added a dish of jam to compliment the butter, and stood looking down at the tea table, wondering what he would do, if she did not come tonight.

The bell rang then, and he hurried down the hall, looking by habit at the screen—and it was Serana standing there, in her Watch uniform, her face in shadow, her posture stiff. He took a breath, and pulled the door open.

She followed him silently down to the tea-room, and stood, silent yet, just inside the door.

He turned, and saw her face clearly for the first time that evening.

"Serana, what has happened?"

She looked at him, her face haggard, eyes red, proud shoulders slumped.

"Come in."

He stepped up to her, and caught her arm, leading her to the table; saw her seated in her usual chair. Then, he crossed the room to the small cabinet, opened it, and poured red wine into a glass. He set it before her, and commanded, "Drink."

She shook herself slightly, and obeyed, downing the whole of it in two long gulps, without appreciation, or even full knowledge of what she did. No matter; it was a common vintage, and it seemed to be doing her some good. Her pale green eyes sparkled; and her shoulders came up, somewhat.

"Good," he said, and took the glass away to refill it, and to pour one for himself.

He came back to the table, and sat across from her.

"Tell me," he said.

She blinked, then, and seemed to fully see. She smiled somewhat.

"Peremptory, little one," she murmured.

"Ah, but I am a manager, and a master baker, and a blight upon the lives of my students," he told her. "Arrogance is the least of my accomplishments."

Her lips bent slightly; perhaps she thought she had smiled.

"So," she said; "I will tell you. Louis LeBlanc died today. Badly."

He blinked, taking in the uniform. Serana did not come to their meetings in her uniform. She came always as Serana Benoit; never as Watch Captain Benoit. He sipped wine to cover his shiver.

"Do you think I did this thing?" he asked.

She laughed, and it was terrible to hear.

"You? No, I do not think that."

She raised her glass and drank.

"No?" he asked. "A man in fear of his life . . ."

She slashed the air with her free hand.

"A man in fear of his life would not have *had time* to do what was done to Louis," she snarled, horror and anger in her voice. "And you, little one—you are not capable of what I saw. You are my student; I know this."

She turned her head aside, but not before he saw the tears.

He took a careful breath.

"Serana—" he began.

"Oh, understand me; I have no love for Louis LeBlanc. But the manner of his death, and the timing of it . . . It is a message, from one Councilor to another, you see; and such a message—it will be war, now, between the ruling houses, but *they* will not bleed! No, they will use us as little toy soldiers, and we will die—for what? The world will not be made better; and when the war is over, or the point is won—another will rise to become the next Louis LeBlanc. It will all be the same, only we will be fewer in the senior and novice ranks, and there will be more orphans from which to recruit replacements . . ."

There was a breathless moment, before she repeated, in a bitter whisper.

"*Replacements.*"

He was an idiot; he could think of nothing to say, to ease her. She had told him the history of House Benoit—told it lightly, as if it were a very fine joke. But now . . .

"I am not a coward. I am not afraid to do my duty," she whispered. "But my duty is to protect the citizens, not to kill fellow Watchmen!"

He did not remember rising, or going 'round the table. He barely remembered putting his arm around her shoulders, and feeling her press her face against his side.

"Of course you are not a coward," he murmured. "You are bold and honorable. Can you not appeal–" Appeal to whom? he thought wildly. If the Councilors were at war, surely the City Council would not rule against them.

"The Common Judges?" he ventured. "Can they not issue a restraint, releasing the Watch from such orders?"

She made a sound; perhaps it was a laugh.

"Don Eyr's twisty mind works on," she murmured. "That is a particularly fine notion–and it was tried, the . . . last time the Councilors went to war. They simply ignored the order, and had those of the Watch and the judiciary who protested killed."

He closed his eyes.

"Don Eyr."

She shifted in his arms, and he stepped back, letting her go as she straightened in her chair. She caught his hand, and looked into his face.

"Don Eyr," she repeated.

"Yes, my friend. What may I do for you?"

She laughed, soft and broken.

"You make it too easy," she said, and drew a breath, keeping her eyes on his.

"I would like to make love with you, little one."

He hesitated. She released his hand.

"I am maladroit," she said. "Please do not regard it."

"No, I *will* regard it," he said, taking her hand between both of his. "Only–to *make love*. I may not have the recipe. But, this I offer–that I value you, and would willingly share pleasure; give and receive comfort. Indeed, I have wished for it, but while we stood as teacher and student–"

"I see it," she said, offering a small smile, but a true one. "We are both fools."

"That is perhaps accurate. I propose that we now teach each other–I will learn to make love . . ."

"And I will learn to share pleasure. Agreed, but–"

She glanced about them, and he laughed.

"No; let us to my rooms; we may be private there."

"Yes," she said, and rose.

* * *

His rooms, at the top of the Institute . . . His rooms were neat, and modest; the bed under the eaves big enough for both, so long as she was careful of her head.

There was a window, which she learned later, after he had risen and left her in order to see to the day's first baking. It was marvelous, this window; one could oversee the entire City, even the Tower of Memories in the heart of the Old City.

Her City, that she loved; her City, that she served and protected.

There would be war; that was certain. A few days, perhaps, of quiet, while the Councilors gathered themselves, and made certain of those Watch Houses which were sworn to them. Benoit's patron was Gargon, of course. Fontaine's patron was Vertoi. It was not to be expected that she would stand shoulder to shoulder with Calvin in this, or with his sister, or any other of her comrades at Fontaine. No, this time, they would be set at each other, like dogs thrown into the pit, while the owners watched safely from above, and perhaps placed wagers on style, and form.

Her stomach cramped, and she turned away from the window, and the view of her City, to survey this place where her little one apparently spent all too few hours at rest.

There was a screen on a small table, under a bright light; a tidy pile of bills or letters placed to the right of the keyboard. Across the room from the bed stood an armoire so large it was certain that the room had been built around it. Beyond the armoire, an archway, through which more light streamed.

She stepped into a small kitchen. A teapot steamed gently on the table next to that sunny window, and the inevitable plate of breads; butter, cheese, and cold sausage. The window overlooked the river, a happy breakfast companion.

After she had eaten, and washed up, and refilled the teapot against his eventual return to his rooms, she showered in the tiny bathroom, and donned her armor, and stood looking down at the bed, recalling what had taken place there.

A sweet lad, indeed; generous and wise; and if he had not made love, then certainly he had given pleasure in full measure.

And Serana Benoit? Serana Benoit was a greater fool than even she had supposed herself to be. What precisely had been the purpose of bedding the child, when she knew he was preparing—as he must!—to flee to his safe future off-world, his small property, his dreamed-for bake-shop? She would miss him—she would have missed him, profoundly, without the sweetness they had shared. All she had accomplished was to make her own loss more poignant.

Yet . . . if she were to die, as it was probable that she would, and soon; she would have this memory in her when she stood to be judged before Camulus in the afterworld.

Mindful of the low ceiling, she bent and made the bed, smoothing the coverlet, catching the lingering perfume of their passion.

A deep breath, and she turned away, moving to the dark corner of the room, to the left, where she recalled the hall door had been.

A piece of paper was pinned to this portal, somewhat lower than her nose. She squinted at it, and found a neat hand-drawn map, guiding her to the nearest outside door. At the bottom of the map, was a note.

It is an interesting recipe, my friend. I would enjoy making more love with you. If you would also enjoy this, let us meet for wine at Paiser's this afternoon when our shifts are done.

She smiled, and tucked the note inside her armor, next to her heart.

#

She brought him flowers, of course. He was worth every rose in the City, and she would not stint him, though it *was* Paiser's and she would shortly be known as a besotted fool in every Watch House and bar in the city. No matter: there were things far worse than to be known as a doting lover.

He rose to take the bouquet from her, dark eyes wide with pleasure. She had exercised restraint, and the flowers did not, quite, overpower him, and in any case it *was* Paiser's and here was the waiter, murmuring that he would place them into a vase for *maysr* and most immediately bring them back.

"I ordered wine," Don Eyr said when they were both seated. "I did not know if you wished to dine, or . . . how you wish to proceed."

Proceed? She thought. She wished to proceed to his rooms–hers were too public for this affair–and undress him, slowly, running her hands over silky, golden skin . . .

Her imaginings were too vivid, and Don Eyr perceptive, as always.

"Perhaps not here?" he murmured, and she laughed.

"Perhaps not."

She paused at the return of the waiter, bearing a vase overfilled with roses, and a second, bearing a small table. This was set at the side of their table in such way that the flowers formed a fragrant screen, shielding them somewhat from the rest of the room.

"*Maysr* has bespoken a bottle," the first waiter said. "Shall I bring it? With some cheeses, and fruit? A basket of bread, perhaps?"

"Serana?" Don Eyr asked and she smiled at him.

"All of it. Let us linger, and make plans."

He understood, and she was delighted to see a blush gild his cheeks with darker gold. She leaned toward him and lowered her voice.

"I have the night watch tomorrow," she murmured. "And you?"

His blush deepened, and his eyes sparkled.

"I," he said, his voice low and sultry, "will ask Chauncey to lead the advanced seminar this evening."

* * *

The war was being fought in skirmishes, at the fringes of the city, and the few injuries sustained thus far were minor. Perhaps the Councilors were being discreet; perhaps they sensed a reluctance among their toy soldiers. They were positioning for advantage; feeling out the temper of the streets; searching for the flashpoint that would ignite violence.

Lots had been drawn at House Benoit, as at the other Watch Houses. Short straw placed you on the Council Watch, which had the duty to protect the City, and whose loyalty was to the Council. This was by necessity a short-term assignment, the Council not being plump in pocket, and was in any case a moot point.

Serana had drawn a long straw.

She did not tell him this. Of course not. There was no need to concern the child, who would be well out of everything in a matter of two weeks. Instead, she listened to him talk about his plans for this bakeshop he would build on the world that was not Lutetia, far from the City, far from Serana, safe from the war brewing on the streets.

"Serana, only listen!" he said, looking up from his latest letter with eyes sparkling.

"I have kin on Ezhel'ti! My father's clan acknowledges the connection, and the delm has written to Mr. dea'Bon to say that they will give me a place as a Festival child among them, if I should wish it. Also–"

"*Do* you wish it?" she asked him, from her lazy slouch in his reading chair. She had pulled it over to the window–the window that looked over her City, and sat bathed in sunlight, her cotton shirt opened over her breasts, her hair blazing like living fire.

With difficulty, Don Eyr removed his attention from the picture she made there, and looked back to the letter, thinking about her question.

"I do not know," he admitted. "I am not accustomed to being in-clan. It would be a change, certainly; but it is all of it a change! And these people–my father's clan–they are long-time residents of Ezhel'ti, and in a very good place from which to introduce me . . ."

"Yes, so long as they are not scoundrels," she said; then wished the words back. Why blight his joy? And these people wanted him, which that wretched old man who had sent him away had never done, as she had heard in the spaces between the words in the tales he had told her of his childhood . . .

Don Eyr was smiling.

"You are suspicious, Watch Captain. You will therefore be pleased to know that Mr. dea'Bon is of a like turn of mind. He has put inquiries into motion, and assures me that there is no need to rush into an association until the facts are known. I may, he says, quite properly be busy with my own affairs for some time after my arrival."

"You are correct," she told him sincerely. "I am pleased, and relieved. Count me as an ardent admirer of Mr. dea'Bon."

"I will be jealous," he said lightly, and she laughed.

"An admirer *from afar*," she amended. "*Far* afar."

"I am soothed," he assured her, and tipped his head. "And now you are sad."

He was *far* too perceptive, she thought, and did not seek to lie to him.

"I will miss you," she said; "very much, Don Eyr."

"And I, you." He rose from the desk and crossed the room to kneel at her side and look up into her face.

"Serana," he said, softly–and she leaned forward to kiss him thoroughly, before he said the words that would bind them both.

He was made for fine things, her little one; for peace, which her own small researches had revealed was the general state of Ezhel'ti. No one knew what *she* had been born for. An orphan, she had been taken in by House Benoit, to be trained in arms and in violence.

His hands were on her breasts, strong fingers kneading . Good. She stood, bringing him with her to the bed, there to make such love between them that neither need utter a word.

* * *

They were to meet at Paiser's mid-afternoon for a glass of wine and a small luncheon. It was her free hour from patrol, and his, between test kitchen and seminar.

Serana arrived first, proceeding toward the outside tables, when she caught a movement from the side of her eye.

She continued her stroll, curving away from the cafe, now, finding two familiar faces on her left hand, moving toward her with precisely as much purpose as the two approaching from her right.

So, the Councilors had decided, she thought, calmly assessing the situation. And Serana Benoit was to be the flashpoint.

She continued to move away from Paiser's, toward the center of the small square, where there were fewer innocents to be caught in the action.

"Watch business!" she snapped at those few. "Move on, move away!"

She touched the weighted stick on her belt, but did not draw it. She did not *need* to draw it; one look at her face, and they moved, rushing away from danger.

There was a shout behind her, which she ignored. Jacques Blanchet could see her in hell. She supposed that she ought to be complimented, that the Councilors found her so provocative that her death would, with certainty, start a war.

Another shout. Serana smiled, grimly. Monique Sauvage could stand in line behind Blanchet.

She had reached the center of the square. She turned, quickly, the stick with its lead core coming up out of her belt, to slam into the extended right arm of Servais Tanguy. He screamed, and twisted aside, weapon falling from nerveless fingers. She spun to intercept Blanchet, kicking him in the knee with her reinforced boots. He was quick, however; the blow did not connect solidly, and here at last was Monique Sauvage, flying at her like the madwoman she was, knife dancing, while Simone Papin stood back, awaiting opportunity.

The world narrowed down to the work at hand. She managed to fell Sauvage with a blow of the stick to her temple, and there was Papin coming in, blade glittering; Tanguy rushing her off-side, shock grenade in hand, and she made the decision to let the armor take the knife-thrust–

Tanguy fell back, baiting her, and there was Blanchet spinning in from her other side. This time, the kick landed well, and she danced to one side as Tanguy triggered his toy, feeling the fizzing tingle as the armor dissipated the charge. She had broken his neck before the fizzing stopped, and turned at last to deal with Papin–

Who was lying on the stones, his neck at an unfortunate angle. From far away came the blare of an emergency wagon. Much closer stood a man in a white coat, knife in hand, point toward the cobbles. He raised his head and looked at her, dark eyes wide.

Serana took a breath.

"You fool!" she snapped.

"He was going to kill you!" Don Eyr snapped in return.

"*I* am wearing armor!" she shouted, and reached out to grab him by the shoulder. "*You* are wearing a baker's smock!"

"Serana," he began, his eyes filling.

Her heart broke; she moved to embrace him—and looked up at the sound of boots pounding cobbles.

From the left came three of House Benoit. From the right, two of Fontaine.

Fontaine was nearer, the senior-most holding binders in such a way to make it clear she knew them for the insult they were.

"Serana Benoit," she said, her voice professional; her eyes sad. "You are under arrest."

She extended her hands to accept the insult, and glanced over her shoulder.

There were now two of House Benoit standing at ready, and Don Eyr was not in sight.

* * *

Once the binders were on, and Fontaine's duty done, Benoit sued for Serana's release to the custody and discipline of her House.

The surprise was that Fontaine released her, in proper form, accepting House Benoit's honor as her bail.

The second surprise, when she emerged from her interview with Commander Mathilde Benoit, and went in search of *Grand-père* Filepe, to tell him with her own voice what had transpired—there was Don Eyr sitting in the sun on the back patio, listening with rapt attention to one of the old man's saltier tales.

She paused, her hand on the warm stone pillar. Don Eyr—someone of the house had given him shirt, vest, and trousers. He had rolled the shirt sleeves above his wrists, and left the top buttons open—in respect of the heat, which was considerable, in this little stone pocket that caught the sun even on rainy days.

Grand-père wore a shawl over thick, well-buttoned shirt and vest, for winter had gotten into his bones on a campaign outside the City when he was a young man, and had never melted away.

Or so he said.

He paused now, on the very edge of the story's bawdy denouement, raised his eyes and gave her a brief nod.

Don Eyr spun out of his chair and rushed to her, hands out, eyes on her face.

"Serana! Are you well?"

In truth, she was *not* well. As of this hour, she was a soldier without a House, in Lutetia, where war was about to erupt, and with her to blame, so far as the Councilors would tell it.

Those shames faded, however, to see him before her, unscathed, beautiful, and concerned for her well-being.

Wordless—for what could she say?—she opened her arms, and he stepped into her embrace.

Eventually, she recalled herself, and lifted her head to meet *Grand-père's* eyes. He smiled, and nodded at the bench on his right side, where Don Eyr had been seated. A 'prentice came out of the cool, dark depths of the house, bearing a tray—wine so cold the carafe was frosty with sweat, cheese and small breads. This, she placed on the table by *Grand-père's* hand, and departed, never once raising her head to see the disgraced soldier on the other side of the patio.

Don Eyr stirred in her arms. She stepped back and let him go, looking down into his face—a face ravaged, and why was that? Ah.

She had shouted at him, and called his actions into doubt. Truly, she was a monster.

She caught his hand.

"*Petit . . .*" she began, but she had reckoned without *Grand-père* Filepe.

"Do not begin this on my porch, unless you intend a threesome!" he said, loudly enough to be heard in the house–or, indeed, at Paiser's.

Serana glared at him, but Don Eyr turned; and approached the bench, bringing her with him by their linked hand.

"Sir, we dare not," he said to the old man; "for certainly you will outstrip us."

A shout of laughter greeted this sally, even as *Grand-père* waved at the tray.

"Serana, child, serve us; then sit, so that we may plan together."

Plan? She thought, but did not ask. One did not ask *Grand-père*; one waited to be told.

She poured the wine, arranged the tray and table more conveniently for all, and settled onto the bench beside Don Eyr.

"So," *Grand-père* said, after they had savored the wine; "Mathilde has done her duty."

"She has," said Serana, matching his careless tone.

"Your lover, here, has explained how it is that he has had training of Benoit; and also how he was able to recognize and counter the particular killing strike Papin had prepared for you."

"The armor–" Serana began, and it was Don Eyr who interrupted her.

"No. Serana–that blade–it was curved. He was coming in low for a thrust and an upsweep . . ."

She stared at him in horror.

"*Under* the armor?"

"Yes," he said, and had recourse to his glass.

"But you–"

"I," he said with irony, "was a child wearing a baker's smock. I doubt he saw me, and if he did, he judged me no threat."

"And he would have been correct," *Grand-père* said, slapping his knee, "had you not learned that disarm so well, my friend! You make our House proud that you are one of our students."

Serana considered him carefully.

"Mathilde acknowledges this?"

"At first, she was inclined otherwise," *Grand-père* said airily. "She may have had hard words to say about bakers and civilians–" He bent a sympathetic eye upon Don Eyr. "You must not regard her, my friend; it was merely a release of her feelings, in order to free adequate room for thought."

"I understand," Don Eyr murmured. "And truly, it was an education."

Serana winced. The House Commander had a strong vocabulary, indeed. The rumor was that each commander logged every curse word in a massive book, kept under lock and key, and that adding to this book had been the sacred duty of Benoit Commanders for centuries.

"When it was put to her that having a half-trained citizen with a strong aversion to having his head stove in walking the street unsupervised was more of a danger to the City than producing a full-trained citizen, Mathilde did indeed rise to the occasion. A file was made, and a certificate produced. My friend here holds the rank of scholar-soldier in House Benoit."

"Scholar-soldier?" Serana repeated.

"There is such a rank," Don Eyr said beside her. "Sergeant Vauclelin would have me know that the last time it was awarded was nearly one hundred local years ago. But the rank was never removed from the lists."

"Indeed. And that rank will keep my young friend well, for the short time he remains on Lutetia. For yourself, Serana . . ."

"For myself," she said, tired now, despite the wine; "I must leave the City and establish myself elsewhere."

"That . . . was unavoidable," said *Grand-père*, sadness in his eyes. "It seems that I am doomed to lose you, child. And I would rather miss you than mourn you."

She stared at him for a moment before she recalled herself, and produced a grin which felt oddly tenuous on her mouth.

"I will miss you so very much, *Grand-père*."

He smiled at her.

"I know, child, but only think–you will never need mourn me, either."

It is true, thought Serana; I will never see him dead; he will therefore live forever.

"It would please me," Don Eyr said softly, "if you would consent to travel with me. Such a course would be all to my benefit, since I am insufficiently suspicious." He gave her a solemn look. "As has been pointed out."

She placed her hand on his knee and met his eyes.

"Little one, I would gladly come with you, but I will not be a burden to you. I have been turned out, with prejudice. To be crass, I have no money, and will have to make my way from the start . . ."

"As to that," said *Grand-père*, putting his glass aside and reaching into his vest. "I have been charged by the commander with a sum of money, which I am to give to my grandchild Serana. It is quite a considerable sum, which surprised me. I had privately considered Watch Captain Benoit something of a spendthrift. It pleases me to have been proved wrong."

He brought forth a fat wallet, and held it out to her.

Serana stared, first at the wallet, then into his eyes.

"Mathilde *agrees* to this?" she demanded.

"My child, Mathilde *proposed* this," *Grand-père* corrected, and smiled his particular, crooked smile. "She's coming along well, I think."

"So you see," said Don Eyr; "you need not be a burden, and, as you are well-funded, you may take your own decision, and not be . . . *beholden* to me."

She looked down into his eyes. His were grave.

"Serana, I would like you to come with me."

She took a breath.

"And I would like to do so," she said. "Do you think there is any possibility that I will be able to buy a berth on the ship you will be traveling on?"

"There is no need," Don Eyr said comfortably. "I hired a stateroom; there is room for both of us."

She blinked.

"You did this—when?"

"When I made my original reservations. All you need do is buy your passage."

Grand-père laughed, and rubbed his hands together.

"I like him, Serana! A man who knows what he wants, and pursues it, though others call him mad! I will miss *both* of you, in truth. And, now—"

The House bell rang—evening muster, that would be, thought Serana.

"Now," she said; "I must go."

"I fear so," said *Grand-père*. "Take the wallet, child. You will find a pack at the service gate—your clothes and other personal belongings. Take that, as well."

"Yes," she said, and rose, Don Eyr beside her.

She slipped the wallet into an inner pocket; bent and kissed the old man's cheek.

"Farewell, *Grand-père*; I will never forget you."

He patted her cheek, wordless for once. Serana stepped back–and Don Eyr went forward, bending to kiss the withered cheek in his turn.

"Farewell, *Grand-père*," he said softly. "Thank you."

"Ah, child, would that we had longer, you and I! Take care of my Serana." A soft touch to the cheek, and a small shove against his shoulder.

"Go, now, both of you."

#

She fitted herself handily into his modest rooms, his quiet life. His associates in the school had long since become used to her occasional presence, and gave no sign that they noticed she was about more frequently these few last days.

She had some idea that she might assist him with his preparations, but there was not much to pack, and only a few things to give away. There was also a study-at-home kit that he dragged out of the bottom of the armoire, and stood for a moment, considering it ruefully.

"What is it?" Serana asked him.

"*The Liaden Code of Proper Conduct*," he answered, his eyes still on the kit. "My clan required that I make a study of it while I was being schooled here, as I would have done if I had remained at home."

"And did you study it?" she asked, eyeing the kit with new interest.

"Oh, yes; I learned and passed every level. Then I put it away, and I fear that I have forgotten everything. There was no one to discuss it with, and I saw no need to continue after I had mastered the basics."

He threw a grin over his shoulder at her.

"Nor any need to make a review. My manner, I fear, cannot but offend."

"You have beautiful manners," Serana said, faintly shocked to hear this estimation. "And your presentation is pleasing."

"Thank you," he said, giving the box one last stare, and turning to face her.

"Will you bring it with you?" she asked, she having taken charge of such packing as there was to do.

"It is a resource, I suppose. Ezhel'ti is a composite world–Liaden and Terran. Were I Terran, I expect my ignorance would be excused. As I am Liaden, I fear I will be held to a higher standard." He sighed suddenly. "I will spend time on the journey, learning Liaden. I have been speaking and thinking in Lutetian for twelve Standards, and I fear I've forgotten the modes entirely."

"We will practice together," said Serana; "I have ordered in a study pack for my own use, and a bundle of what purport to be *genuine melant'i plays*. Between it and your Code, we will be very busy. And here I had dreamed of a voyage spent almost entirely in bed . . ."

He laughed.

"We might study in bed, after all."

"Yes," she agreed, with a slow smile, "so we might."

It was pleasant, living thus; and the best part of the day occurred in the dark hours just before dawn, when he rose to start the day's baking.

She asked if she might accompany him–and succeeded in surprising him.

"There is nothing to see; only me, working."

"But I have never seen you, baking," Serana said, having discovered a desire in herself to observe him at every daily action. "I will be quiet and stand out of the way."

He was silent for so long that she knew the answer would be *no* when he spoke. But he in turn surprised her.

"There are stools, and tea," he told her, and added, perhaps to be clear, "Yes, you may come."

#

It was a pleasure like none Serana had ever known, to sit quietly, and sip her tea, watching him at his work. He was calm, he was competent; he was unhurried and utterly concentrated. The universe held still and respectful while Dan Eyr worked, and during this sacred time, no ill was permitted to intrude upon Lutetia.

She watched him for hours, and never once grew bored. It seemed to her that she might watch him for years, and be nothing other than content.

At the end of it, the sun up, and the kitchen nearly too warm, he would surrender his creations to the over-manager, and Serana would slip out to await him in the hall. They would go up to his rooms together, hand-in-hand, to make and eat their breakfast. Often, they would not care to break the silence, and she felt no lack for it.

This morning, however, the pattern varied.

An envelope had been shoved under the door while they were away. Don Eyr bent to retrieve it, and carried it into the kitchen, leaving it on the table as they put together a simple meal.

It was not until they were seated, tea poured and bread buttered, that he noticed it again—she saw him read the envelope—start—and read it again, more closely.

"Is there something wrong?" she asked.

"Nothing more than unusual," he said, picking the envelope up. "I have a letter from—from my delm."

The old man who hated the fact of him, who had sent him among strangers, careless of whether he might fail or thrive; more surely an orphan than she had ever been.

"Has he never written you before?"

"No, never," Don Eyr said, apparently finding nothing strange in this. "Mr. dea'Bon writes, and once, after I had first come here, Mrs. ban'Teli wrote. No one else."

If he found nothing strange, at least he found nothing dreadful, either. Serana lifted the teapot and refilled his cup.

Don Eyr slit the envelope open with a butter knife, and removed a single sheet of paper.

He stared at it, frowning, and she recalled his concern that he had forgotten his native tongue, having had so little use for it . . .

"I am–called home," Don Eyr said, sounding, for the first time in their acquaintance, uncertain. He looked up to meet her eyes. "Back to Liad, that is. I am to come immediately."

"Why such haste?"

"He does not say, merely to come at once; the clan has need of–oh."

She saw the blush mount his cheeks as his mouth tightened, and he raised his head again to meet her eyes.

"Oh?" she asked.

"Yes. I think I see. He has arranged a marriage for me–I can think of nothing else he might mean by *of use to the clan*."

"He has arranged a marriage?" Serana repeated. Her stomach ached, as if she had taken a punch. "But–would he not at least write you the name of your wife?"

"Not necessarily. In fact, it would be very like him to think it no concern of mine." He glanced back at the letter, mouth tight, folded it, slid it into the envelope, and put the envelope on the table, address down.

He picked up his tea cup.

Serana carefully released the breath she had been holding. He was going to ignore this peremptory and rude summoning. Well, of course he was! What hold had the old man over him, now?

"I think," Don Eyr said slowly, "that we must change our plans, somewhat. You will go to Ezhel'ti, if you would, and see the house put to order, perhaps look about for a proper location for the *boulangerie*."

"Will I?" she said, watching him. "And where will you go, little one?"

He blinked at her.

"I? I will go to Liad, as my delm has ordered, and be of use to the clan. When the marriage is finished, I will join you on Ezhel'ti."

He said it so calmly, as if it made perfect sense. As if the scheming old man was his patron, and must, therefore, be obeyed!

"When do you expect that the marriage will be finished?" she asked, calm in her turn.

He moved his shoulders.

"If I recall my Code correctly, which is not very likely; a contract marriage lasts a Liaden year, on average. It ends when the child is born, and has been accepted into the receiving clan."

He sent her a shrewd glance.

"It is an alliance the delm wants. An alliance that would be good for the clan, else he would not pursue it, but not . . . grand enough to marry out the nadelm."

He was so certain about this marriage, she thought, as if there were no possibility of it going wrong. Well, she had promised to be suspicious for him, had she not?

"I will go with you," she said, nodding at the letter.

Don Eyr blinked at her.

"Serana, I do not think that you would . . . like . . ." he began, and she leaned forward to lay a finger across his lips.

"I would not like that you were bedding another woman? You are correct. However, we have not promised each other monogamy, and if you must marry to seal a good alliance for your clan; I believe I may accommodate that. It will be far better if I am with you, little one. You have lost the way of the homeworld, and will need someone on your off-side."

His lips bent into an ironic smile.

"I have undoubtedly forgotten much. But Serana, I have forgotten things you have never known!"

"Ah, but *I* do not need to know! I am a barbarian, as anyone can see by looking at me. In fact, I am your bodyguard, such being the custom of Lutetia."

She leaned forward, and put her hand over his, holding his eyes with hers.

"Don Eyr. *Petit*. Can you not ignore this . . . *summons*?"

He drew a breath.

"I think not–no."

"So, you will go to Liad, and accomplish this duty your delm demands of you?"

"Yes," he said, though not with any eagerness.

"Very well. If that is what you will do, then I will come with you."

Silence.

Serana took a deep, quiet breath.

"If you do not want me, only say so, little one."

His free hand came to rest atop hers.

"But I *cannot* say so, Serana," he said. He leaned forward and brushed his lips across hers.

"Come, then," he murmured; "I want you."

Three

Liad

The *melant'i* plays that Serana had purchased had proved a valuable resource, giving insight into how the *Liaden Code of Proper Conduct* might—and might not—be used to one's own advantage.

For instance, the *Code* stated only that a child of the clan summoned home by the delm may enter the house by the front door, which would seem adamantine.

However, the *melant'i* plays illustrated the power of *may*.

May permitted choice, and thus Don Eyr paid off the taxi at the corner, and walked round to the servant's door, where, as a child, he had been accustomed to going and coming, so as not to risk affronting the delm with his presence.

Serana, in her guise as his bodyguard, walked half-a-step behind his left shoulder.

He found the small door in the wall, and pressed his palm against the plate. There came a small click, and he stepped inside, Serana ducking in behind him.

He made certain the door had sealed, then paused to take his bearings.

"The kitchen," he said, looking up at her, "is to the left."

She gave him a smile, and he started forward—and stopped as a woman stepped quickly out of the left-hand hallway.

She was a neat, elderly woman, her grey hair in a knot at the back of her head. She was wearing a house uniform of puce and green—Serat's colors.

"Who–" she began; and stopped, staring.

"Mrs. ban'Teli," he said, showing her his empty hands. "It is Don Eyr."

"So it ever was, Don Eyr," she said, coming forward to put her hands in his. "You look well, but–Child, whatever are you doing here?"

"The delm has called me home," he said, smiling at her.

"Has he?" This seemed to concern her; her fingers tensed on his. "Why?"

"He forgot to put down the reason in his letter," he said lightly, noting that she was trembling slightly, and also that the collar of her uniform was somewhat frayed, and her apron had been carefully mended with thread that did not quite match.

"You are a son of the House," Mrs. ban'Teli said then. "You should come in by the front door."

"Yes, and so I would have done," Don Eyr assured her, "save that I wished to see you first, and also to ask if you will give my poor Serana some tea in the kitchen, while I go to the delm."

He stepped slightly aside, and Serana came forward, offering a very nice bow.

"Madame," she said, gently, in her Letitian-accented Liaden. "I have heard much about you, and am pleased to meet you at last."

Mrs. ban'Teli performed a quick inventory, eyes bright, and bowed in her turn.

She looked back to Don Eyr.

"I will be pleased to bring your companion to the kitchen and see her comfortable," she said, which was also, he thought, a promise to ask many questions. That was expectable; he and Serana had agreed between them that all such questions would be met with truth. The kitchen staff did not bore the delm with the business of the kitchen.

"Come," said Mrs. ban'Teli, "both of you. We will see Lady Serana settled, and for you, sir, we will call Mr. pak'Epron, who will guide you properly to the delm. He is in his study with the papers, so it is likely that he would not have heard the bell in any case."

#

Serat sat behind a desk covered in the racing papers. So much was unchanged from Don Eyr's memories of the delm. He looked up with considerable irritation when Mr. pak'Epron said quietly, "Master Don Eyr, sir."

"Go away," Serat said, and Mr. pak'Epron did so. Despite his inclinations, Don Eyr did not go away, but walked toward the desk and the two chairs set there. One was piled high with even more racing sheets, but the other was–

"Stop there!" snapped Serat. "I have not given you leave to approach!"

Don Eyr stopped, and stood, hands folded neatly before him. He took a deep breath, and waited for further instructions.

"Does your delm merit no bow?"

Ah, yes, thought Don Eyr; he was in violation of courtesy. No wonder the old man was testy.

He produced the required bow–clanmember to delm–and straightened, murmuring, "Serat," in as neutral a tone as he could manage.

The old man glared at him.

"Why are you come?"

Don Eyr felt a tremble along his nerves. Had the old man forgotten? Could he, in fact, have merely ignored that peremptory letter and gone about his life?

Too late now to know the answers to those questions. Don Eyr inclined his head slightly, and said, quietly.

"You sent for me, sir."

There was a sniff.

"And you came. Remarkable. Your mother refused to come home when our delm sent for her. He froze her accounts, but she continued to disobey. Afraid, of course; she had already lost most of the clan's investments." He paused, looking Don Eyr up and down.

"You might have dressed to the delm's honor, but I suppose this is the best an impecunious student might do. Also, your accent is deplorable, which I suppose is expectable. However! I will have the proper mode from you, sirrah! That, at least, you will produce correctly. Abra is a stickler for such things and you will not give him insult! Am I plain?"

"No, sir," said Don Eyr, perhaps unwisely.

Papers crinkled as the old man's fingers closed on the sheets layering his desk.

"Are you defying me?"

"I do not see how I might do so, sir. Surely defiance may only follow comprehension," Don Eyr answered, keeping the mode in mind.

"Stupid, too," said Serat, and Don Eyr took a breath, thinking of Serana in the kitchen, sharing tea with Mrs. ban'Teli.

It was not, he told himself, unjust. He *had* been stupid, and Serana had been correct: He need not have come.

He thought then of the portions of the house he had seen on his way from the kitchens. It seemed that everything was shabby–worn, and that in at least one room there were signs that a rather large painting had been removed from the wall, and a piece of furniture, as well.

Serat needs this marriage, he thought then, not for alliance, but for money.

"What is it that I am required to do for the clan?" he asked, rather as if he were addressing a recalcitrant student than the delm of Serat.

The old man across the desk stared him up and down.

"You are required to go to Abra's house in the city and place yourself at his service. You are to say that you stand the payment of Serat's debt, which is now cleared."

"Am I to be married, then?" Don Eyr asked, his recent perusal of the Code having given him the very distinct notion that there were proprieties to be followed, papers to be filed . . .

"Married? No. Go away."

Serat was bent over his papers again; Don Eyr was already forgotten. Or perhaps not.

He bowed to the delm's honor, turned and let himself out of the study, closing the door quietly behind him.

He closed his eyes, took three deep breaths, opened his eyes and saw a figure hovering discreetly near the archway into the main hall.

"Mr. pak'Epron."

"Yes, Master Don Eyr."

"Is my cousin Vyk Tor in the house?"

"Yes, sir."

"Good," said Don Eyr. "Please take me to him."

#

"Cousin Don Eyr."

Like his uncle, his cousin Vyk Tor was also found behind a desk smothered in paper–though these seemed to be business documents, and files, some on the letterhead of Mr. dea'Bon's office.

"May I give you a glass of wine?" his cousin asked, rising.

Don Eyr sighed.

"Thank you, a glass of wine would be most welcome," he said.

"You've been to see Father, then," said Vyk Tor, crossing the room to the wine table.

Don Eyr considered the small office, finding the same signs of shabbiness and deferred maintenance that were apparent elsewhere in the house.

His cousin turned from the table, glasses in hand, and moved toward the table and chairs set before the large window.

"Let us sit here," he said. "The prospect is slightly more pleasing than my desk."

Don Eyr joined him, took the offered glass, and sipped, automatically judging the vintage, and finding it—surprisingly—mundane.

He frowned slightly. His memory was that Serat had demanded expensive wines at table. A vintage such as this . . .

"The wine offends?"

He gave his cousin a frank look, remembering too late that to stare boldly into a man's face was to be rude.

"The wine—surprises," he said, and sank into the chair. His cousin stiffened, then relaxed and took his own chair.

"Understand," Don Eyr said, "I have spent the last dozen Standards learning wines and foods, in a culture that values wine and food . . . very much."

Vyk Tor tipped his head.

"I thought we had sent you to be a baker."

"That, too," Don Eyr said composedly. "One must certify for three specialties before one is permitted to graduate."

"I had not known the curriculum was so . . . rigorous," said his cousin, drinking deeply.

"The Lutetia *École de Cuisine* is a premier school. Their graduates go on to become chefs in the houses of queens, and in the great restaurants of the universe. Or," he raised his glass, "they found great restaurants."

"And you, have you founded your restaurant?"

"I was on my way to found a *boulangerie* on Ezhelt'i when Serat called me home. Now that I am here, I am bewildered. It seems I am not to marry for the advantage of the clan, but what I am meant to do eludes me."

Vyk Tor sighed.

"You must forgive Father," he began, and stopped at Don Eyr's sharp movement.

"No," he said, taking a deep breath against the growing anger; "I am not required to forgive Serat. Indeed, I begin to question whether I am required to obey him."

"Surely you are required to obey him!" his cousin said sharply. "He is the delm! The clan has brought you into adulthood; and seen you educated, and nourished!"

"So it has," said Don Eyr, dryly, and decided upon a change of topic.

"I missed a painting in the withdrawing room, when Mr. pak'Epron guided me to the delm; and it seemed also a divan had been removed. Is the house being remodeled?"

"The House," his cousin said, on the sharp edge of a sigh, "is foundering. I found by going through the clan's past finances that Father has always gambled. In fact, he lost his private fortune some years ago. That was when he began gambling with Serat's fortune."

Don Eyr stared at him.

"The *qe'andra* did not prevent him?"

"The *qe'andra* are in the clan's employ. Mr. dea'Bon withdrew himself, when it became apparent that Father would not abstain, but his heir . . . did not. We are not quite run off our legs, but we have had to embrace–" He raised his wine glass–"economies, as well as selling off certain items of value."

He drank, finishing the glass, and put it on the table.

"Thank the gods, we have not yet been required to sell our business interests."

Don Eyr put his glass on the table.

"Can you not curb him?"

His cousin looked at him with interest.

"How would you suggest I do that?"

This was familiar ground; many of the plays he and Serana had watched turned on points of honor between delm and nadelm.

"You are the nadelm. Surely, if the delm is not able–or endangers the clan . . ."

He stopped because his cousin was laughing.

"I have been able to move some of the businesses, and some of our stocks, into the nadelm's honor. I made a bolder throw, for all of our finances, and Father felt it necessary to tell me that he would declare me dead if I continued in my grasping ways."

He moved a hand–wearily, thought Don Eyr.

"Dead, I can do nothing. If I remain, at least I can do . . . something."

There was for the moment, silence. Don Eyr looked at his half-empty wine glass. Did not pick it up.

"In any case, that is where you come in, Cousin. Our funding is insufficient to pay off Abra's amount, but he agrees to accept one of Clan Serat to do such errands as might be assigned, at the compensation rate for unskilled labor, minus the costs of food and lodging, until such time as the debt has been balanced."

Don Eyr sat, feeling the blood roar in his ears, thinking of the house on Ezhel'ti; the clan of his father, which had been willing to acknowledge him.

Of Serana.

Gods, Serana.

"The delm has sold me to pay off his gambling debts," he said, his voice flat, and without mode.

"In a word," his cousin said; "yes."

* * *

They were taken in to Mr. dea'Bon without delay; the butler announcing them in soft, respectful tones.

"Lord Don Eyr fer'Gasta Clan Serat. Captain Serana Benoit."

The old man rose from behind his desk and bowed, to Serana's eye, with proper respect for her small one.

"Your Lordship," he said, and there was respect in the soft voice, too; a certain fondness in the gaze that she might have missed, had she not seen the *melant'i* plays.

Don Eyr raised a hand.

"Certainly, I am no lordship," he began, and the old gentleman raised a hand in turn.

"Certainly, you are; and I am delighted to be at your service. You're looking well, sir."

He might have argued, save his temper was already fully engaged, and the old gentleman was in no way its target. Serana was informed; she had not previously been privileged to see Don Eyr *angry*. To know that he was not only capable of righteous rage, but remained its master–those things were good to know.

So, no argument, but a bow, less deep than the one he had received, because, so Serana deduced, the old gentleman would have it that way.

"I am pleased to see you again, sir; I only wish it might be under happier circumstances."

"Ah." The old gentleman looked wise. "You come to me from Serat."

He glanced at the butler, who remained in the doorway.

"Wine and a tray, if you will, Mr. ben'Darble. Lord Don Eyr and Captain Benoit are doubtless in need of refreshment after a trying afternoon."

"Sir." The butler bowed and was gone, closing the door silently behind him.

"I am remiss," her small one said then, and extended a hand to bring her forward. "This is Serana Benoit. You may speak to her as to myself."

It was a phrase from the plays. They had supposed, between them, that it had signaled a trust that went beyond mere clan connections, and thus seldom found favor with the delms of drama. Certainly, it meant something more than mere words to the old gentleman.

He was not so unsubtle as to raise even an eyebrow, but he considered her now with interest, rather than merely courtesy. She bowed, as would a Watch Captain to a solid citizen.

"Sir."

"Captain Benoit; I am honored," he said, returning her bow precisely.

Straightening, he spoke again to Don Eyr.

"By your goodness, my lord–Captain–sit; take your ease. I know something of why you have come, I think. Be assured that my service is to you; not Serat, nor the nadelm. You may speak frankly to me. Everything you say will remain in this room, in the memory of we three; and recorded in my personal client files, which I share with no one, except on those same terms of confidentiality."

Don Eyr sighed; moved toward the chair at the right side of the old gentleman's desk, and paused to look to her.

She gave him a smile and a nod.

"I am well, here," she said, sliding into the too-small chair, and folding her legs expertly under her.

He smiled, faintly, and seated himself, whereupon the tray arrived and was disposed. The butler, assured that they could, indeed, look after themselves, left them, closing the door silently behind. The old gentleman poured wine; they sipped, Serana noting Don Eyr's shoulders softening somewhat as he tasted the vintage.

His glass set to one side, the old gentleman leaned back in his chair, looked to Don Eyr, and said, simply, "Tell me."

\#

Don Eyr wilted somewhat in his chair, weary with the telling. The old gentleman steepled his fingers, his gaze abstracted. Serana, not wishing to disturb a genius at his work, but unwilling to see her *petit* in need, rose, refreshed all three glasses, and placed two of the delicate sandwiches on the plate at Don Eyr's hand.

He smiled up at her.

"Thank you," he murmured in Lutetian.

"It is nothing; do not exhaust yourself before the battle."

She laid a hand on his shoulder, pressing for a moment before returning to her own chair and meeting the old gentleman's eyes.

He inclined his head gravely and turned to Don Eyr.

"Serat's actions are by Code. They are deplorable, but the Code does not disallow. The resources of the clan are for the delm to dispense. I will mention that this is the precise paragraph which Serat quotes . . . often . . . to justify his use of the clan's funds."

The old gentleman reached for his wine glass.

"Therefore, there is nothing for either the *qe'andra* nor the Council to take up."

Serana felt her own anger, well-banked against the hour when it would be useful to her–and to him–flicker and flare. In his chair, Don Eyr drew a breath, but said nothing.

The old gentleman inclined his head.

"We do, yes, have hope that the contract may be broken–not by you, but by Abra."

"You think that Delm Abra will not accept my service?" Don Eyr said, the accent of home gilding his mode. "I will be delighted to present myself in the worst possible light."

The old man smiled.

"Indeed, you must present yourself as you are–a lord in the delm's line, second only to the nadelm of Serat. You are an honorable man."

He sipped his wine, and set the glass side.

"Abra, I fear, is *not* an honorable man. For proof, we have the record of his many fines paid to the Council for violations of Code. You must be vigilant. When he breaks with the Code, as he will do, you must relay this breach to me, so that I may act on your behalf."

"Is it so certain that he will violate the Code?" Don Eyr asked, brows drawn.

The old gentleman smiled.

"With Abra, it is as if the Code is an enemy he must strike at again and again. He is no more able to help himself than Serat can refrain from placing wagers. All you need do is wait, and be vigilant."

Serana stirred. Don Eyr and Mr. dea'Bon turned to her.

"Is he dangerous, this man?" she asked.

"One of the fines Abra paid was to the Guild of *Qe'andra*, for the death of an apprentice. The child had found a second set of books, and was, as required by the protocols of his house and those of the Guild, in the process of documenting the incident. Abra ordered him to stop; the child stated that he was not able to do so. Abra struck him . . ."

There was a small pause; the old gentleman extended a hand to toy with his glass.

". . . and killed him. Abra paid the life-price without protest, which I think is telling in itself."

"Yes," said Serana. "I have known such men. Thank you."

"Of course."

Don Eyr had gathered himself once more, sitting alert in his chair.

"Thank you, sir. I am grateful for your time and insights. I ask."

"By all means, sir. I will answer to the best of my ability."

"I am long away from the Code, alas, but it is my understanding that I may become dead to the clan. I wish this to occur as speedily as possible."

"Ah."

The old gentleman's smile was edged with regret.

"The only person who may declare a clan member dead is the delm. In this case, I think we may agree that Serat will do no such thing. Also, having obeyed the summons to return, you are now in the position of having accepted the Delm's Word. If you should simply leave, after having been instructed in your duty by the delm, you will be pursued, arrested, and brought back."

He paused, and spread his palms.

"The Council has much precedent for this, I fear."

Silence, before Don Eyr bowed his head and gathered himself to rise. Serana ached to hold him; the busy mind had produced the best solution for this absurd situation–and it had been checked and blocked. Don Eyr was not accustomed to losing, Serana realized abruptly. The relative modesty of his goals had kept this aspect of his nature hidden, until now.

"I think your lordship was not given his suite at Serat's clanhouse for the night?" said Mr. dea'Bon delicately.

Don Eyr tipped his head to one side.

"I was not. Apparently, Abra is to provide all things for me."

"Yet, as little as Abra values virtue, he does value courtesy, though neither so much as his own comfort. If you will allow me to advise you once more, I would suggest that you send a note around by one of my house's staff, stating that you will wait upon Delm Abra tomorrow in the early afternoon. This will insure he is not wakened too early in the day, which may lead to bad temper. Also, if you wish, you and Captain Benoit may partake of the hospitality of *this* House, where you may rest easy tonight."

Don Eyr bowed, abruptly. Serana thought it might have been done to hide an excess of emotion.

"You are far too good to us, sir."

"That would be difficult. Now, if you please, I will call Mr. ben'Darble to show the way to your . . ."

He paused, delicately, and Don Eyr murmured.

"Room, if you please, sir."

"Indeed. Mr. ben'Darble will show you to your suite. I very much hope that you will join us for the prime meal, but if you prefer, it will be brought to you."

He stood and bowed.

"Please," he said, and Serana felt tears prick her eyelids. "Be welcome in our House."

* * *

If Abra's house was too fine for the street it graced, Abra was too fine for the house. Or, Serana thought darkly, so he wished to appear. Certainly, he dressed well, with many small jewels glittering about his person, and rings on his fingers. His hair was pale brown, as if he had left it too long in the sun; extravagantly curled, and perfumed. His face was long, his mouth cruel, and his chin weak. At the moment, he was . . . amused; coolly so. It must seem to him, Serana thought, that Don Eyr was the merest sweet morsel, which he must be careful not to consume too quickly.

"Now, it seems to me that Serat and I had agreed that I would accept the service of Telma fer'Gasta's by-blow in payment for his debt. I do not recall mention of a . . . *pet*, and I can assure you that I will neither feed it nor pay it."

Don Eyr remained calm in the face of these insults, which were of course meant to touch him and try him. It was well, Serana thought, that he did so, though it would only mean that Abra would strike harder, next time.

"Sir," she said, stepping forward, and speaking as if she had much less of the language than she did. "I am Serana Benoit. I am Lord Don Eyr's bodyguard, and I have been paid, sir, with the money upfront, for a contract of seven years. There are yet five years remaining on this contract, and so I am here."

He stared at her, the cruel mouth thin with distaste. Serana returned his regard, mildly, until at last, he turned away and spoke to Don Eyr.

"A bodyguard?"

Don Eyr bowed.

"All high-ranking Lutetian persons employ a bodyguard."

"I was told you were a baker."

Don Eyr said nothing.

"I repeat that I will not feed it," Abra said after a moment.

"You need not feed me, sir," said Serana. "I account my expenses, and my lord pays them. It is in the contract. Perhaps sir would like to see it?"

Abra drew a hard breath, but did not turn his head. Once more, he addressed Don Eyr. "You will instruct it not to speak to me."

Don Eyr bowed, briefly, and Serana thought she saw the flicker of a knife in that gesture.

"Serana," he said, turning to face her, and speaking in the mode known as Comrade. "You are relieved of the burden of his lordship's conversation. Please do not speak to him directly, as it agitates his *melant'i*."

He turned back to Abra, and met his eyes.

"His lordship will naturally refrain from addressing you," he continued, "as I am certain that doing so must also distress him extremely."

Abra's eyes were cold, his beringed fingers were tight on the arm of his chair. He inclined his head gracefully, however.

"We come now to the matter of your domestic arrangements. As you are my servant, a room has been set aside for you in the servant's wing."

He paused, perhaps to savor an anticipated protest, as this was, Serana saw, yet another insult.

Don Eyr inclined his head slightly, face attentive.

"You will take your meals with the servants," Abra continued after a moment, his cruel mouth tight.

"As I am your servant," Don Eyr murmured. "Exactly so."

That was perhaps an error, to have shown so much spirit. Abra's eyes gleamed, and he gave a curt nod.

"You are dismissed. I will be going out this evening. You will wait upon me. I will summon you when I am ready to leave."

With that, he turned his back on them, pretending to busy himself at his screen.

Don Eyr bowed, turned and let them out, closing the door very quietly behind them.

"Now the question becomes," he said softly in Lutetian, "which is more amusing, to have us caught as thieves in his house, or showing all the world his new possession?"

"Surely," Serana answered, "he will go for the long game, that man."

"Indeed. Now–ah."

He stepped quickly to a small side hall, and looked inside. The woman who had let them in stood there, impassive, but clearly interested.

"Good day to you," Don Eyr said easily in Comrade. "I am new in his lordship's employ. He has graciously granted me and my household a room in the servant's wing. Will you teach me how to arrive there?"

The butler stirred slightly, and Serana saw her weighing which course would anger her master more–to aid the newcomer or to allow him to wander the house. Commonsense decided the day, or a realization of proper duty. In any case, she offered a small nod.

"I will show you," she said.

* * *

It was a small room, though not nearly as rude as he had prepared himself to entertain. It was not, however, kind to Serana's proportions.

"Well," she said, good-naturedly, "at least here I may lose myself entirely in passion."

He considered her.

"How so?"

"Why, I will not have to constantly be aware of the eaves, and their proximity to my head. Only think how we may soar, now that my attention will not be divided."

"Of course," he said, politely. "But, consider, Serana, the size of this room, not only of the bed. It is not a hovel, but I would not see you here. We shall ask Mr. dea'Bon to find you a more fitting apartment..."

"If this place fits you, it fits me," Serana interrupted him. She leaned forward and touched his cheek. "Little one, accept that I will not leave you alone in that man's hand. He does not want a servant; he wants a whipping boy. It will please him to taunt you. Already he insults your birth."

"No," said Don Eyr; "he is nothing more than factual. I was not born from a proper contract, nor was I caught at Festival. I am the product of an affair of pleasure, whom my mother decided to regularize."

"In fact, you were born of love," said Serana.

He smiled.

"In fact, you are a woman of Lutetia," he answered her. "And, indeed–it is Abra's error, that he attempts to diminish my *melant'i*. As the plays teach us–we each know the value of our own *melant'i*."

He took a breath.

"I am not, however, certain of my answer, the next time he insults *you*."

"But he will not insult me again! I have been instructed not to speak to him, and he has been instructed not to speak to me."

"He takes my instruction exactly so much as you do," he said, sounding bitter in his own ears. "Serana, this . . . this *gallimaufry* is nothing of yours. I would not see you waste your life. You are made for–for bold ventures, and fair. This is . . . drab and dreary, and–wholly unworthy of you."

She smiled at him, and he knew he would not win this argument. Oh, he could send her away. All he needed do was tell her that he did not want her and she would remove herself immediately. The words settled on the edge of his tongue. He would tell her–*Serana, I do not want you.* She would leave him to pursue her own life, free of this stupid circumstance he had brought her to . . .

And, yet . . . he could not bring the lie to his lips.

"Come," she said cheerfully, "let us find the kitchen, and see what arrangements might be made."

"Arrangements?" he asked, his heart aching.

"Indeed. You have not had your luncheon, and if that man is feeding you, he can begin now."

#

The kitchen they found easily enough by following their noses. Don Eyr paused on the threshold, Serana at his back, and surveyed the area, pleased to find it clean and well-appointed, with proper stations, staffed appropriately.

He felt some of the tension leave him, soothed by this display of orderly busyness.

"May I help you . . . sir?"

The grizzled over-chef was approaching, wiping his hands on a towel, looking from him to Serana. Plainly, he had not been told about the new servant and his bodyguard, Don Eyr thought. And, plainly, it suited the master's whim to make the assimilation of the new servant into his household as difficult as possible.

"I am Don Eyr fer'Gasta," he said, bowing to the chef's honor; "newly arrived to serve Delm Abra. This is my companion, Serana Benoit. One was told that the house would feed me, and I have come to speak with you regarding the necessities of the kitchen, so that I do not impede your work."

The over-chef was . . . puzzled, but gracious.

"I had not been informed of your arrival," he said. "The house is sometimes not so forthcoming with the kitchen as one would wish. We are preparing Prime, but surely there is food at the staff table. I will show you. My name is Mae Nir vas'Urbil."

"It was Abra's word," Serana said as they crossed the busy kitchen toward a window at the back, "that he will not feed me, as I am not employed by the house, but am here on Don Eyr's account."

Chef vas'Urbil frowned.

"I recall now," he said, looking closely at Don Eyr's face. "You're the lad Serat lost at cards."

Don Eyr bowed gently, not slackening his pace.

"Here. We keep this area stocked for staff; you may eat at any hour that duty does not claim you." He glanced at Serana. "*Both* of you. Abra has not given me any instructions regarding new servants in the house, and this kitchen can feed two more as easily as one."

"You are kind," Don Eyr murmured.

Chef vas'Urbil moved a hand.

"I am efficient, and I keep within budget. That is what Abra cares about. Now–"

A lamentation rose from a far corner of the kitchen.

"The bread!" cried a voice. "Ah, the bread!"

Don Eyr was moving before he recalled that this was not his kitchen to oversee, and by then, he had arrived at the ovens, and the lamenting under-baker there.

"What is the difficulty?" asked the chef, who had arrived at Don Eyr's shoulder.

"The bread, sir; it did not rise. And there is no time to begin again. I–"

"When is Prime?" asked Don Eyr.

"In two hours," said Chef vas'Urbil.

"May I assist?" Don Eyr asked. "I do not wish to disorder your kitchen. This, however, is my work; I am trained in bread."

"Who trained you?"

"I have graduated from *École de Cuisine* at Lutetia."

Chef vas'Urbil blinked.

Then, he waved a hand.

"If you know what to do, Baker, by all means, do it. I have a kitchen to oversee."

"Yes," said Don Eyr and turned to the weeping under-baker, feeling very much in his element, even to the point of calming an overwrought student.

"What we shall do is make *petit pain*," he told her. She stared at him.

"Sir?"

"Small breads," he said briskly. "They rise once, and bake quickly. We have time enough; and they will arrive pleasingly hot at the table."

"I do not–"

"I will demonstrate," he told her, moving around the station, and plucking an apron from a hook.

"What is your name?"

"Zelli, sir."

"Well, Zelli, my name is Don Eyr. I have done this many times before, and can assure you that we are in no danger of failing. Is the mixer clean and ready?"

"Yes, sir."

"Good. Now attend me . . ."

* * *

Serana started up from the chair where she had been reading.

"Tell me he did not do this."

Don Eyr sat on the edge of the bed. His face hurt, and his pride, though he had not been struck in public. He was not accustomed to being struck. Worse, it had taken every ounce of his will, not to strike back.

"Of course, he did it," he said now to Serana. "It is his right, is it not? The Code and the plays teach us that a delm may do what the delm pleases to all members of the clan, including taking their lives. My delm gave me into Abra's care."

"He will not live to strike you again," Serana said calmly.

He looked up sharply.

"Go," he said, his voice harsh. "Leave me now."

Shock etched her face.

"Don Eyr–"

He held up a hand.

"I will not be the instrument of your ruin! I will not see you tarnish yourself. I will not–"

His voice broke, and to his own horror, he began to cry.

Serana turned abruptly, and left the room, the door closing behind her.

Don Eyr gasped.

"Good," he said raggedly, and bent over until his forehead rested on his knees. He tried to regulate his breathing, to master the tears, to–

Serana was gone. He was alone. It was well; he ought to send to Mr. dea'Bon, to be certain that she had passage wherever she wished to go. The house on Ezhel'ti was hers, he would make it so, if she wished to establish herself there, or to–

The door cycled. Gentle hands were on his shoulders.

"Sit up, *petit;* allow me to examine this bruise. Here. Here is ice, and I have also some salve which is recommended to me by the night cook. A tray will be brought, wine, cheese, and fruits. We shall make a merry feast, eh?"

He jerked under the soft pressure of her fingers.

"He did not withhold himself, I see. First, the ice, then the salve. . ."

The cold stung, then numbed.

"Serana—you must go."

"Indeed, little one, I must not. You have the right of it; to kill this man would not be at all clever. I give you my word that I will not kill him. May I remain?"

He reached out, half-blind with weeping, and touched her lips.

"I am weak. Yes, Serana. Please stay."

* * *

For the first relumma of service, Abra was content to take Don Eyr on his evening rounds of pleasure, explaining to everyone he met who his servant was and how he had come into Abra's service. This generated much gossip, which Abra was certain would discommode his new toy, especially the betting pool regarding the exact day and time when Serat crumbled under the weight of its own debts and was written out of the Book of Clans, and the rumors regarding Don Eyr's mother.

After that sport had worn thin, Don Eyr was given various menial tasks that took him to the borders of Low and Mid-Port, Abra having ownership of many of the most disreputable houses on that border. He was always glad to have Serana with him, but especially so on these errands, where he felt her long, competent presence was everything that prevented him being robbed.

There were periods when he was "on-call"–constrained to remain in the house and await the master's word. These might have lain heavier on him had there not been the kitchen, and the beginning of a friendship between himself and Mae Nir vas'Urbil. He was welcome in the kitchen at any time, to teach, or to create whatever pleased him. Those creations went to the staff room, and thus he won the goodwill, if not the friendship, of staff.

On the occasions when they both had an hour free, Don Eyr and Mae Nir would sit at study, the over-chef having produced a book of recipes from the *Lutetia École de Cuisine*, translated to Liaden from Lutetian. Serana gathered that the translation was inadequate to the utmost, and Don Eyr spent much time explaining–and occasionally demonstrating–certain techniques which had not translated *at all*.

For her part, Serana taught those of the staff who wished to learn disengages, and feints. It seemed Abra's guests were not always of impeccable *melant'i*, and sometimes went so far as to touch that which was not theirs. It would not do to provide lasting harm to Abra's guests, so Serana told her students; however, no one could possibly object to receiving a small lesson.

In this manner, two relumma passed, and Abra had not yet, in their sight, done one bit of violence to the Code.

On the morning of the first day of his third relumma of service, Abra called Don Eyr to his office.

"I have acquired a piece of land in Low Port, at the corner of Offal Court and Pudding Lane. Before it can be put to use, it needs to be cleared of debris. See to it."

Four

Low Port

The enforcers were coming. That was the word on the street.

Abra's enforcers.

He had put the most able on the outer walls, the least able inside walls. There was a risk there, that those inside would be easy meat, once he had fallen. He had thought to send them away. If there had been any place safer than this place that he had made, he *would have* sent them away.

But, this was Low Port. There was no safety in Low Port, save being stronger than everyone else.

There were bolt holes from the inner room—tunnels too small for an adult to use. They would be able to get away, when . . . if . . . *away*. Out into Low Port, where they would be prey.

And he would be forsworn.

"Here they come," he heard someone say as feet hurried past his huddling place.

Jax Ton peered carefully around the edge of the wall, his cheek rubbing the gritty old stone.

Yes, here they were, just coming 'round the corner. Not Low Porters, you could tell by the clothes, and by the walk. Up Porters, they walked firm, like they could take anything on the street. A lot of them, they didn't look, and that got them in trouble. These two, though . . .

These two walked alert, and he'd seen them, he realized. Both of them, together, just like now. A dark-haired man, walking light and watchful; at his back a giantess, with cropped red hair, who walked even lighter, her eyes sweeping the street like beacons.

They were coming this way. Of course, they were coming this way.

Jax Ton made sure of his grip, and said, in a piercing whisper.
"*Now*."

* * *

Low Port was where the clanless, the criminal, and the mad
collected. There was no place for them in Mid-Port, and certainly
not in High Port. Rats strolled the broken streets at their leisure;
buildings sagged, and occasionally fell down, from lack of care. The
people were hungry, and shabby, and, most of them, hopeless. There
were predators on every street, and a man might be murdered for a
good pair of boots.

That had been Don Eyr's judgment of Low Port from his
previous visits on Abra's behalf. He realized now that he had not seen
the worst of it.

The street was lined with basic shelters, from ragged tents and
sagging inflatables, to huts built from scavenged bits of plastic, stone,
and cardboard.

In fact, there was one building on the entire street–a stone pile
that would likely survive a meteor strike.

Abra's property.

"Are we to bulldoze the walls," he asked Serana, "or merely pick
up the trash?"

In fact, there was remarkably little trash around the walls, unlike
the rest of the street. There were also remarkably few pedestrians,
though Don Eyr could feel the pressure of eyes watching from those
tattered shelters. No one challenged them, which happened often
on the . . . better streets of Low Port, a circumstance that made his
nerves tingle.

"Softly, little one," said Serana. "There is a door. Let us approach
from either side, so that we do not tempt anyone into an
indiscretion."

"Yes," he said and swung to the right, as Serana went to the left–

Directly into a hail of stones, and sticks.

He hit the ground, rolling on a shoulder, and rising to one knee, arms over his head to protect it.

Serana . . .

Serana had continued forward as if the missiles were made of whipped cream. She went down on her knees some distance from the doorway, and held her hands up, palms showing.

"Peace," he heard her say, in a calm, carrying voice. "Child, stand down. We are not here to hurt you."

#

It was a terrible tale the lad, Jax Ton, told them—starting with his own family's ruin and destruction—a small clan, a small business located on the edge of Mid-Port and Low, in the section known as Twilight. To throw suspicion off of themselves, a neighbor had given information against them for smuggling and human trafficking. It wasn't true, Jax Ton said hotly; his delm would never have stood for it, but the Port Authority didn't care to hear the truth, so long as they put the fear of retribution into guilty and innocent alike. The clan was broken; the elders arrested, and Jax Ton—Jax Ton had fled. Into Low Port. Growing up in the Twilight, he had friends in Low Port, or so he thought, until his friends tried to sell him and he ran again, not to Mid-Port, where the Proctors waited, but deeper into Low Port, where he found two children, starving, and spent his last coins to feed them.

Over time—Jax Ton wasn't entirely clear on how much time—three relumma? A year?—more children had gathered to him, usually an elder child with a younger in their care. They were eight, now, and Jax Ton; they had needed a safe place, a place that they, that was—

"Defensible," Serana said with a nod, looking 'round at the ring of tense faces. "You have done well. These walls will stand against a siege engine."

In fact, Don Eyr thought, looking at those same tense faces, they *had* done well. The faces were grubby, perhaps, but not distressingly so, and while they were dressed in a motley of garments, those were, by local standards, clean. Thin, yes, but not desperately so. Wary, but not feral. Or not quite feral. No doubt, the elder ones were accomplished thieves.

There was nothing here that he had not seen before. Lutetia had its poor, after all, and the Institute, sitting in the shadow of the Old City, saw them often.

"As much as this place meets your needs," he said now, speaking softly so as not to startle any of them, but Jax Ton, particularly. It was Jax Ton they must win to trust. The others would follow him.

"I regret, but you cannot stay here. The man who owns this building is both acquisitive and cruel. Best for all to relocate. Is there another place, perhaps not quite so well arranged, where you might go?"

Jax Ton frowned, and one of the older children leaned forward.

"There's the Rooms," she said, speaking to Jax Ton.

"Need money for the Rooms," another child protested.

Don Eyr held up a hand.

"Money need not concern you at the moment. Is it a place where you might keep together and in safety?"

Jax Ton looked at him, eyes wide.

"Money no concern?" he repeated. "Will *you* pay for us?"

Plainly, he disbelieved it, and Don Eyr could not blame him.

"Indeed, I will pay for you. More, we will escort you to this place, and see you settled and provisioned."

The boy was wary of a trap. Of course he was. Don Eyr waited.

"My friend, you cannot stay here," Serana said. "What my partner has told you is true. If we turn a blind eye and report this property clear, Abra will learn soon enough that we lied. Aside from what may be done to Don Eyr for such transgression, you will again be exposed and in danger. Best to retreat in good order, and establish a base elsewhere."

Jax Ton took a hard breath, looked around at his band of eight, wordlessly gathering their input. His gaze moved to Don Eyr, to Serana, and he inclined his head, jerkily, as if the gesture were not much used.

"Yes," he said. "We will go with you."

#

The Rooms was a rambling and ramshackle building that had, Don Eyr thought, once been half-a-dozen buildings, now connected by catwalks, ladders, and impromptu lifts. It looked a veritable fire-trap, and the manager no better than she ought to be. Still, she showed them a suite of rooms on the top floor, accessible by a stair, a woven rope walkway, and a catwalk connecting them to the next building.

Jax Ton inspected it, and Serana did, Don Eyr standing with the manager at the door.

"That's a twelfth-cantra for a relumma," she said. "No business done up here, though if they wanna work, I can put 'em in touch."

Don Eyr feared he did not misunderstand her, which did nothing to reconcile him to this place. To leave children here? And, yet, they were capable children, and they had been surviving very well, snug inside their rock walls. This . . . he looked around—plasboard walls, plasboard floor, plasboard ceiling with discolorations, here and there, which hinted that the rain came through.

"Yes," said Jax Ton, arriving with Serana. Don Eyr looked at her over the boy's head, saw doubtful eyes in a grim face.

"That is well, then," he said to Jax Ton. "Go and bring the others up."

"My money, sir," the manager said.

He turned. Perhaps he moved too quickly; perhaps something of his thoughts showed on his face. In any case, she stepped back.

"Your money," he repeated moderately. "Of course. Let us go to your office and settle the account."

#

The rent was paid for two relumma, and it did occur to Don Eyr that it was perhaps not quite wise to have exposed himself as a man who had so very much coin in his pocket. Still, it was done, while Serana stood aside with Jax Ton, handing over a card, and speaking with him most earnestly.

The boy slipped the card into some inner pocket, and made sober reply, then extended both hands to catch Serana's.

"Thank you," Don Eyr heard him say as he left the manager's office. "I am—grateful."

"Be wary, and take care," Serana told him. "That is our thanks. And remember—if there is trouble you cannot turn aside, send or come to that address. I will help you."

It was on the tip of his tongue to correct that, but, there, Serana, as ever, had the right of it. *He* could not promise *we*. His life was ordered at the whim of Abra, who would surely do his utmost to thwart any assistance Don Eyr might offer.

"Sir, thank you." The boy grasped Don Eyr's hand, his grip strong, and perhaps, a little, desperate.

"You are welcome," he said, smiling into the worried eyes. "Be well, Jax Ton."

The boy left, climbing the swaying stairs like a squirrel. He and Serana walked out to the street, and turned their steps toward Mid-Port.

They walked a block, and those pedestrians they encountered did very little to set his mind at ease regarding the fate of those eight children.

Don Eyr stopped, and looked up at Serana.

"They cannot be left there," he said. "Capable as they are, they are too soft, too easy. There are too many against them. That woman–offered to guide them to a brothel, in case any wished to work."

"I agree," Serana said softly. "They are too vulnerable. I will return, and guard them. You, with your twisty mind, will consider how we may do better for them. Come, I will escort you to safer streets, and–"

"I need no escort," Don Eyr said, recalling the last group they had passed on this street.

"Go back to them, now, Serana. I will . . . think of something."

She gazed into his face, hers showing wonder and no little irony. At last, she raised a hand and touched his cheek.

"I will see them safe, *petit*. Guard yourself close."

And with that, she turned and left him on the street.

#

"Children in the Low Port, my friend?" Chef vas'Urbil looked doubtful. "What would you have me do?"

"Advise me," Don Eyr said. "Surely, there must be some safe place to which we can deliver them, where they can receive an education other than how to survive on the streets."

"As I understand it, that is the highest class available in Low Port," returned the chef. He moved a hand. "Understand me, I am not unsympathetic; children ought not to be in danger, and yet, Low Port . . . you will not find many in Mid-Port or High who will care to discuss Low Port. It is widely held that those who live there deserve no better, else they would not have fallen so far. There is no . . . agency

... to support them." He paused to sip his tea, and looked at Don Eyr with curiosity.

"Was it not thus at Lutetia?"

"At Lutetia there were slums, surely, and the poor. But the city and the citizens provided some support. Orphanages, clinics, schools."

The chef looked aside.

"We on Liad are not so kindly. The clan is all and everything, as you have found. What recourse is there for you, ceded to Abra to cover your delm's markers?"

"None that I am aware of," Don Eyr said, and considered his friend with weary amusement. "Is my delm an idiot?"

"That and more!" the chef said heatedly. "He might have paid off Abra and gained income for the clan. Only, he would have had to find investors for a restaurant, which would have been easy enough, with an *École de Cuisine* chef to manage it, not to say provide the breads and desserts!"

He looked thoughtful.

"Of course, investors would demand that the profits be safe from Serat, which he would not like, at all. And, yet, this! It is to throw you, and every hope of Serat ever coming about into the wind!" He blow out a hard breath.

"Fool and son of a fool."

Don Eyr raised his eyebrows.

"Did you know my grandfather?"

"I am older than you, though not so old as that. No, it was a tale to amaze all of Liad, that Serat chose to send his daughter outworld–"

"I have heard the tale," said Don Eyr, and the chef threw him a wise look.

"You have heard the gossip, I'll warrant, and the most malicious of it, at that. Serat's daughter was sound; the son was a fool, but the son had not defied the father, nor called his judgment into question. For those crimes, she was sent to mind the clan's faltering fortunes off-world, since she was wiser than her delm in finance. The boy–your delm, now–grew up with the fixed notion that any competition for the ring was dangerous, and his intellect has plainly deteriorated from there." He drank off what was left of his tea.

"Forgive me if I offend," he added.

Don Eyr laughed.

"Yes, well. Returning to your children in the Low Port . . . I cannot advise you, save to walk away. Life is cheap in the Low Port, and children's lives cheaper than most. Rabbits among wolves, if they are without a clan or a . . . a group of some kind."

"And would you walk away from children in need? Children in danger?"

His friend moved his shoulders, turning empty palms up.

"Gods grant it never comes to me, because, in truth, I do not know what I would do."

#

It had been Don Eyr's intention to return to Low Port within a day–two at the most– though his vaunted twisty brain had not yet produced a solution for the children. Surely, there must be something . . . and Serana . . .

Serana was a warrior; she was cautious, and canny, and fully capable.

But Low Port was a killer, and he did not intend to leave her there without backup . . .

It was Abra's genius to know precisely how best to do harm. For the next twelve-day, he kept Don Eyr busy from dawn to dawn, with errands all about the city and the port, and then to stand as his trained monkey, trailing him from party to gaming table to an assignation.

At the latter, the lady considered him with interest.

"Does it perform?"

"One supposes so," Abra said, voice languid and eyes glinting. "Will you try it?"

"Perhaps I will–unless you do not care for competition?"

Abra raised his head at that, and there was a look in his eye that did not bode well for the lady, should she persist in this vein. She ignored him, or perhaps she did not see. Instead, she crossed the room to Don Eyr standing where he had been left, near the bureau. He lowered his eyes, and recruited himself to stillness.

"I believe he is shy," said the lady, and he felt her stroke his hair. "Serat's sister's child, you say?"

"It is what Serat says, in any case," said Abra, carelessly. "Will you have him?"

"While you watch?"

"I fear so, as I own him, and must therefore be certain that he comes to no harm."

The lady snorted delicately.

"Surely, the Code forbids slavery," she said, trailing a slim hand down Don Eyr's arm, and raising his hand to her lips.

He stiffened as she blew lightly across his knuckles–before releasing him to toy again with his hair.

"But this is not slavery; it is the payment of a rather considerable debt. In essence, I own him until such time as he has worked out the amount Serat owes me. Which, given the leisurely pace at which he pursues his duties, will be some years into his second lifetime."

"You might call the debt paid," said the lady.

"Now, why would I do that?"

"Ah, of course; I forget myself," said the lady, and slid her hand under Don Eyr's chin.

"Look at me, little one," she murmured.

His temper flared, and he raised his head, meeting her eyes, which widened slightly, eyebrows rising. She tipped her head to one side, as if considering his merits.

"Insipid," she said after a moment, and turned away.

"Come, Har Per, send the child home, and let us continue our explorations."

"Perhaps he needs an education, if he is as insipid as you say?"

"I am not a school," the lady said tartly. "Nor do I desire an audience this evening."

"But perhaps on some other evening? I tremble with anticipation," Abra said, placing his hand over his heart.

"Yes, very likely. Perhaps you would care to leave, also?"

Abra stiffened, and Don Eyr feared for the lady, who, perhaps did not know the limits of her power.

. . . or perhaps she did. Outrage melted into something else, and Abra raised a hand to cup the lady's cheek. He bent as if to kiss her—and paused in the act to look over her head.

"Go home," he snarled. "Tomorrow is rent day. Mind you find tal'Qechee in his office. I want no missed payments."

Don Eyr bowed, and turned, finding the door opening before him, and the lady's butler there to guide him away.

#

tal'Qechee's office was not in Low Port. Not *quite* in Low Port, though it danced with the boundary. His business interests were definitely based on the other side of the line, and the persons he employed were questionable at best. He was also difficult to find in his office, as Don Eyr had discovered on the previous occasions when he had been sent to collect tal'Qechee's "rent". The best hour to find him was early–*very* early–in the morning, when he was counting his own receipts from the night before.

Don Eyr therefore arrived early.

Night Port had not quite given over to Day; dawn teased the horizon, but had not yet committed to a fuller embrace. The streets were damp, it having rained somewhat in the night time. The gambling hells, bars, and other night side entertainment would be calling *last bid, last drink, last start*, and Mr. tal'Qechee would surely be in his office, now or very soon, in order to receive the couriers bearing the night's gleanings.

His reasoning was correct, though his arrival did not please Mr. tal'Qechee, who required him to tarry until all of the night's receipts were in and counted, so he was later than he wished to be, leaving for his next errand, which was much on his mind as he finally departed, his inside pocket heavy with cash.

The second errand was not so difficult as Mr. tal'Qechee, who made difficulty an art, but it would require some finesse to extract the "rent" when he was so far beyond his appointed hour. The second appointment pretended to grandeur, and a missed appointment was an affront worthy of a duel.

Still, he managed the thing, ruthlessly sacrificing Mr. tal'Qechee's character in the process, so that they both had a common boor to deplore, and left the office with a hurried step. If he went quickly, he might arrive at his third destination very nearly at the proper time.

Hurry and distraction almost saw him murdered.

As it was, he glimpsed the attacker from the corner of his eye in time to duck, and kick, feeling a kneecap go under his boot, even as he spun to engage the second, who had a cudgel . . .

#

"Not broken," said his friend the chef. "Mind you, it *ought* to be broken. You have the Dragon's own luck, Don Eyr."

"I was stupid," Don Eyr protested, wincing as Zelli wrapped an icy towel around his shoulder. "He should never have touched me."

"And he?" asked the chef.

"One has a shattered kneecap; the other–the one with the stick–I think I broke his wrist."

"You think." The chef stared.

"I was distracted," Don Eyr told him. "Happily, I kept hold of Abra's rent money, or I would be hurt, indeed."

"I will tend this, Zelli–see to the small breads," the chef said, and looked closely into Don Eyr's face.

"He strikes you? Abra, I speak of."

"When he feels able," said Don Eyr. "After all, he owns me; why should he restrain himself?"

"He may *say* that he owns you, my friend, but that is not the truth. I grant that the difference is subtle, but Serat did not *sell* you. He contracted with Abra for one of his to work off his debt. *Serat* might beat you, all by the Code and proper. But *you are not* Abra's; and he ought to be careful–very careful, I might say–with Serat's asset."

Don Eyr stared at him, took a breath. This–Abra's lover had said much the same; giving him a hint that he had been too ignorant to take up.

"I wish to send a note around to Mr. dea'Bon," he said abruptly. "Can you spare someone to take it? I would do so myself, but I'm to wait on him tonight."

"Cho Lin will carry your note, as soon as you write it. You are in no condition to go anywhere tonight, save bed, after a good meal, and wine."

"If I do not go, I will break faith with the contract."

"Surely, the contract does not say that you will accompany him when you are ill, or injured."

"It says that I am his to command in all things," Don Eyr said. "Is he likely to cede me an evening?"

The chef was silent, and Don Eyr sighed.

"Yes, far more likely that he will derive a good deal of pleasure from dragging me here and there until dawn, and explaining to all and sundry how I happened to be clumsier than usual this evening."

"My friend, this is not a life for you."

"I agree," Don Eyr said. "Of your kindness; may I have a pen and a blank page?"

#

The note was dispatched.

At the chef's insistence, Don Eyr had spent a half-hour with his shoulder in the grip of the kitchen's first aid kit, which did little more than administer an analgesic, and a therapeutic massage. Had the bone been broken, it might have done more; bruises, though, had to take their own time.

He showered, and changed his clothes, and was sitting down to a bowl of soup, cheese, and a small bread–Zelli had become proficient with small breads–when there came a clamor at the delivery door, which Vessa scrambled to answer.

"Don Eyr? There's a . . . young person wanting to speak with you."

A young person?

He shoved back his stool and all but ran to the back door.

The child–not Jax Ton, but one of the older children. To his shame, he had not learned their names. He had not thought it would be needful.

"Forgive me–you are?"

"Ashti, sir." She bobbed her head, and swallowed. "Jax Ton sends that Serana had been injured."

#

Abra be damned; and Serat, and their soulless, legal contract, too.

"You have not seen me," he told his friend the chef. "You have no idea where I am."

"He will not ask; but yes—if he does so, that is my tale."

Don Eyr bundled Ashti into a taxi, got out when the driver balked at going any further, and fair ran along the broken streets.

He followed the child up the rattling stairs to the ramshackle suite at the top of the building. She paused at the landing, and a shadow stepped out of darker shadows—Jax Ton, holding his pipe at ready.

"He came," Ashti said, and Jax Ton looked beyond her, to his face, his own pale and worried.

"Go in," he said, and stepped aside.

Don Eyr inclined his head, and paused a moment to steady his breathing. Serana was injured; he must not come to her in disorder.

Calmer, if not calm, he opened the door, and stepped through.

The first room was crowded with solemn-faced children, who stepped aside to let him through, to the back room, bathed in the uncertain light of emergency dims. There was a long form stretched out what might easily have a been a bed or a table, and another, sitting on the stool beside.

That figure rose at his entrance, and moved forward, to the place where the light was strongest. She was whip-thin, and dark, wearing the usual Low Port motley, with a soldier's jacket over all. There were two deliberate, diagonal scars down her right cheek.

She bowed.

"I am Fireyn, sir. The medic."

A medic. Of course. Serana was wounded. Jax Ton was a sensible lad; he would have called for a medic. Though it made his blood run cold, that she had needed one.

"How badly . . ." he began, but at that point, the bed spoke.

"A scratch only, *petit*; I swear it to you. And my own fault, to add to the sting."

"You cannot see around corners," Fireyn the medic said, in a comfortable, mild way, as if she and Serana were long known to each other. "And it is rather more than a scratch, my friend, though not nearly as bad as it could have been."

She stepped aside, and moved a hand, waving him to the bed and the stool.

"Please—you are Don Eyr, are you not?"

"Yes. Forgive me. I am remiss."

"You are, I expect, worried. Satisfy yourself, I beg. I will be outside, with Jax Ton."

The medic left. Don Eyr sank down to the stool she had vacated.

"So," he said, his voice shaking, despite an effort to sound appropriately stern. "This scratch of yours."

"I was careless, and met paz'Kormit at the corner. He took offense more quickly than I could mount a defense." She sighed.

"But as Fireyn says, it is not so bad as it could have been—he was thrusting for the gut, and I made very sure to break his arm."

"Serana . . ."

"Hush, small one; it is done, and already I am mending. Fireyn was trained as a field medic; she is very good."

"Where did she come from?"

Serana smiled at him.

"Where should she come from, save Low Port? And now it is your turn."

"My turn?" He blinked at her.

"Yes, your shoulder; there is some stiffness there; I marked it when you came in."

His shoulder, gods; it seemed a hundred years ago.

"It is a day to be careless, I suppose. I went to collect the rent today—"

"Alone!"

"Of course, alone," he said gently. "In any case, I went early to Mr. tal'Qechee, who was annoyed by my impertinence, and made me wait until all of last night's winnings had been counted out to pay me. So that he did not have to open the safe, you see."

Serana muttered in Lutetian.

"I object, as it casts curs in a bad light. But, yes; I was therefore late for my second appointment, and was in addition required to soothe ruffled emotions, before I could collect what was owed. Leaving that appointment, I saw that I might almost be on time for the third, if only I hurried . . ."

"So you hurried, and you did not look."

"Exactly. Two in Mr. tal'Qechee's employ sought to recover the rent, plus a bonus. I disabled the first, but the second had a stick. He was almost too quick."

"Almost," said Serana, with satisfaction.

"I believe that he has a broken wrist. In any case, I had the stick until I threw it away in Mid-Port."

"And your shoulder. Broken?"

"Merely deeply insulted."

She smiled in the dimness.

"It seems obvious to me, little one, that we each do better when we have the other nearby."

"I have also reached this conclusion."

He raised his hands; lowered them.

"Serana, forgive me. I had not meant to leave you alone so long, but Abra has kept me busy every hour since I returned."

"It is fortunate that he did not require you tonight," she said.

"He did," Don Eyr said. "But your need was greater."

She drew a hard breath.

"I am flattered, but he will hurt you, little one."

"No," said Don Eyr. "He will not. I am done with this sham. And I will not leave you, Serana. Not again."

"Peace." She placed a hand on his knee. "The children, Don Eyr . . ."

"I have no notion about the children; my famously twisty mind has failed me."

"Then it is fortunate that I have had a notion," she said. "What is wrong, Don Eyr, with Low Port?"

"Aside from being lawless and blighted by poverty and ignorance?"

"You put it so succinctly! Yes, exactly. We can, with these children—we can make a beginning."

"A beginning of what?"

"We may establish a Watch house, in the grand tradition of Lutetia. I may teach; and you may. We shall gather to us also a handful of senior officers . . ."

"From whence will these senior officers come?" he wondered.

"As Fireyn, they will come from Low Port. There are those who were abandoned, as she was, by her merc unit, and others, who are not naturally lawless, and who resist a devolution into brutes. They are intermittently forces of law, order, and protection, but they perhaps lack motivation, or opportunity to do more."

"And we offer them motivation—the children?"

"Indeed, little one. What master does not wish for an apprentice to carry her work on when it is come time for her to sit on the back porch, drink wine, and tell bawdy stories?"

He smiled.

"And you—I have seen how you leap to teach, who rejected the role of a teacher at the Institute. Would it not please you, to teach, as well as to nourish?"

"You paint a picture," he said slowly. "But, Serana—in Low Port?"

"In fact. Fireyn knows of a place—an old barracks, not far from here; perhaps a block nearer the Mid-Port. There is, she tells me, a kitchen, with ovens. She not being a baker or a cook, she cannot tell me if they would meet your needs. In front, there is what had been a recruiting office, which may be well for a bakery. It is tentative; I have not seen it. Indeed, I was on my way to meet her so that I might inspect it today when I fell into error. It is how she came upon me so quickly."

"Serana . . ."

"A scratch, I swear it to you. I will be perfectly fine on the morrow."

"More lives than a cat," he said softly, putting his hand over hers.

"Just so."

"What will happen, now that you have broken Serat's agreement?" Serana asked after a time.

"I think . . . nothing," he said, slowly, the other events of the evening beginning to return to him. "I must, tomorrow, leave you—for a few hours. I sent 'round to Mr. dea'Bon; it is possible that Abra has broken Code, or at least defied the terms of the contract, on the occasions when he struck me. I have had it pointed out to me that he is not my delm, who may kill me as the whim takes him, and nothing in the contract cedes a delm's authority over me to Abra."

"So," said Serana with satisfaction.

"It may not suffice; my word against his—"

"And mine," she said, fiercely.

"And yours. But, tomorrow, I must go. Also . . ." he hesitated, unwilling to raise hope prematurely.

"Tell me."

"I may have found a way to release myself from Serat, at least in part."

She stirred.

"What has Don Eyr's twisty mind produced this time?" she wondered softly.

"Do you remember the play—*Degrees of Separation*?"

There was a pause before Serana laughed softly.

"Do you think it will suffice, the clever nadelm's scheme?"

"I think that I will lay it before Mr. dea'Bon and allow him to determine that."

He leaned forward suddenly.

"Do you, indeed, wish to remain here, to establish a Watch, and raise these children to the tradition?"

"I do. We cannot abandon them; therefore, we must teach them. They will then teach others, and so it will spread, wider with each new generation of teachers."

"A long goal, Serana."

"But worthy."

"As you say."

Silence fell; he may have dozed, for he waked to her pulling on his hand.

"Come and lie down by me. I have missed sleeping with you, *petit.*"

He needed no more persuasion than that, and so they arranged themselves, careful of their injuries, and fell asleep in each other's arms.

#

His account as an honorable man, with Law Officer Serana Benoit corroborating, was, indeed, enough.

"You need not return to him, my Lord," Mr. dea'Bon said, with stern authority. "While this matter is under examination by the Accountant's Guild, you may return to the safety of your clanhouse."

"Ah," said Don Eyr; "you anticipate my next topic. But, first, if I may–how much could I expect to realize from the sale of my property on Ezhel'ti?"

"As it happens, I have an offer on my desk, from your father's clan. Their offer, so my colleague on Ezhel'ti tells me, is low, though not insultingly so. We may be able to negotiate upwards somewhat. Have you instructions?"

"Yes," Don Eyr said, "sell it for as good a price as you can reasonably get. Do not endanger the sale by attempting to wring every bit from the buyer. My need is cash, in the very near future."

Mr. dea'Bon made a note on his pad.

"I will see it done, my Lord." He looked up. "I remind that you have complete control over the account which is fed by your rents. If your need exceeds those funds, I am prepared, personally, to advance you a portion of the money you will certainly realize from the sale of your property."

"Thank you; that may be necessary, but for the moment, let it remain a possibility."

"Yes, my Lord."

"Excellent; we now address the likelihood of my return to the supposed safety of my clanhouse. Under no circumstances will I do so. My intention is set up my own establishment. I will remain on-planet, for I think that may be required, but I wish to file an Intention to Separate, immediately."

Mr. dea'Bon raised his eyebrows.

"That is . . . quite old."

"Is it disallowed?"

"Disallowed? Oh, no. No, not at all. I will have to do some research, but there is nothing to prevent you from filing such an Intention. However, you must, if memory serves me, set forth the conditions by which you would return to the arms of your clan."

"Yes. I will gladly return if and when Serat agrees to accommodate my household. Which at this moment includes Captain Benoit, nine children, and a calico kitten. I anticipate the household will grow, as we establish our base. Also, I insist that the monies belonging to my household shall be kept separate from the clan's accounts, and the delm shall be specifically barred from access."

Mr. dea'Bon had a dreamy look on his face. Very nearly, he was seen to smile. He made a brisk series of notes on his pad, and looked up once more.

"I believe I may work with this. May I ask, when we have achieved a successful outcome, that I be allowed to share the work with my colleagues? An Intention of Separation is rare enough, but these terms..."

He blinked and emerged somewhat from his dream state.

"You do understand, my Lord? You must be prepared to return to Serat's care, if your terms are met."

"I understand," said Don Eyr.

"Excellent. There is one more detail. While the investigation into Abra's breach of contract is taking place, your delm may freeze your quartershare, and your personal accounts." He paused.

"I advise that, in the case, Serat long ago emptied your accounts. The monies you received while you were attending school were from the rent of your house on Ezhel'ti."

He glanced once more at his note pad.

"Is there any other way in which I might serve you, my Lord?"

"I think–yes. There is an old barracks at Crakle and Toom in the Low Port. Can you find for me who owns it, and how I may acquire it?"

Another note.

"Yes. Is there a comm code I may have, in order to report my progress?"

"I will have it for you ... tomorrow, sir. For today, we are wanted in our household."

"I understand, sir."

The old gentleman rose, and bowed.

"Until soon, my Lord. Captain Benoit."

Five

Some Years Later

The morning rush was over, and Don Eyr stepped out onto the porch to bask in the mid-morning sunshine. The porch faced the exercise yard, and there was a self-defense lesson in progress. Cisco and Ail Den were pushing the older children hard, and they were rising to the challenge.

The younger children were at their ethics lesson, taught by Serana. Later, he would meet them in the kitchen, and they would collaborate on making the mid-day meal for the household. A household that had expanded, from the original nine children, to a dozen, guarded and educated by five very capable adults, supported by a veritable army of cats–fierce mousers, and interested companions.

There was more–a small neighborhood had grown up around them; an area of relative peace, in which the neighbors assisted each other, and kept watch for each other. The bakery provided bread, and sweets, and a gathering place, and the children of other households often attended lessons with the children of the bake house.

Don Eyr sighed, and stretched, and, hearing the step behind him, turned into Serana's embrace.

"Is it well, little one?" she asked softly.

He laughed softly.

"It is well, Serana. Very well, indeed."

UNE PETITE LISTE DE MOTS ÉTRANGES
A small list of strange words

chouquettes (f): cream puffs

commis (f): junior chef

dacquoise (f): almond and butternut meringue cake

delm (l): the head of a clan

École de Cuisine (f): School of Cooking

grand-père (f): grandfather

Lutetia (g): . . . in our timeline, Lutetia was the capital city of the Parisii, a Gallic tribe. It was renamed *Paris* back a few years ago–Wikipedia says 360AD.

masyr: monsieur

melant'i (l): who one is, in whole or in part, depending upon circumstances

merde (f): damn. More or less.

nadelm (l): the heir to the delm

on-dits (f): "they say" aka gossip

boulangerie (f): bakery

petit (f): small

qe'andra (l): a person of business; sort of an accountant-lawyer

relumma (l): one-quarter of a Liaden year

Key:

f: French

g: Gallic

l: Liaden

About Fortune's Favors

"Fortune's Favors" arrived, titleless, at the Worst Possible Time–when we were rushing for the finish line on Liaden novel *Accepting the Lance*. Sharon wrote a couple pages, to set up the character, along with a detailed outline, and–sent the story to the back of the line.

Now, there's always the risk, when you tell a story it has to wait its turn, that it will come surly, and go away. That used to bother us, that we would lose a story. On the other hand, we can't write *all* the stories, and we certainly can't write *all* the stories *at the same time*.

So, we've learned to take the risk, and work on the stories in order of importance, and/or deadline. It's a sad truth of the writer's life, for instance, that the demands of a novel will always override the needs of a short story.

So, the nameless story with the new character we really wanted to meet, was sent to the back of the line, and we hoped it would still want to play with us, after we finished the novel.

The good news is that the story waited. It had changed a little while it was waiting, but that was expectable, and we were pleased to see the inclusion of a couple of characters we'd worked with previously. We'd been *wondering* what they'd been getting up to!

We also welcomed the opportunity to explore a little more of the geography and people of Low Port, so, in all, we were very glad the story waited for us.

Sharon Lee and Steve Miller
Cat Farm and Confusion Factory, April 2019

Fortune's Favors

One

It was to the gayn'Urlez Hell in lower Low Port that his feet finally brought him, over the objections of most of himself.

There were those who dismissed Low Port as a miserable pit of vicious humanity where lived predators and prey; the roles subject to reversal without notice.

Those contended that there was nothing of value in Low Port; that it was worth the life of any honorable person to even attempt to walk such streets.

They . . . were not wrong, those who lived in the comfort of Mid Port and the luxury of High; and who bothered to give Low Port half a thought down the course of a Standard Year.

They were *not* wrong.

But they lacked discrimination.

It was true that there were very many bad and dangerous streets inside the uneasy boundaries of Low Port, and then—

There were worse.

The gayn'Urlez Gaming Hell occupied the corner of two such thoroughfares, and the best that could be said of them is that they were . . . somewhat less unsafe than the Hell itself.

Mar Tyn eys'Ornstahl had made it a policy—insofar as he was able to make policy – not to enter gayn'Urlez, much less work there.

Today, his feet had trampled policy, and Mar Tyn only hoped that he would survive the experience.

So anxious was he for that outcome, in fact, that he took the extreme action of . . . arguing . . . with his feet.

On the very corner, directly across from the most dangerous Hell in Low Port, Mar Tyn—turned to the right.

His feet hesitated, then strode out promptly enough, even turning right at the next corner, with no prompting from him, toward the somewhat safer streets where he was at least known.

Another might have assumed victory, just there, but Mar Tyn had lived with his feet for many years. It thus came as no surprise when they failed to take his direction at the next corner, bearing left, rather than right, until they stopped once more across the street from Hell.

He sighed. That was how it was going to be, was it?

Best to get on with it, then.

#

The barkeep was a thick woman with cropped grey hair and a prosthetic eye. She gave him a glance as he approached and leaned her elbows on the bar.

"Got reg'lars on tonight," she told him, pleasant enough. "Two days down there's a bed open, if you want to reserve in advance. Reservation includes a drink tonight and an hour to study the layout. The House takes six."

Mar Tyn smiled at her over the bar.

"I'm not a pleasure-worker," he said, gently.

She frowned.

"What *are* you, then?"

"A Luck."

She might have laughed at him; he expected it. She might equally have accepted him at his word; most did. Who, after all, would claim to be a Luck, if they were not?

He did not expect her to be *angry* with him.

"A Luck! Are you brain-dead? Do you know what happened to the last Luck who worked here?"

He did not. Not actually. Not *specifically*. He could guess, though.

"Her winner beat her, and robbed her of her share?"

The barkeep looked dire.

"Her winner followed her home, beat her, raped her, murdered her, took the money, her child–and for good measure, fired the building."

She paused, and took a breath, ducking her head.

"They say she was lucky to the last–no one died in the fire."

Mar Tyn took a breath.

"Ahteya," he said.

That earned him another hard glare, the prosthetic eye glowing red.

"You knew her?"

"No. We–Lucks–we know . . . *of* each other, in a general way. I had heard that a Luck named Ahteya had been killed–" Rare enough; most who hired a Luck didn't care to court the *ill*-luck that must come with such an act, though Lucks were still regularly beaten and robbed. Mar Tyn supposed that it was a matter of necessity. Violence was Low Port's primary answer to hunger and want, and it could be reasoned that a Luck whose gift did not protect them was *meant* to be robbed.

"I hadn't heard where she'd been working," he told the barkeep. "Or that she had a child."

"Well, now you know, and I hope the knowledge improves your day. You can leave."

"No," he said, with real regret–for her, and for him. "I can't."

Another red glare.

"*Can't?*"

"Despite appearances, I'm not a fool. When I saw where I had come to, I tried to walk away. With what success you see."

He produced an ironic bow.

"I believe the choice before us is–will you allow me to sign the book, or will I freelance?"

The color drained out of her face.

"You poach here and gayn'Urlez will break all of your bones. Slowly."

"I understand," he told her.

She sighed, then, hard and defeated.

"You're *certain*?" she asked.

"Rarely have I been more certain," he said, and added, for the wounded look in her natural eye. "I don't like it, either."

She reached beneath the bar.

"Here's the book, then; sign in. House's piece from your cut is twelve."

He glanced up from the page, pen in hand–"Not six?"

"Six is for whores; they comfort the losers, and convince them to try again, which is good for the House. If a Luck's good, they're bad for the House, 'cause their winner's going to go big."

"I'm good," he told her, which was neither a lie nor a boast. "The Lucky Cut is–?"

"Thirty-six."

"*Thirty-six*?"

Great gods, no wonder Ahteya's winner had wanted her share. Even after she had paid the House its twelve percent . . .

"House rules," the barkeep told him. "gayn'Urlez wants them to think before they hire. Better for the House, if they don't hire."

"Of course."

He signed, and sighed, and pushed the book back to her. She glanced at his name.

"All right, Mar Tyn. The House pays for your winner's drinks. You get a meal before you start work, and as much cold tea as you can stomach. I'll show you the back way out, too."

That last was truly kind. He wondered how well she had known Ahteya.

"Thank you."

"Stay alive, that's how you thank me," she snapped, glancing over his head at the clock.

"Let's get you to the kitchen for your supper. It's near time for the earlies to get in."

#

His supper long eaten, and his third cup of cold tea sitting, untouched, by his hand, Mar Tyn sat behind the small red table, within good view of both the door and the bar. His winner had not yet arrived, and he might have been inclined to wonder why his feet had brought him here, were it not for the certainty that he would find out soon enough.

He had, very occasionally, been delivered to this place or that, only to find that . . . something–perhaps the simple act of obeying the compulsion of his gift–had altered circumstances sufficiently that he was no longer required in that particular place and time. On every one of those occasions, however, he had felt . . . a release. His feet lost their wisdom halfway down a busy thoroughfare, or his sudden thought that it would be pleasant to have a cold treat resulted in his arrival at the ice vendor's stall.

This evening he felt no such release, and a trial thought–that it would be pleasant to go back to his room in the attic of Bendi's House of Joy–did not result in his standing up from behind the table, approaching the bar, and informing the 'keeper that he was quit.

Mar Tyn sighed.

No, his winner was taking her time, that was all. His gift *did* prefer to be beforetime in these matters. His part was to recruit his patience, and be vigilant.

He looked at his cup of tea, then around about him. There was something that was said on the streets–that *like called to like*, and here in gayn'Urlez Hell one could see ample evidence of that small truth.

Those who framed the residents of Low Port as brutes and less would need only to look through gayn'Urlez's door to be vindicated. Gambling was the primary draw–and those it drew ranged from the desperate, willing to do anything for a meal, to those who had the means to oblige them. Opposite his corner was another table, like his, clearly visible from both door and bar. The woman sitting there was the current local power to contend with. Her name was Lady voz'Laathi, and she held six entire blocks under her protection, with gayn'Urlez Hell being the center-point. Two bullies stood behind her, guns and knives on display, and those who dared approach the table did so with hunched shoulders and bowed heads.

As if she had felt his glance, the lady turned her head and met his eyes. For a moment, they regarded each other. The lady spoke over her shoulder and one of her two protectors stepped away from the table, and crossed the room.

Mar Tyn drew a deep breath. Surely, he thought, *surely* not . . .

"Luck," the man said, standing on the far side of the red table.

"Gun," he answered, politely.

"My lady asks you to look aside. She's got no need of your gift."

Mar Tyn bowed his head, pointedly averting his eyes.

"My regards to your lady. Please assure her that I am here on other business."

"I'll tell her that. She says, too, that you're on her ticket. Eat, drink, whatever you want. My lady's no enemy of luck."

"I honor her," Mar Tyn said, not entirely without truth. There were those who would have had an audacious Luck shot for his incautious glances. "The House feeds me this evening."

"I'll tell her that, too," said the lady's Gun, and turned away, but not before he had dropped a coin to the tabletop.

Mar Tyn's reactions were Low Port quick. His hand flashed out, covering the bright thing while it was still spinning and pinning it flat to the table.

He glanced quickly around the room, careful to avoid the lady's eyes, though he could feel her attention on him. He pulled the coin to him, and slipped it away into a pocket. It was a valuable thing, and a dangerous one, and he wished it had not been given.

Well, but given it had been; and, once accepted, it couldn't be returned, unless he wished to risk offering the lady an insult that would certainly be Balanced with his life.

He took a breath.

That he had been given no chance to refuse the favor . . .

. . . that . . . was disturbing.

Mar Tyn closed his eyes, drew a deep breath, held it for the count of twelve–and exhaled.

There was no tremor from his gift; nor sizzle of anticipation in his blood.

He opened his eyes, and turned his head to make a study of the room behind the bar.

Try, he told himself, considering the greater room, and the crowd at the card table . . . *Try not to be a fool.*

The Luck's Table was set as far as possible from the games of chance. That was prudent; proximity *was* a factor in the working of his gift. He personally felt that he was not situated quite far *enough* from the games to avoid influence, if his gift was feeling playful–which, fortunately, it was not.

He did not, of course, say this to Sera gayn'Urlez when she came to his table, shortly after the Gun had left him.

"You're the Luck Vali signed in, are you?"

"Yes, Sera. Mar Tyn eys'Ornstahl, Sera."

"Why choose to come here?"

"Sera, forgive me; I did not *choose* to come here."

That earned him a grin, unexpected and attractive on a broad face with one short white scar high on each cheek.

"So, you've been here before?"

"Twice, Sera. Once, when I was a child, with my mentor. Again, when I was newly my own master."

"Not since?"

"No, Sera."

"Why not? Didn't earn enough?"

"Sera, I earned well that night. My winner was killed by a wolf-pack, three paces from the door, and I swore that I would not help someone to their death again."

The frown was as fearsome as the grin had been attractive.

"I don't allow wolf-packs on my corner, or on either street, for the length of the block."

Mar Tyn had heard about this policy, which was enforced by the lady at whom he had been bidden not to stare. Such enforcement benefited both, after all, and gayn'Urlez *did* sit at the center of the lady's base.

"Sera's brother was gayn'Urlez," he said. "When last I worked here."

Interest showed in her face.

"My brother died six years ago. You're older than you look."

In fact, he did look younger than his years, and had in addition come unusually young into the fullness of his gift. Which gayn'Urlez had no need to know.

He therefore inclined his head, acknowledging her observation.

"Vali told you the rules and the rates?"

"Yes, Sera."

"Questions?"

"I collect my commission, less the House's fee, from the floor boss?"

"That is correct. Your winner will also collect, minus the House's fee, from the floor boss." She paused, seeming to consider him.

"If you feel that you're in danger from your winner, or from anyone else on the floor, you have Vali send for me, understood?"

This was an unexpected courtesy. Mar Tyn inclined his head.

"Yes, Sera."

"Yes," she repeated, and sighed. "I'm in earnest, Luck eys'Ornstahl. Vali would have told you about Ahteya. I don't necessarily want Lucks operating out of my premises, but that doesn't mean I want them beat and killed for doing what they were hired to do."

"Thank you for your care," he said, since it seemed she expected a reply, and it was good policy to be polite to the host.

She stood another moment or two, studying him. He gave her all his face, feeling no twinge from his gift. His was to sit there, then, and wait, until waiting was over.

#

The room had filled and the play had grown raucous before Mar Tyn felt a shiver along a particular set of nerves, and looked up to see a man approaching the Luck's Table. He wore a leather jacket of a certain style, though to Mar Tyn's eye he was no pilot. His face, like so many faces in Low Port, bore a scar–his just under the right eye, star-shaped, as if someone had thrust a broken bottle, edges first, at him.

"Luck for hire?" he demanded, voice rough, tone irritable.

"Ser, yes," Mar Tyn said.

"Stand lively, then! I've work for you tonight!"

Mar Tyn rose, looking over his prospective winner's shoulder to Vali at the bar. He caught her prosthetic eye, and she inclined her head, teeth indenting her lower lip.

"Gods, you're nothing but a kid! Do you think this is a joke?"

"No, Ser," Mar Tyn said truthfully. "I'm not so young as I seem."

"You can influence the *kazino*, can you?"

Well, no, not exactly, but there was no coherent way to explain how his gift operated to someone who did not also bear the gift. And this man did not want an explanation—not really. He wanted a guarantee that Mar Tyn would make him a big winner, which, Mar Tyn realized, considering the warmth of his blood, he would very likely do. Barring stupidity, of course. Not even Luck trumped stupidity.

So.

"Ser, the *kazino* is a specialty," he said, which was almost true. Wheels, machines, and devices were the easiest touch for his Luck. Cards were more difficult, and Sticks the most difficult of all. His win average for Sticks was fifty-eight percent, only a little over what native probability might achieve; while his success rate with the machines was very nearly seventy-three percent. Keplyr had found his affinity for *kazino* amazing. But Keplyr's gift had favored cards.

"All right, here."

The man grabbed his shoulder and pulled him to a stop by the *kazino* table.

"Get busy," he said, and leaned close, voice low and full of threat. "If I catch you slacking off, I'll break your fingers. You don't need your fingers to give me a win, do you?"

"No, Ser," Mar Tyn said quietly. "But pain will disturb my concentration."

"Then keep your mind on the job," snarled his soon-to-be winner. He reached into his jacket pocket and withdrew two quarter-cantra, which he gave to the croupier in exchange for a small handful of chips.

Mar Tyn closed his eyes, the better to see what his gift might tell him.

"Well?"

He answered without opening his eyes.
"Everything on red three."

#

His winner had done well, though he did not seem pleased with either his success or Mar Tyn's obvious diligence on his behalf. He did not win all of the spins, of course; chance simply did not operate that way. However, he won very nearly three-quarters; and his losses were—save one—minor.

The big loss—Mar Tyn had felt it looming, and directed that a prudent bet be set on green eight. It wouldn't have done to cash out of the table entirely; not with the rolling waves of plenty he sensed hovering just beyond the loss. Besides, it put heart in the other players to see that even a man augmented by Luck was not immune to a set-back, and he owed at least that much courtesy to the House.

So, he had directed that prudent placement, but his winner—his winner had not been drinking. Perhaps he was drunk with success; certainly he was arrogant.

In any case, he turned his head, met Mar Tyn's eye, and placed twice the requested amount on the square.

It could have been worse; at least the man had not let everything ride on the spin. Also, the loss had the happy outcome of demonstrating that Mar Tyn knew his business far better than the man who had engaged him.

After that, his winner placed his bets as directed by his Luck, though he did so with ill-grace, and continued to win. The table lost players, and filled again, in the way of such things, until—two hours before the day-port bell forced even gayn'Urlez to close—the man abruptly swept all his winnings off the table, and carried them to the floor boss' station.

It was gayn'Urlez herself at the desk, which ought not have surprised him, Mar Tyn thought. She tallied the chips, did the conversion to coin, and counted out the whole amount.

That done, she paused, the money on full display until the winner stirred and growled, "Agreed."

"Excellent," she said. "We will now pay your just debts. Thirty-six percent to the Luck."

She counted it onto the desk before him, fingers firm.

"Agreed," said Mar Tyn in his turn; "and twelve percent to the House."

She smiled faintly.

"Indeed."

The appropriate amount was subtracted. He accepted the remainder and slid it away into various pockets.

"You are done here for this night, Master Luck," gayn'Urlez said then. "The House can bear no more."

"Sera, yes. My thanks."

She did not even look at him, her fingers already busy with the remaining money.

"You will of course share a drink with me," she said to the winner. "On the House."

Mar Tyn was already through the bar's pass-through, on his way to the back exit, but he heard the winner clearly.

"No."

#

He ran, his feet and the rest of himself of one accord.

Fleetness was a survival skill in Low Port, and Mar Tyn had thus far survived. Still, his winner, though heavier, had longer legs, and a great motivator in the money in Mar Tyn's pocket. If it came to an outright race, the larger man would overtake the smaller.

Happily, the race was not nearly so straightforward.

Mar Tyn's goal was not his attic room at Bendi's. No, he was flying full-speed toward one of his bolt-holes, a cellar window left off the hook beneath a pawn shop in Litik Street. He was a bare two blocks from that slightly moldy point of safety, confident that he could reach it handily.

In fact, he had the pawn shop in view, and was veering to the left, aiming for the alley that unlatched window opened into . . .

When his feet betrayed him again.

He hurtled past the pawn shop, even as he flung out a hand to snatch the post at the corner of the building, intending to swing himself 'round and into the alley.

"Hey!" he heard a man shout behind him. "You! Luck! Stop!"

Dammit.

Mar Tyn took a hard breath—and let his feet take him.

#

His winner caught him at the corner of Skench and Taemon, when a speeding and overburdened lorry lurched into the intersection as he started through. He missed his stride, staggered, threw himself to the right—and was lifted from his feet by a grip on his collar.

His winner tossed him, casually, into the wall of the building on the corner. Luckily, the wall was plas, not stone, and Mar Tyn bounced, ducking out of the way of his winner's fist.

The second punch connected, knocking him back into the wall. Mar Tyn used the slight give, and kicked out, hard and accurate. His winner yelled, doubled over—and Mar Tyn was gone, hurtling across the intersection, guided by feet or fear, it hardly mattered. He had no taste for being beaten, nor did he care to buy out of a beating by surrendering the evening's earnings. He had a far better use for—

His feet dashed down an alleyway, a dark tunnel with a light at the end.

A courtyard, he saw, and the gate standing, luckily, open. Much good it would do him. A dead-end was still a dead-end, and his winner would have him.

He saw it, as his feet threw him into the yard–a window, there on the second floor, showed a light.

He might get lucky, after all.

"The house, the house!" he shouted, as his feet sped him forward. "Thieves and brigands! Be aware!"

The grip this time was on his shoulder, and the wall he connected with was stone.

The light flared and fragmented; he twisted to the left, dodging the next blow, hearing his winner curse as his fist struck the wall, and the grip on his shoulder loosen.

He tore free, intending to run back through the gate, but his own feet tripped him, and he went down to the cobbles on one knee. His winner spun, face shadowed, light running like quicksilver along the edge of the blade as he raised it.

Mar Tyn took a breath and shouted.

"The house! Murder!"

. . . and dove to the cobbles between his winner's feet, rolling, knocking him off-balance.

He heard the metal cry out as the knife struck stone, its brilliance swallowed in the shadows, and lurched to his feet, turning this time toward the house, where more lights had come on. He heard shouting–and his collar was gripped.

He was thrown against the wall again, and held there as his winner slapped him hard, driving his head against the stone.

All the lights went out; he felt his jacket torn open, a hand exploring the pockets, heard a grunt of satisfaction, and release of the punishing grip that held him upright.

He slid to the cobbles, the light coming back, smeared and uncertain.

The first kick broke his arm, and he screamed, earning a second kick, in the ribs.

A distant noise broke on his befuddled ears, and a woman's voice, speaking with authority.

"Who is brawling in my yard? Her Nin bey'Pasra, you rogue! Have I not told you often enough to stay away from here?"

A shadow loomed in the smeary light, snatching his winner and spinning him about as if he were nothing more than a child's toy made from twisted rags.

A blow landed; his winner staggered, and it occurred to Mar Tyn that this was his final chance to live out the night.

Run, he told himself, but he had no strength to rise.

Instead, he lay there on the cobbles while a large red-haired woman, briskly efficient, dealt with Her Nin bey'Pasra, slapping him into the wall as an afterthought, stripping him of his jacket as he slumped; at last picking him up by scruff and seat, frog-marching him to the gate, and pitching him into the alley.

Metal clashed–perhaps, Mar Tyn thought muzzily, she had thrown him into the garbage cans.

The woman turned, grabbed the gate and pulled it to, leaning down as if to get a closer look at the latch.

Perhaps she swore; her voice was low, the words nonsensical. She pulled a piece of chain from somewhere in the shadows, and wrapped the latch, muttering the while.

Then she crossed the yard, and squatted next to Mar Tyn. He blinked up at her, the light making a conflagration of her hair.

"Can you rise?" she asked him.

"I believe so," he said, and found that, with her arm, he could, though he crashed to his knees when she withdrew that kind support.

"My head," he muttered, raising his good hand, only to have it caught and held in firm fingers.

"I see it," she said, and raised her voice, "Fireyn!"

He flinched.

"There is nothing to fear here," she told him, her large voice now soothing and soft. "You were lucky that our gate was open."

"And why was that?" came another voice, this one male.

"The latch was broken again," the woman answered him. "We are in need of a solution there."

"Tomorrow," said the man, kneeling beside her and looking into Mar Tyn's face.

"You may put yourself in our care," he said with a gentleness rarely given even to children. "You have come to the safest place in Low Port."

He smiled, wry in the smeary light.

"I understand that is not so very much to say, but, for now, at least, you are safe. My name is Don Eyr; this lady who succored you is Serana. Fireyn, who is coming to us now, is our medic. May we know your name?"

"Mar Tyn eys'Ornstahl," he managed, as the medic approached him down a long tunnel edged with fire. He wanted only to close his eyes, and surrender to that kindly dark, but he owed them one more thing. They must be told of their peril.

"I am . . ." his breath was coming in short, painful gasps, but he forced the words out. "I am . . . luck . . ."

The darkness reached out. He embraced it, sobbing. The last thing he heard before he was taken utterly was the man's voice, murmuring.

"Indeed, you are that."

Interludes

Mar Tyn woke to a multitude of aches, and opened his eyes upon a thin, fierce face. Two achingly straight scars traced a diagonal path down her right cheek, white against tan skin.

"Medic?" he whispered. There had been a medic—or at least, a medic on the way. He recalled that, particularly, for a medic in Low Port was a wonder of herself.

His observer dipped her chin in approval, and added, "Fireyn. Tell me your name."

"Mar Tyn eys'Ornstahl."

Another dip of the chin.

"Your right arm is broken; your ribs are accounted for. You have proven that your head is harder than our wall, so you need not make that experiment again. I used a first aid kit on the ribs, the head, and the arm, and injected you with an accelerant, which will speed healing. The arm is your worst remaining problem. You will need to wear a sling, even after your other wounds allow you to leave your bed."

He licked his lips.

"How long–" he began, but the darkness rushed up again, swallowing the thin, clever face, amid all of his sluggard thoughts.

#

He woke feeling tired, and opened his eyes to a different face, not quite so thin, nor yet so fierce, with a clear golden complexion rarely found in Low Port. The features were regular; cheeks unscarred; eyes brown, and serious.

"Do you know me?" he asked. His Liaden bore an accent–tantalizingly unfamiliar.

"You are Don Eyr," Mar Tyn answered. "I recall your voice."

Don Eyr smiled.

"It was rather dark, wasn't it? You may be pleased to learn that Fireyn wishes you to rise, and walk, and afterward make a report of yourself. She will also be observing you with her instruments."

He tipped his head, and Mar Tyn followed the gesture, finding the medic standing at a tripod across the room.

The room—it was small, but very light. He turned his head, finding a window in the end wall; a clean window, through which the afternoon sun entered, brilliance intact.

"When?" Mar Tyn asked.

"Now," Fireyn said. "If you are able. If you are not able, then I will be informed."

He marked her accent this time, and noted the way she stood, balanced and alert. One of the Betrayed, then, which made sense of her paleness, and the precision of the cuts that had formed her scars.

"What she means to say is that, if you are not able, she will immediately intensify your treatment," Don Eyr said, rising from the chair next to Mar Tyn's bed. "She was military, and believes in quick healing."

"A necessity, on a battlefield," Fireyn said.

And also on Low Port, thought Mar Tyn, putting the coverlet back with one hand. His right arm was in a sling, and he was wearing a knee-length robe.

Carefully, he put his feet over the side of the bed, situated them firmly—and rose.

He paused, but his head was quite steady; his balance secure. Looking up, he saw Don Eyr leaning against a wall, perhaps a dozen paces from the side of the bed.

Mar Tyn walked toward him, steps firm and unhurried.

Reaching Don Eyr, Mar Tyn bowed. Finding his balance still stable, he turned and walked to the window, where he paused to look out.

Below him was the yard his feet had carried him to in his race against his winner. It was a tidy space, seen in decent daylight. He particularly noted the tiered shelving, filled with potted plants.

"I hope I brought no harm to your garden," he said, turning to face Don Eyr.

"Not a leaf was bent," the other man assured him.

"Good."

He walked back to Fireyn.

"I report myself able. Shall I go?"

He heard Don Eyr shift against the wall–but Fireyn was shaking her head.

"I fear you are guilty of under-reporting," she said, and glanced over his head.

"I recommend an additional round of therapy," she said, to Don Eyr, Mar Tyn understood.

"You are the medic," came the answer. "Friend Mar Tyn."

He turned.

"This choice is yours. I stipulate that the therapy is not without risk. I also stipulate that none of those under my keeping–or, indeed, myself–have taken harm from it. If you wish my recommendation, it is that you allow it. This house will stand for your safety, while you are vulnerable. If you do not care to risk so much, that is, of course, your decision. It is understood that you may have business elsewhere."

It was gently said, and Mar Tyn was somewhat astonished to find that he believed that he was safe in this house, in the care of Fireyn and Don Eyr. Which left only the question . . .

Do I, Mar Tyn inquired with interest of himself, *have business elsewhere?*

There came no restless fizzing in his blood; it was as if his feet were rooted to the floor. He was, he realized, at peace, which was very nearly as dangerous as believing himself to be safe.

And yet . . . his feet had brought him here; his feet were content that he remain here.

He was curious to learn why.

He turned to Fireyn.

"Additional therapy," he said. "I accept."

Two

He woke feeling hale and bright, and more well than he'd been in his life. Opening his eyes, he discovered himself alone. The chair beside the bed had a shirt–not his–draped carefully over the back, and a pair of pants–likewise not his–folded neatly on the seat. The boots on the floor by the chair were, indeed, his, though someone had cleaned them, and even produced the beginning of a shine.

Mar Tyn sighed. His blood was effervescent, and his feet were itching to move.

Apparently, he had business to tend to, and he'd best be about it quickly.

#

He had managed the shirt, the pants, the socks–even with the sling–but the boots had proved beyond him.

Sock-foot, then, he danced lightly out of the room, along a short hall and down a metal staircase. At the bottom, he turned right, down a longer hallway, and found himself in a kitchen, warm, bright, and smelling of baking.

There was a large table along the right-hand side of the room, much be-floured, and holding a large bowl, well-swathed in toweling. Across the room, a light glowed red above what he took to be an oven, set into the heavy stone wall.

Despite the evidence of previous industry, the kitchen was at this moment empty.

Mar Tyn spied a teapot on a counter, holding court with a dozen mismatched cups. His feet assumed; he poured, bearing the brightly flowered cup with him to the window overlooking the courtyard, and got himself onto one of the two high stools there.

He waited, sipping tea; his feet at rest; his blood a-sizzle.

123

Footsteps in the hall heralded the arrival of Don Eyr, who bent his head, cordial and unsurprised, before crossing to the teapot, pouring, and returning to the window, slipping easily onto the second stool.

He said nothing, nor did Mar Tyn. Indeed, there was scarcely time enough for a companionable sip of tea before more footsteps sounded in the hall, overhasty, and desperate.

A girl burst into the kitchen, lamenting as she came.

"Oh, the bread! It will be ruined!"

She dashed to the worktable, snatching the towel from the bowl, shoulders tense–and loosening all at once, as she erupted into a flurry of purposeful action, a sharp punch down into the bowl before upending it and turning an elastic mass out onto the floured table. The bowl was set aside, as with her free hand she reached for a wide, flat blade . . .

"I wonder," Don Eyr said quietly from beside him, "what you did, just now."

Ah, thought Mar Tyn, and turned to face his host.

"Forgive my ignorance, but first I must know what happened, that went against your expectations."

Don Eyr glanced to the girl, who had divided her dough into two even portions, and was busily shaping the first with strong, sure fingers.

"The bread–the dough in the bowl, you see–it *ought* to have been ruined–*fallen*, as we have it. She left it too long at rise." He sipped his tea, and added.

"These matters are delicate, and . . . not always precise. Bread-making only pretends to be a science."

"Ah."

Mar Tyn sipped his tea, and met Don Eyr's eyes.

"I am a Luck. You say that this—" he used his chin to point at the busy worker— "is an art, and not a science. That there is some element of imprecision inherent in the event."

"Yes," said Don Eyr, "but in the case, she had left it beyond the point of recovery."

"You know your art, and I do not," Mar Tyn said gently. "I only say that, given what we have seen, there must have been some small probability that the bread would *not* be ruined, and my presence . . . gave that probability an extra weight."

Don Eyr sipped, eyes fixed on some point between the stools and the work table.

"In fact," he said eventually; "you altered the future?"

Mar Tyn sighed.

"So it is said. It's the reason we're banned from Mid and High Ports, and why the Healers and *dramliz* spit on us."

Don Eyr frowned slightly, his eyes on the baker, who had finished shaping the second loaf. She transferred the pans to the shelf by the oven door, covered them with the cloth, and wiped her hands on her apron.

Mar Tyn took a careful breath, surprised to find an ache in his side, as if one of the ribs had not entirely healed.

"I will leave," he said softly. "An escort to the gate—"

"There's no need for haste," Don Eyr murmured. "Drink your tea."

The baker approached them; bowed.

"The loaves are shaped, Brother," she said to Don Eyr.

"So I see," he answered. "Mind you do not neglect them in their rising. You cannot count on good fortune twice."

Which was, Mar Tyn thought, finishing the last of his tea, very wise of him.

The baker blushed, and murmured, and turned to clean the work table.

"I wonder," Don Eyr said, turning on his stool to face Mar Tyn, "if you will come and eat breakfast with myself and Serana." He raised one hand, fingers wide. "If you feel that you must go, I will not detain you, though I will ask for a moment to fetch those things which belong to you."

Mar Tyn paused, considering himself, and his condition.

His feet . . . were content. His stomach . . . was in need, noisily so.

He inclined his head.

"I would very much like to share a meal with you and Serana," he said.

He slid off the stool onto his quiet feet, and followed Don Eyr out of the kitchen.

#

They ascended a short staircase to a room half-a-floor above the kitchen. A table set for three was under the open window. Mar Tyn glanced out over the courtyard, and realized that the light he had seen, the night his winner had caught him, had come exactly from this room.

He turned his attention to the larger apartment. A bureau stood against the wall next to the table, laden with dishes of biscuits, vegetables, and cheese; and a teapot, gently steaming.

Shelves lined the walls, overfull with books and tapes, and where there were not shelves, there were . . . pictures–flat-pics, hand-drawings, swirls of color . . .

Along the wall opposite the table was a screen, a double-lounge facing it. In the far corner, two more chairs sat companionably together in an angle of the shelves, a light suspended from the ceiling over both. A red-haired woman sat in one of the chairs, reading. There was a door in the wall directly behind her, almost invisible in the abundance of . . . *things*.

Mar Tyn's feet had taken him to larger rooms, and longer tables. But he had never been in so comfortable–so *welcoming*–a room. Indeed, by the standards of the rooms he most usually frequented, this cluttered chamber was . . . he groped for the word, and had only just achieved *luxurious* when the woman looked up from her book.

"Ah, here he comes, on his own two feet!" she said cordially, rising–and rising some more.

Her height was not so much of a surprise–she had cast the shadow of a giantess in the courtyard. No, what startled was her . . . fitness; this was not a woman who knew want, or who went often without her dinner. From her part in his rescue, he had assumed that she was a soldier, but he saw now that she was not. Fireyn–*there* was a soldier, from squared shoulders to flexed knees. This person–was upright, and strong, and–*proud*, thought Mar Tyn.

Just as Don Eyr was proud. And well-fed.

As the baker of breads, in the kitchen below: well-fed, strong. Embarrassed, but not abused.

"I strike him to silence," Serana noted, drily.

Mar Tyn bestirred himself and produced, having seen such things on tapes, a bow of gratitude.

"I mean no disrespect," he said. "I was overcome for a moment, recalling that I owe you my life."

"Glib," came the judgment from high up.

"But truthful," Don Eyr said, stepping to Mar Tyn's side.

"Serana, I make you known to Mar Tyn eys'Ornstahl, who is a Luck. Ser eys'Ornstahl, here is Captain Serana Benoit."

Well–a soldier after all?

Serana smiled down at him.

"My rank comes from worlds away, where I was one captain of many in the city guard. Security, not military."

Security, thought Mar Tyn, recalling her bent over the broken lock. *House* security. She would have questions for him. How not?

He took a breath and met her eyes–pale green and knowing. She smiled faintly.

"Come," she said, sweeping a large hand out, as if to show him the buffet and the table, "let us eat."

#

In general, Mar Tyn ate more regularly than many residents of Low Port–a benefit of his gift, which would have no use for him, if he were too weak to obey its whims.

The breakfast he was given at Don Eyr and Serana's table was beyond anything he had ever eaten; something other than mere food, so nuanced that he felt his head spin with the multiplicity of tastes and textures.

His attempt to eat sparingly was defeated by his host, who monitored his plate closely, and immediately replaced what he had eaten.

At last, though, he sat back, dizzy and replete, and looked up into Serana's eyes.

She smiled at him, fondly, or so it seemed, and leaned back comfortably in her chair.

"Tell us," she said.

He sighed slightly, unwilling to face the inevitable results of having told them. But–he owed them no less than his life, and nothing but the truth would pay that debt.

Also–they had children in their care–he had heard their voices round the house and yard as he had eaten. Well-fed, strong, and prideful children, like the girl whose bread he had preserved. If the purpose that united this house was the protection of children–a purpose nearly unheard of, in Low Port . . .

The house needed to know about Lucks and the particular perils attending them–not only so that they might be more careful of who they let behind their protections, but to know the signs, should one of those in their care prove to be Lucky.

So, he sighed, but he told them–quietly and calmly, beginning with the day he found the woman he supposed to have been his mother lying on the floor of their basement room. He had thought her asleep, but she hadn't woken, not even when there came heavy footsteps and loud voices in the hallway.

That had been the first time his feet had moved him, away, *not* to the front of the house, where the voices were loudest, but down a back hallway, and into a pipe scarcely large enough to accommodate his small, skinny self, which, after some small time of crawling, led into a deserted, rubble-filled alleyway.

He had climbed out of the pipe, half-turned back toward the place he had just quit–but his feet took him, and he walked for many blocks, up and down streets he had never seen before, until he came to Dreyling's Tea Shop.

His feet took him into the shop, and marched him to the backmost table. He hoisted himself into one of the two chairs–and waited, for what, he could not have said. No one took any note of him. He tried, once, to wriggle out of his chair and go away, but some force he did not understand kept him where he was.

Eventually, a man with grey streaking his dark hair, wearing fine and neatly patched clothing, joined him at the table, called for tea and a plate of crackers, and when they had come, asked what was his name.

He disposed of the years with Keplyr as mentor and master with a simple– "He took me in, and taught me how to survive my gift. He had lived a long time as a Luck in Low Port. It was his belief that his gift had called mine."

Keplyr's death, the stuff of nightmares that *still* woke him–he did not mention, only saying that, in time, he came to be his own master.

He spoke of the nature of his work, the particular risks found in gaming houses, and told the story of Ahteya as a caution for them, before finishing with is own misadventure, from which Captain Serana had so kindly extricated him.

"So," said that same Captain Serana, when finally he came to an end. "It seems to me that the first question we must ask is–*why*."

Mar Tyn blinked at her.

Beside him, Don Eyr laughed softly, and rose, taking the teapot with him.

"Nothing occurs to you?" Serana prodded gently.

"Why," Mar Tyn said slowly, "so that you might save my life."

But Serana shook her head.

"You would have been safe at your first bolt-hole, but your feet bore you past," she pointed out. "Running on is what put you in danger."

Mar Tyn took a breath. He was not accustomed to questioning the motives of his gift, even after the instance was over. His chest was suddenly tight, and his breath somewhat short . . .

"Surely," Don Eyr said, returning to the table and leaning on the back of Serana's chair, "Aidlee's loaves were not worth so much."

The pressure in his chest dissolved in laughter.

"A shattered arm, and a broken head? No, I think we can agree there," he said, and looked again to Serana.

"Perhaps," he offered tentatively, "it was necessary that I alert the house that the gate was standing wide?"

Don Eyr and Serana exchanged a glance.

"Certainly," she said slowly, "it would have been no good thing, had some we can both name found us open. Yet . . ."

She looked again to Mar Tyn.

"There was no sign, after, that any had come back to complete their work, and been surprised to find the gate in force."

Mar Tyn moved his shoulders, uneasy once more.

"The fact that the gate had been relocked–the noise alone, when my winner caught me– might have changed intentions."

There was a light knock, and Don Eyr went away again, to the door. He returned with another teapot, newly steaming, and poured for all three before sitting down.

"Your *winner* . . ." Serana said, her mouth twisting with distaste. She took a sip from her cup, lips softening.

"We unfortunately know of your winner," Don Eyr said. "His name is Her Nin bey'Pasra. A very bad man. A thief, and also a murderer, many times over."

Mar Tyn nodded, unsurprised.

"I saw the jacket," he said. "There are those who take particular pleasure in damaging pilots, but they will take easier meat, if they must."

"Yes."

Serana sighed.

"I should have left him the jacket, perhaps . . ."

Don Eyr reached across the table, and put his hand over hers.

"It is done," he said, firm and quiet. "Serana. It is done."

"True," she said, and slipped her hand away, giving him a crooked smile.

She rose, then, and moved to the bureau. Opening a drawer, she removed a packet, which she brought back to the table, and placed before Mar Tyn.

"We will allow you to tell us," she said, sitting down and picking up her tea cup, "if that might be worth shattered ribs, a broken arm, and a cracked head."

The packet was sealed. Mar Tyn ran a thumbnail down the seam–and sat staring as the coins rolled and danced along the table.

Here was not only the Luck's portion from gayn'Urlez, he thought, but the winner's, as well.

"A considerable sum," Don Eyr murmured.

Mar Tyn took a breath.

A very considerable sum, as he was accustomed to count money. Was it worth a beating that had nearly killed him?

Maybe, he thought. Maybe not the money, particularly, but what the money might *buy* him?

Oh, yes.

. . . but there was . . . a problem.

He glanced down at the sling cradling his right arm.

"Where may I find Fireyn?" he asked.

"She has a short-term outside of the house," Serana said. "It is possible that we might be able to answer your question in her stead."

He nodded.

"I only wonder how much longer the arm must be restrained–and if," he added, as the next thought came to him– "if it *must be* restrained, or that is only *advisable*."

Serana laughed.

"Hear him! *Only* advisable! Fireyn would gut him where he sits."

"Perhaps not so much," Don Eyr protested, "though she would certainly avail herself of a teaching moment."

Mar Tyn considered them both, wondering if he might receive an answer, after their laughter had died.

"Ah, he glares. I ask pardon," Serana said. "I have myself made the error of inquiring of Fireyn if a certain protocol was necessary or *merely prudent*. And I will tell you that it is well I keep my hair thus short, for she would have surely snatched me bald."

"From this you learn that Fireyn's advice is immutable," Don Eyr said. "I am also able to tell you that she felt another three weeks would see you completely healed and whole."

Three weeks?

Mar Tyn looked at the coins on the table, seeing their worth in terms of his life.

"Might I . . ." he said slowly, "be given another dose of accelerant?"

Don Eyr shook his head.

"No more accelerant for you, my friend. It is not without cost, and you have had three doses." He held up a hand, first finger extended, "One, to keep you with us, for you were in a perilous condition, and more likely to die than to live."

Mar Tyn blinked, recalling Fireyn's wry assurance that his head had proved harder than the wall.

"The skull injury?" he asked.

"The ribs," Don Eyr said. "Several had broken; at least one compromised your lungs. Fireyn immediately saw how it was, used the first aid kit, and employed the accelerant."

Mar Tyn drew a breath and bowed his head.

"I understand. The other occasions?"

"After you had wakened the first time and fainted almost immediately."

Mar Tyn eyed him.

"I held conversation with Fireyn; she told me her name, and asked for mine."

Don Eyr smiled, sadly.

"That was not the first time."

Mar Tyn took a breath.

"And the third time you surely recall, as you agreed to the dose."

"That, yes," Mar Tyn admitted, and asked. "Was I still so ill?"

"No more than you are accustomed to being, I think. Fireyn, however, took into her calculations that Her Nin bey'Pasra is still alive, and inclines toward holding a grudge."

"That was prudent of her," Mar Tyn said slowly. "I wonder—how long have I *been* in your care?"

"Two weeks."

"So long as that?" Mar Tyn murmured, hardly surprised; scarcely dismayed.

He let his eyes rest on the money again. *His money.*

Plus, the winner's share.

Knowing what he now knew, he asked himself again: was the money–the brighter future the money would assure him–*was* it worth a beating which, absent luck, and Fireyn, would have meant his death?

No, certainly not . . . except, he had *not* died, because neither luck nor Fireyn had been withheld from him.

That meant, then . . .

Well, and what *did* it mean?

"We have created more problems than we have solved," Serana remarked. "I regret that. Tell us what we might do, to ease your burden."

But Mar Tyn was thinking, now that Serana had put him on this unaccustomed path. His luck had brought him here. Why? Why *here*? Why had he been so badly damaged? Why put him in debt to these people–a debt he could never repay–

Repay.

He touched the money with just the tips of the fingers of his good hand.

The house cared for children, who were constantly at risk in Low Port. There would be those who would see the prosperity of the house and seek to steal it, and make it their own– witness the broken gate lock. To maintain such an establishment, with proper security–these things did not come cheap. That they existed at all in Low Port was . . . almost beyond belief.

He looked up.

"This," he said, meeting Serana's eyes, since he did not think he could meet Don Eyr's. Serana was the hard-headed one, he thought.

The ruthless one.

He cleared his throat.

"This," he said again. "I believe this is yours."

Serana's eyes opened wide.

"No, my friend, that it is not! We are established here in Low Port, but we strive—we strive to do better. There are children in the house, whom we have taken it up to educate, and so we must stand as an example to them."

Involuntarily, he glanced to Don Eyr, who nodded, solemnly.

"Indeed, that is your money. Very nearly you gave your life for it. Is it that have you no use for it?"

Almost, he laughed.

"I have good use for it," he said, and sighed. "But I cannot use it, with my arm thus."

"Why?" asked Don Eyr.

Mar Tyn sighed.

"In the Low Port, there are three houses—guild houses, you may call them—which offer a measure of safety to those Lucks who can afford the buy-in, and the monthly dues."

He took a breath.

"From least to greatest, they are: the House of Chance, the House of Fortune, and Prosperity."

"And you have here . . ." Serana placed her fingertips lightly against the coins, "enough to buy into Prosperity."

It was a question born of honest ignorance, and he did not laugh at her.

"The only way to join Prosperity is to be born there," he said gently, and nodded at the riches on the table. "That, however, will buy me a place in the House of Fortune, and pay my dues for a year or two."

Serana frowned, and looked beyond him, to Don Eyr. Mar Tyn waited, and presently, her eyes came back to him.

"These are princely prices, for Low Port."

"Yes. It is why most of us are freelances."

"But tell me why you cannot go inside of this hour and buy yourself safety. If it is for the need of a guard, perhaps one of us may accompany you."

"As it happens, it is for this." He rocked his arm in its sling. "I will be asked if I am accident-prone. That would make me a bad risk for the House."

"I see," Don Eyr frowned. "They must, of course, tend to their profit."

There was no answer to that, and Mar Tyn made none, merely frowning down at the table, and trying to work out the moves.

"What would you have us do?" Serana asked.

He stirred, and looked up at her.

"I have lodgings," he said. "But I cannot have such a sum with me, there, or on the streets."

"But, that is easy!" Serana said, looking over his head to meet Don Eyr's eyes. "We can hold it in the safe."

"Yes;" he agreed; "that is no trouble at all."

A safe. Who possessed such a thing? Well. Carmintine the pawnbroker would very likely hold this dragon's hoard for him, as she already held the greater balance of his money. She would, of course, charge him interest. With such a sum, that would be no small expense, and he was still left with the problem of transporting it through the streets.

No, best to leave it where it was.

"You understand," Serana said softly, "that there *are* children in the house, and they are our priority."

"Therefore your money is lucky," Don Eyr said, "for it will receive our same protection, though it is of far less value."

Mar Tyn stared at him, but he seemed to be serious.

"I will be pleased to leave my money under the protection of your house," he said slowly. "What interest will you charge?"

Serana half-laughed.

"What a place this is!" she exclaimed. "We will hold your money for love, my friend. Or, if you will have your Balance, we will hold it in payment for having brought more trouble into your life."

"After *saving* my life," Mar Tyn added, but there seemed to be no arguing with her, and he was suddenly aware of a small twitching in the soles of his feet.

"I feel that I must go," he said, looking between them; "now."

Don Eyr rose immediately.

"Allow me to help you with your boots," he said.

Three

His feet took him home.

Which was to say, to the customer entrance of Bendi's House of Joy. He tried to bring his meager influence to bear; to force his purposeful march past the front and round to the back of the house, the delivery door, and the stairs to the attic room where he slept, which he was let to have so that his luck would shield the house.

Of course, his preference counted for nothing.

Cray was on the front door, a man big even for a Terran, and who thought more quickly with his fists than his head.

Still, they had never fallen out, nor had much to do with each other, beyond a nod, and a murmured greeting.

Today, however, Cray saw him approaching, and shifted to stand in the center of the door, muscled arms crossed over powerful chest.

"Go away," he said.

Mar Tyn stopped just out of grabbing distance.

"I need to see Bendi."

"Go away," Cray repeated, and Mar Tyn was wondering if his feet were so eager that they would try a dart around the big man, and through the door.

Possibly, he would be fast enough, even with the odd balance lent by the sling.

It was not put to the test however, for here came Bendi out of the house, to stand beside Cray, fists on her hips, and her face flushed so dark that the ragged gash along the left side of her face stood out like ivory.

"You! Find a cush job somewhere else, did you, Luck? See what's happened to *me* while you were gone! I've got three hurt, and a broken water pipe, because *you* couldn't be bothered to pay your rent! Do you think I'm letting you back in here now?"

"I–" began Mar Tyn, but Bendi had noticed the sling.

138

She stiffened, her fists fell to her sides.

"*Get out,*" she snarled.

"Bendi–"

"Get out! Your luck's broken, hasn't it? Get away from me and mine before you bring down worse upon us!"

"I'll go," Mar Tyn said; understanding that this was not an argument he could win. "Only let me get my clothes from upstairs, and the money I had asked you to hold– "

"The money went to repair the pipe," she interrupted, "and I know better than to let broken Luck into my house. Go away, *now*, or Cray will kill you."

That, Mar Tyn thought, was possible. Bendi was beyond angry; she was terrified. Terrified that his broken luck would visit more grief on her house.

He was inclined to mourn the money he had given to bind her trust, and his other shirt–nearly new! But . . . he had money, he reminded himself. He could buy another shirt.

So, he went away; his feet walking him to the right, down the long block of fallen-in buildings, and right again, round the corner, and up the alley that ran between Bendi's house and the grab-a-bite next door. That was where the bolt-door was, and there–there stood Jonsie, Bendi's partner and sometimes worker, holding a sack, which he held out as Mar Tyn came near.

"Your stuff," he said, even the Low Port patois bearing the accent of his native speech. "Nothing to do for the coins, I'm feared; long days them're spent."

"I'm grateful," Mar Tyn said, taking the sack. There was a slight rattle, which would be his sewing kit–all he had left of Keplyr–and the weight suggested that Jonsie had rousted out his second pair of pants, as well as his extra socks and small clothes.

"'s'all right," said Jonsie. "Jes' don't be seen, gawn out. Bad for both of us, that."

"Yes," Mar Tyn said feverently.

His feet turned him around, back to the mouth of the alley, and up the street, away from all of Bendi's doors.

#

The sack made walking . . . awkward.

Not that people carrying sacks were anything unusual in Low Port. In his particular case, however, he had only one good arm to use for defense–and it was occupied with the sack. He supposed he might simply push the thing into the arms of anyone who tried to take it, and make good his escape when they fainted in astonishment.

A small tremor of nerves disturbed him at the thought of giving away his clothes, even as a tactic for survival. He could, he reminded himself again, buy more clothes. *Better* clothes, though he always tried to promptly mend any tears, and to wash himself and his clothing, regularly. That was Keplyr's training, Keplyr having been Mid House, before he came of age a Luck, and his clan of respectable Healers cast him out into Low Port.

As it happened, no one tried for Mar Tyn's sack, and he turned into Litik Street where the pawnshop was located with something like a spring in his step–

His feet faltered–and stopped moving altogether.

There was smoke in the air, and a crowd down toward the middle of the street, where the pawnshop was located. The pawnshop, where he leased space in Carmintine's safe, for his money–his savings. His *considerable* savings, which had been very nearly enough to buy himself a place in Chance . . .

He walked, carefully, through the smoke that got thicker the nearer he came, until he was on the edge of the crowd staring at the burnt ruin of Carmintine's shop.

There was something going on at the front of the crowd, that he was too short to see. With a sigh, he carefully slipped into the mass of bodies, and squirmed forward.

It was slow going, and surprisingly painful, as his not-yet-healed arm in its sling bumped against solid bodies–and the solid bodies pushed back, or, at best, did not yield.

Finally, though, he made it to the front edge of the crowd, and there was Carmintine, sooty and grey from head to boot soles, and four others who were known on the streets as enforcers for hire. It would appear that Carmintine had just finished paying them to stand as guards on the gutted shop, and keep away those who might risk burnt fingers for the silver and gemstones they might find among the ash.

Such protections did not come cheap, and Carmintine had hired a good team that stayed bought, once they had accepted their money–at least until the first payment was missed.

Mar Tyn slipped back into the crowd, and, once beyond it, turned away. There was no use trying to speak to Carmintine now, with her livelihood gone to ash, and the hungry crowd pressing 'round. He would try again later, maybe, but he thought he knew what would happen, if he asked after the money the pawnbroker had been holding for him.

He paused in the street, changed his grip on the sack, and started away back up the street, when he heard his name called.

Glancing to the side, he saw Pelfit the Gossip in her rickety roost, waving urgently at him. He thought he would ignore the summons, then thought better of it, just before his feet turned him toward her.

"Yes?" he said, when he had arrived, and all she did was look at his arm in its sling, and the sleeve of his jacket pinned up out of the way.

She dragged her eyes up to his face, and held out one unsteady, bony hand.

"Word on the street, Mar Tyn Luck."

Pelfit's ears were large. If not intelligent, she was at least shrewd, and more often than not her gossip was worth the price.

Mar Tyn set his sack down between his feet, reached awkwardly into a jacket pocket and pulled out the packet of bread and jam that Don Eyr had insisted he take with him.

"Fresh bread," he said, "and berry spread."

Her hand darted, and the neat packet was gone, vanished into layers of rags.

"Word on the street," she said again. "A dozen days now I've heard it. Mar Tyn's luck is broken, and he's a danger to all who knew him."

Mar Tyn frowned. That sort of Word could be got out on the street easily enough, a matter of whispering into the ear of this Gossip and that one, with a protein bar slipped into a receptive hand as proof of the news . . .

"Word on the street," Pelfit said again, her hand extended.

He considered her.

"If you would tell me that Bendi's house has taken hurt, and the pawnbroker burned out, I have those Words, I thank you."

She sighed, her hand falling away.

"That's everything, then," she said slowly, and turned away from him. She did not wish him well.

Of course not. She'd already taken a risk, speaking to a man who wore his broken Luck plainly visible in a sling.

Mar Tyn took a breath, picked up his sack, and waited a heartbeat, to see if his feet would move him.

When they did not, he walked away up the street, taking care how he went, until he turned down a short dim alley, and slipped into a niche in the crumbling stone wall.

When he was satisfied that no one had followed him, he proceeded down the alley, until he came to a set of metal stairs, which he climbed until he reached a ledge of that same crumbling stone, that made the beginning of a graceful arch across the alley–and ended not quite halfway across.

He settled himself carefully in the shadow against the wall, made certain he could see the alley below in both directions, and set himself to think.

Mar Tyn Luck was a danger, to himself and all who know him.

That was a warning. A warning that Mar Tyn was being hunted, and those who knew him would do best for themselves by thrusting him away.

It was . . . interesting, in its way, that *he* had been given a warning. That sort of courtesy was reserved for the disagreements that might fall between Lady voz'Laathi and her rivals. Not merely a warning, but an invitation to choose sides in an upcoming war.

Mere Lucks did not go to war, though some were *brought* to war by those who sought to insure their victory.

No.

His blood ran cold, with nothing of his gift in it; merely his own reasoned certainty.

'ware, Mar Tyn Luck, whose friends will suffer.

The small mischiefs at Bendi's house; the greater one at the pawnshop–those had

been . . . surety. Proof that whoever had put that Word out was in earnest.

Deadly earnest.

And, further . . .

He closed his eyes.

The warning was not *for him.*

It was for his friends–Bendi, Carmintine.

Don Eyr. Serana. The children.

The bakery, with its broken gate latch.

The bakery, where Her Nin bey'Pasra had lost his winnings—and his jacket of honor, too.

Someone—the likeliest being Her Nin bey'Pasra—was going to war against the bakery. He was calling for allies, who would share in the profits gained, which would include the children, so carefully kept, so proud, and so soft.

Mar Tyn's mouth dried. He thrust himself clumsily to his feet, the elbow of his slinged arm banging against the wall and sending a thrill of pain through his bones.

He waited, panting, until his vision cleared, then began to pick his way across the rubble, back to the top of the metal stairs.

He must return to the bakery, at once.

Four

For a wonder, his feet remained obedient to his will, walking his chosen route at a prudent pace. He therefore arrived at the bakery as he chose to do–at the front door. His decision was influenced by the certainty that Serana would have long ago managed the difficulty with the lock on the back gate, and that whoever kept the front door would have instructions on whether he was to be admitted.

What he would do, if the house would not admit him–he hadn't . . . quite . . . worked out.

But, as it happened, he need not have wasted any thought on that question.

He had barely gotten his foot on the lower step when the door sprung open and Fireyn leapt down to grab him 'round the waist, hoisting him and carrying him up the rest of the flight. A second of her kind, also bearing the scars of those who had been Betrayed, stood in the doorway, gun not quite showing; sharp eyes parsing the street.

He swung out as they reached him, clearing the way for their entrance; and swung back behind them, pulling the door closed.

Locks were engaged. Mar Tyn heard them snap and sing into place even as Fireyn set him on his feet in the hallway, and looked down at him, eyes squinted; an expression on her scarred face that he could not, precisely, read.

"Are you hurt?" she snapped.

"No. Not hurt. Is Don Eyr to house? Serana? I have news."

"They are teaching. We heard the whisper on the street. We were afraid, that you had heard it too late."

Mar Tyn sighed and sagged against the wall.

"Aidlee!" Fireyn raised her voice slightly, and there came a stirring down the hall in answer.

The girl who had not lost her breads appeared, wiping her hands on an apron. Fireyn nudged him forward.

"Ser eys'Ornstahl wants some tea, and a quiet place to sit until Don Eyr's class is over."

"Yes," said the girl, and smiled at him. "This way, Ser. You may rest in the book room. I will bring a tray."

#

The tray had held not only tea, but several fist-sized rolls which Aidlee named cheese breads. She filled his cup, asked him if he wanted anything else, and when he said that he was very well fixed, told him that he might find her in the kitchen if he went left down the hall from the doorway to the book room.

She left him then, and he sat in the chair she had shown him to, and drank his tea in small, appreciative sips. Such good tea, that pleased the nose as the cup was lifted, and the tongue as the sip was taken.

He closed his eyes and savored that small wonder, and when he had done, he put the cup back on the tray, stood up and looked around him.

Book room, he thought, and it was so—an entire room full of books. Upstairs, in the quiet room where he had shared breakfast with Serana and Don Eyr—he had thought *that* room held a wealth of books. But here . . .

It was not much larger than the upstairs room, but of more regular proportions. Several long tables marched down the center, bracketed by benches. Each table held four notepads—two at the top of the table, and two at the foot. At the wall nearest the door was a small table, supporting a computer. Light strips along the ceiling made the place bright, in the absence of windows.

Mar Tyn went to the nearest shelf and began to read the titles.

He had not made much progress before he heard the door open behind him.

He turned as Don Eyr entered, a white cap on his head, and an apron over all. His eyes looked tired, but he smiled when he saw he had Mar Tyn's attention, and came quickly to his side.

"We were worried," he said, grabbing Mar Tyn's good arm in both of his hands. "I am glad that you came back to us."

"You may not be glad, very soon. Have you heard the Word on the street?"

Don Eyr frowned.

"It is said that Mar Tyn the Luck is lucky no more, and has become a danger to his friends."

"Yes!" said Mar Tyn. "I ought not to have come back, only–"

Only, his money, enough to buy his way to Fortune, and, belatedly, the thought that, after all, his gift had not played him false.

First, though, to be certain.

"I had not thought to ask before–who is your protector?"

"Our protector?" Don Eyr shook his head. "We protect ourselves, here."

"That will not do," Mar Tyn said. "Not in this. They–Her Nin bey'Pasra, is my belief– has put out a call for allies. He has declared war on this place–on you, on Serana, and everyone you mean to keep safe here. He will see all you have built destroyed. You cannot stand against him alone. Here–"

He had realized on his way back–realized at last why his gift had guided him here that night; understood why he had been given no opportunity to refuse . . .

He reached into his pocket, and brought the thing out.

"Here!" he said again, and opened his fist to show Lady voz'Laathi's token.

Don Eyr glanced at his palm; his shoulders moved in a silent sigh even as the door worked and Serana strode into the bookroom.

"What have we, a tableau?" she asked, stopping behind Don Eyr's shoulder, and glancing down at Mar Tyn's palm.

"Our Lady of Benevolence," she said, softly. "She is not so well-named, that one."

She raised her eyes and met Mar Tyn's glance.

"Are you one of hers, my friend?"

"I am not, but you ought to make haste to become so!" he said sharply.

He should have waited for Serana, he thought, wildly. Serana, who was ruthless, and practical–and who would surely grasp the weapon that he had brought to her hand . . .

"Now, why, I wonder?" she asked, still in that soft tone.

"Because Her Nin bey'Pasra calls openly for allies on the streets. He means to break the bakery, Serana, and destroy it all!"

She said nothing, merely continuing to wait politely, her eyes fixed on his face.

Mar Tyn took a breath, found he had no more words, spun and slapped the coin on the table.

"Use it," he said, harshly.

"Of a certainty, we will treat it as it deserves," Serana told him.

She reached out and gripped his shoulder. "You are concerned for us. It says much, and we love you the more for it. Tell me, what will *you* do?"

"I?" he stared, at a loss for a moment, though he had thought of that, thought it straight through. He would–he would . . .

Oh, yes.

"I will take my money, that you hold for me, and buy myself safety."

"This is intriguing," Don Eyr said. "But I beg you will rethink that plan, if only for the moment. Ail Den and Cisco have been keeping the streets under eye, and there are loiterers where usually there are none. They are not yet an army, but they would be able to visit a great deal of trouble upon a one-armed man, especially if he were slowed by the weight of so much money."

Mar Tyn looked at him bleakly.

"I cannot stay here."

"Because you will bring bad luck down on our house?"

It was said gently; without mockery. Mar Tyn drew a hard breath.

"There is no such thing as *bad luck*," he said straitly. "There is no such thing as *good luck*. There is only Luck, which is an . . . energy. A field. Some of us are focal points for the field, but make no mistake, *it* uses *us*. Lucks who attempt to force their gift die more quickly than those of us who are receptive, and hold ourselves ready to act in defense of our lives."

If we are allowed so much, he added silently, Keplyr's death flickering behind his eyelids.

"My gift sent me to gayn'Urlez Hell; it drew Lady voz'Laathi's coin to me; and granted my winner what would be a fortune even in Mid Port. Luck led me here, to this place, to you, and those you protect, with this token of the lady's protection. To preserve you and your works. You had asked me *why here*? *This* is the answer. It would not have served so well, had I been killed, because you might not have found the token in my pocket, or known it for what it was."

He took a breath, looked from Serana's face to Don Eyr's.

"I beg you, do not cast this aside."

Serana looked at Don Eyr. Don Eyr looked at Serana.

They both looked back at Mar Tyn.

"It is a kindness," Don Eyr said gently. "I—we—accept that you offer us this from the fullness of your heart. We are grateful, for your regard, and for your courage, which brought you back, knowing your danger."

"You worry that we are soft, and easy to crack," Serana said then. "But you have not considered—perhaps you do not know!—that we have kept our place here for nearly four years. This is not the first time a mob has attempted to break us. We are not complacent, but we are, I think, not in as much danger as you believe us to be. Stay and stand with us. Will your gift allow it?"

He considered himself–feet at rest, blood a little quick, but without the sizzle of the field manifest. Truth told, he was doubtful that he *could* leave, if it came to that . . .

"My gift . . . insists upon it," he said, wryly.

Five

The streets fought for them.

He had not realized–had not been part of the life of the bakery long enough to . . . *see it.*

The bakery's influence did not stop at its reinforced stone walls. And it was a bigger place, of itself, than he had understood: a huge stone square, that Fireyn had told him had once been a barracks and military offices. One such office had a large window onto Crakle Street, which was now a shop, that sold bread, and other foods, which the . . . *neighbors* purchased with coin, or barter, or labor. Children who lived on those surrounding streets attended classes with the children who lived inside. Adults also came for classes, for meetings, for sparring sessions.

Serana and Cisco taught courses in self-defense. Fireyn taught strategy and first aid.

All taught a curriculum of self-esteem, and . . . ethics.

Ethics . . .

Mar Tyn had tried the word on his tongue in Don Eyr's hearing, and had been given a book tape for his trouble. He'd tucked it into his pocket, promising to read it after the current event was done.

For, despite the startling fact that its protectors were more than four adults and the children themselves, the war was going . . . not well for the bakery.

To be fair, neither were matters proceeding as quickly as Her Nin bey'Pasra and his allies doubtless wished.

Which was probably why they decided to bring fire into it.

The first thing they gave to the flames was the Gossip Roost at the corner of Toom Street. It was only made from cardboard and plas–and burned too fast to serve as a rallying point. Nor was anyone hurt, since the Gossip himself had taken shelter inside the bakery.

When news of his loss reached him, he had sighed, and sat, tight-lipped and silent, glaring at nothing in particular, until one of the older children came to him with a notepad.

"Bai Sly, help me sketch what the Roost looked like," the child said earnestly. "How big was it? Were there any drawers or cupboards?"

"That is so, when this is over, we can rebuild quickly," Cisco said to Mar Tyn, when they stopped at the kitchen for jelly-bread to have with them, in case they should become hungry during their shift as door guards.

"Rebuild," Mar Tyn repeated, as they moved to take over their post from Don Eyr and Ail Den.

"Yes."

"What if the invaders win?"

"They won't." Cisco threw him a grin. "If this plays like the other attacks, what's going to happen is they'll get bored in a couple days, when they find out we're not as easy as they thought we'd be, and start fighting among themselves."

They turned into the hallway that led to the side door post.

"Why don't they fire the street?" asked Mar Tyn.

There were signs of fire on every street in Low Port. Not all–or even most–had been set by bullies intent on smoking out their prey. But such tactics weren't unknown.

"They may try to fire the street," Don Eyr said as they reached the door. "But they will have a hard time of it."

"Why?"

"Fireyn and Dale–" Dale was the other one of the Betrayed attached to the bakery– "produced a flame retardant, and all the neighborhood helped to coat the buildings."

"Most of the buildings," said Cisco. "A couple are still vulnerable, like the Gossip Roost, but the most aren't."

He stepped forward.

"The Watch changes. Go get something to eat, and some rest."

"It has been quiet," Don Eyr said, and produced a weary smile. "The watch changes, brothers."

He and Ail Den passed up the hall. There was a small *boom*, which was the far door closing behind them.

#

The riot arrived exactly two hours after Mar Tyn and Cisco had taken over the door.

Dozens of bullies came storming down the street, throwing stones, breaking doors, engaging with the defenders of the street. Knives and pipes were in evidence, employed by both sides. There were no guns–not yet . . .

Cisco swore, and pulled a comm from his pocket, stepping back to call Serana.

Mar Tyn stood his post, breath caught in horror. It came to him that the allies had gotten bored already and this rolling wave of destruction was Her Nin bey'Pasra's way of keeping them to his cause.

He sighed, then, relieved to be safe behind closed doors, rather than scrambling for cover inside the erupting mayhem–and swore aloud.

His feet–his feet were moving, and there were locks on the door; locks a one-armed man could not manipulate, even if he did know the codes.

He thrust his good hand out, bracing himself against the wall, but his feet kept walking, inexorable, toward the locked door.

There was a snap, and a flicker, as if Low Port's spotty power grid had achieved one of its frequent overloads.

Mar Tyn put his good hand out to grip the handle–and pulled the door open.

His feet marched him out into the riot. He pulled the door closed. Behind him, he heard Cisco yell.

#

His feet turned left, determinedly moving into the teeth of the riot. He was, Mar Tyn thought dispassionately, going to die. He was going to be torn into pieces, like Keplyr had been, trying to use his Luck–and who had known better than Keplyr that Luck was *no one's* to use!– trying to *use his Luck* to turn aside a mob raging down on a band of Mid-Porters, who had crossed the line with no purpose other than to bring food to the hungry.

He dodged a knife half-heartedly thrust at his belly, ducked away from a blow that would have knocked his head from his shoulders–all without a break in stride. In fact, he had gotten past the worst of the confusion and fighting before the expected hand closed 'round his collar and he was jerked backward, into a thin space between two houses.

"You!" Her Nin bey'Pasra shook him like a mongrel with a rat. "Where's my money?"

"I don't have it, Ser." The sound of his own voice astonished him. He sounded utterly calm and unafraid.

A hard slap across his mouth; his head hit the plas wall. He stood, head turned half-aside, waiting for the next blow.

Which did not come.

"Do you want to live, Luck?" snarled his captor.

What game was this? Mar Tyn turned his head slightly, watching the other out of the side of his eye.

"I want to live," he said flatly.

"Then earn your life from me!"

Another blow–and the world went black.

#

Pain brought him back to consciousness. He was lying in the dirt, his head throbbing, and Her Nin bey'Pasra looming above him, smiling.

Mar Tyn closed his eyes, seeing his own doom in that smile.

"Look at me! Unless you've decided you no longer want to live."

He opened his eyes and stared into the smile, which seemed to please the man.

"Give me victory in this war, Luck, and I will let you live."

A terrifying promise. Let to live, in Low Port, with all his limbs broken? Or with a knife wound to the gut?

Still . . .

"I will try what I may do," he said, which was not a lie, and added, "Ser."

Teeth glinted.

"Try," his winner advised. "Try hard."

The shift of balance warned him; he rolled, but he could not avoid the boot that came against his weak arm in its sling. Lightning flared through his head, and he screamed.

Curling around his damaged arm, he heard Her Nin bey'Pasra speak again.

"Give me the delm of flour and all of his treasures, or you *will* know pain, Luck.

"Now, *try!*"

There came the sound of steps, retreating, of a door being heavily slammed into place and the song of a lock being engaged.

Mar Tyn lay in the dirt, and wondered if, after all, there was such a thing as bad luck.

#

He might have passed out again. He woke to a touch. A touch from a soft, very cold hand, against his cheek.

Carefully, he opened his eyes.

A small, exceedingly dirty, child was kneeling next to him. Her hair was a dusty snarl, bruises and cuts were clearly visible between the rents in her rags.

"Hello," he said, very softly, feeling Luck burning in his blood.

She continued to stare at him out of light eyes surrounded by black bruises.

"You are like my mother was," she said, her voice gritty and low. "I can see the colors all around you."

He took a breath, deep and careful, and slowly, without taking his eyes from hers, he uncoiled until he was flat on his back.

"Was your mother Ahteya?" he asked her softly.

She closed her eyes, and turned her face away.

Mar Tyn waited, his bones on fire.

The child turned back to him, desperation in the gaunt, scratched face.

"I can fix it," she said.

"Fix what?"

"This," she said, and leaned forward, putting her two small hands against his newly-shattered arm.

Pain—no. Something far more exalted than mere pain flowed into him from the two cold points of her hands. He couldn't scream; he had no breath; and it continued, this strange, clear, not-pain; his arm was encased in it, and he imagined he could feel the broken bones grinding back into place.

Above him, the child whimpered, and he tried to tell her not to hurt herself, but he had no voice, until—

She lifted her hands away, and sat back on her heels. Tears made streaks of mud down her face. There was a sound, and she snapped around, gasping, but whatever—whoever—it was passed by their sturdy locked door.

Mar Tyn remained where he was, feeling nearly transparent, now that both pain and anti-pain had left him. Carefully, he raised his recently re-broken arm, turned it this way, that way; flexed his fingers.

Everything operated precisely as it should.

A Healer, he thought. *The child is a Healer.*

Awkwardly, he rolled into a seated position, and put two good arms around his knees. The child turned to face him again, and he saw that she was shivering.

He reached into his pocket and pulled out the packet of bread and jam, worse for its recent use, but certainly still edible.

"Eat," he said, offering it to her on the palm of his hand.

She stared at it; he saw her wavering on the edge of refusing, but one grubby hand snatched out, as if of its own accord, and she was unwrapping the treat.

"He'll be back," she whispered. "He'll beat me, unless I make the bakery unlucky. I can't make the bakery unlucky–can you?"

"No," he said softly, watching her cram the bread into her mouth. "I can't. There is no such thing as good luck or bad luck. There is only Luck."

She swallowed, somewhat stickily, and he wished he had water for her.

"He says I'm a Luck," she said. "A bad and *stupid* Luck."

"He knows nothing. What is your name?"

"Aazali."

"Aazali, my name is Mar Tyn, and I *am* a Luck, as your mother was. Thank you for healing my arm. I will take you away, and I swear to you, on my mentor's honor, that Her Nin bey'Pasra will never beat you again."

She looked up at him.

"You can promise this?"

He paused, listening to his blood.

"I can," he said, with absolute certainty. "I will take you to a safe place, to rest and to heal." That first, and most importantly. The rest of what must happen—that could wait until she was safe with Don Eyr and Serana.

"Where will you take me?" she asked him. She had stopped shivering, he saw. That was good.

"I will take you to the bakery. Will you come?"

"When the bakery falls and he finds me there, he'll kill me," she said matter-of-factly.

"The bakery is not going to fall," Mar Tyn said, certain again, as he was so rarely certain.

She considered him for a long moment.

"He killed my mother," she said.

"I know. He will not have you."

Another pause, as if she were looking very nearly at those colors she claimed to see spiraling around him.

"I'll come," she said at last.

"Good."

He rose, effortlessly, to his feet. She rose less easily, and wavered where she stood.

"It will be best," he said, "if I carry you."

Another ageless stare from those bruised light eyes.

"Yes," she said.

He bent and took her into his arms. She weighed nothing.

"Arms around my neck," he told her. "Head down. Eyes closed."

She did as he asked. Her hair scratched his chin.

He took a breath, standing quiet; and felt his feet begin to move.

"We go," he said, as they marched toward the door. "Hold firm."

There came a snap, and a fizzle, as if Low Port's spotty power grid had achieved one of its frequent overloads.

Ahead of them, the door sagged on its hinges.

Mar Tyn extended a hand and pushed it out of his way.

#

The riot had dissolved into isolated pockets of violence along the street–and what looked to be a full-fledged brawl across from the bakery.

Mar Tyn's feet walked steadily and with assurance down the littered street, detouring around rocks, and bodies, and other debris. The child in his arms scarcely seemed to breathe.

He had the side door of the bakery in his eye before the shout he had been expecting came from behind. His feet did not falter; he walked, not even looking aside.

"I'll kill you both!" Her Nin bey'Pasra roared. Heavy footsteps thundered from behind.

Ahead, the bakery door burst open. Fireyn had a gun in her hand, and her face was terrible to see. Cisco held the door, also showing a gun, and Don Eyr was scarcely behind him, shouting.

Mar Tyn's feet deigned at last to run. A shot sounded from behind; a second, and a thud, as if a sack of rocks had hit the street. His foot struck a rock, and he stumbled, throwing himself forward, into Don Eyr's arms.

The three of them pulled back into safety of the hallway; Fireyn leaping in behind.

Cisco slammed the door.

"Done?" he asked.

"Done and dead," she answered.

"What happened?" Don Eyr asked nearer at hand. He straightened slowly, one hand on Mar Tyn's shoulder; one hand on Aazali's narrow back.

"I'll tell you everything," Mar Tyn said. "But first–the child."

"Yes," Don Eyr said. "First–the child."

Six

The streets were recovered from the war; the rubble had been cleared away, the Gossip Roost rebuilt. Repairs had been made as needed. Classes had resumed.

Aazali sen'Pero and Mar Tyn eys'Ornstahl–well-fed, well-washed, well-dressed–stood in the large parlor, with Don Eyr, and Serana, and Fireyn.

"You should have a third," Serana said, not for the first time, "to guard your back."

It was prudent, but Mar Tyn's feet, rebels that they were, would have none of it.

"Myself, and Aazali," he said. "We cannot arrive as an armed delegation. Mid Port wouldn't understand."

Don Eyr stirred, and sighed, and spread his hands, meeting Serana's eyes with a small smile.

"He is correct, my love; accept it."

She sighed, her answering smile wry.

"In fact, I am over-protective."

"We share the fault," Fireyn said. She turned a stern eye on him. "Mar Tyn. You will be *prudent*."

He smiled at her with new-learned tenderness.

"Now, how can I promise that?"

Almost, she smiled in turn. Almost.

"Do what you might, then," she said.

"I will."

Serana dropped to one knee and opened her arms.

"My child, remember us. If you have need, come. You will always have a place with us."

"Thank you," Aazali said, and threw herself into the large embrace. "I might stay here," she whispered, but Serana put her at arm's length and shook her head.

"We cannot train you, and training you *must* have, for your own protection and that of your friends. If, when you are trained, you choose to come back to us, we will have you, gladly."

"Yes," said Aazali. They had, after all, been over this, many times.

She turned, then, to hug Don Eyr, then Fireyn, and at last came back to his side, slipping her small warm hand into his.

"Mar Tyn," she said, looking up into his face with grey eyes still shadowed from all she had endured. "It is time for us to go."

Seven

Some hours later, and they were in Mid Port. Thus far, no one had taken notice of them, neatly dressed and cleanly as they were. Mar Tyn was at one with his feet, as they walked into the pretty court, with its flowers and fountains, and the house just there, as if waiting for them.

Aazali's grip on his hand tightened on his as they climbed the stairs.

"Mar Tyn," she said, when they had finished the flight, and stood before the polished wooden door.

"Mar Tyn, what if they don't want me?"

This was not a new question, either, but he did not fault her for asking again.

"They would be fools, not to want you," he said patiently. "If it happens that they *are* fools, we will return to the bakery, and make another plan."

"Yes," she breathed, and he raised his free hand to touch the bell-pad.

Three notes sounded, muted by the door.

They waited.

The door opened, revealing a halfling with wide blue eyes and curling yellow hair. Doubtless, his face was pleasing enough when he smiled. But he was not smiling. He barely glanced at Aazali, his attention was all for Mar Tyn, or, rather, whatever he saw just beyond Mar Tyn's shoulder, which plainly pleased him not at all.

"We want none of your sort here," he said shortly. "Go, before the hall master comes."

It might, Mar Tyn thought, have been kindness, of its sort. He chose to believe so.

"You want none of my sort," he agreed. "But this child is one of yours, Healer, and the Hall holds an obligation to train her."

The boy's frown grew marked.

"Tainted . . ." he began–and spun as a shadow flickered behind him, and a plump woman, her pale red hair pulled into a long tail behind her head, stepped to his side.

"I will take care of these gentles, Tin Non," she said.

"Yes, Healer." The doorkeeper bowed and left them.

Mar Tyn met the Healer's pale blue eyes. She was, he thought, with a small shock, no older than he was. Surely, this was not the hall master.

"Tin Non gives you good advice," she told him. "You should be gone before the hall master arrives. We have perhaps twelve minutes."

With that she turned to the child standing very still beside him, her grip bruising his fingers.

She bent, her eyes on the child–and abruptly went to her knees, as if what she saw there were too much to bear, standing.

"So young," Mar Tyn heard her whisper, before she extended a plump hand.

"My name is Dyoli," she said softly. "May I know yours?"

"Aazali," the child said, ignoring the outstretched hand. "I am Aazali sen'Pero. And this is *my friend*, Mar Tyn eys'Ornstahl."

There was a small pause, during which the Healer slanted her eyes at him, before returning her attention to Aazali.

"I see that he is your good friend," she said, softly. "He is very brave to bring you here, placing himself so much at risk. I see that you honor him. I honor him, too."

She paused, as if she were scrutinizing something visible to only herself.

"We in this Hall will take care of you," she said, after a moment.

"Serana said you would train me," Aazali answered.

Healer Dyoli bowed her head.

"We will do that, also. But first, we will take care of you," she said softly, and offered her hand again. "Will you come with me?"

The child stiffened, her fingers tightening. Mar Tyn dropped to his heels, so that all of their faces were level.

"Aazali, this is what we had talked about," he said gently. "This is the *best* outcome to our plan."

"Yes," she said, then, and of a sudden threw herself around his neck.

"Stay safe," she said, her voice breaking on a sob. "Mar Tyn, *promise* me."

"Child, as safe as I may. You know that is everything I can promise."

"Yes," she said again, and he felt her whole body shudder as she sighed.

She moved her head, and kissed his cheek, then pushed against his shoulder.

He let her go, and watched as she stepped forward and at last took the Healer's hand.

"Thank you," she said, subdued, but willing.

"Thank you, Sister," the Healer answered, rising slowly. "I will do my best to be worthy of you."

Mar Tyn rose, as well, and cleared his throat. She looked to him.

"I have," he said, reaching toward an inner pocket. "Funds for the child's keep. Her mother is dead. She has no clan, no kin."

The Healer frowned, glanced past his shoulder, then looked into his face.

"The Hall will keep her, and I will myself take her under my care. You—use your money to secure your fortune, Mar Tyn eys'Ornstahl. I . . . feel, *very strongly*, that you ought to do so."

He blinked at her, momentarily wordless, but there—it was said that some Healers saw ahead in time.

"Thank you," he said. "I will take your advice."

She glanced behind her suddenly, the long tail of her hair swinging, and stepped back into the hallway, drawing Aazali with her.

"The hall master. Go, quickly! Stay as safe as you are able, Mar Tyn."

The door closed, and he turned, at one with his feet–down the stairs, and out of the courtyard, into the wide street, walking brisk and light, away from Mid Port–back to Low Port and his fortune.

Block Party

The lights were on at the Wayhouse, which was still enough of a novelty that Algaina paused after she'd unlocked the shop door to look at it. Wasn't many got up as early in the day as she did, an' the Wayhouse . . . well, it was a *wayhouse*, wasn't it? Always had been, back to when the Gilmour Agency ran Surebleak. Wasn't meant but to give a newbie on the street someplace in outta the snow to sleep while they got themselves sorted an' settled.

This new batch of folks'd been in maybe four, five days, an' every morning, when Gaina opened the shop, there was the light. Made her feel a kinda warm pleasureableness, that she wasn't awake alone in the dark.

Well.

She shook herself and turned back to the shop, her thoughts still half on the Wayhouse. According to the neighbors, there were at least four kids living there, but not one of 'em come in to her shop for sweets. Might be they was shy. She wondered if she oughta take a plate o'cookies up, whatever was left over, when the shop closed. Introduce herself. Find out who was awake so early, every day, and what they did in the dark hours.

#

Algaina was in the back, getting the batch of sparemint cookies outta the oven, when she heard the bell on the front door ring out, which would be Luzeal, comin' in for her hot 'toot and warm roll before headin' down to Boss Conrad's territory an' the archive project. Luzee was always her first customer, ever since the first day she opened up.

"Be right out!" she called. "Got somethin' I want you to taste."

Wasn't no answer from the front room, which was typical; Luzee needed a cup o'toot to make her civilized.

Algaina closed the oven door, and stepped back into the shop, sliding the tray onto the counter, and looking 'round.

It wasn't Luzee who was her first customer this morning; it was Roe Yingling, who wasn't zackly a stranger–she let him run a ticket, after all–but nowhere near a reg'lar.

Algaina wasn't that fond of Roe, but he was a neighbor, and aside from having loud opinions at inconvenient times, he didn't stint the street.

"Mornin'," she said, giving him a nod. He'd already drawn himself a cup and was sipping it gingerly, wanting the warmth against the cold, but not wanting to burn his tongue. "You're up early."

He nodded around a sip from the cup.

"Word on the street's they're hiring over Boss Kalhoon's territory, long-term labor. Gonna go over an' see what I can get."

"Hadn't heard that," Algaina said; "good luck with it."

"Need it all, an' then some," Roe said, leaning over the pot and topping off his cup. "Body's gotta be quick if they wanna grab a job before a newbie gets it."

That was Roe's biggest and most frequent complaint, right there, Algaina knew. Not that there'd been that much work, the way things'd been fixed before Boss Conrad showed up to sort Surebleak out, which it–and they–surely had needed. Breaking up the old ways hadn't made work so much as it made time and room for 'bleakers to be able to roll up their sleeves and get on with what needed doin'.

The newbies, they'd followed the Boss to Surebleak, and they were a point of contention. So far's Algaina knew or saw, they was just as willing to work as any 'bleaker, an' somewhat more'n others. They come in with off-world skills, certain enough, but they wasn't 'bleakers. They didn't know what work needed done before that other piece o'work could get done, or necessarily how the weather played in–stuff that 'bleakers knew by instinct. Mostly, the work was team-based, 'bleaker and newbie, and plenty too much for everybody.

Still, there was a certain class of streeter, of which Roe Yingling was one, who wanted to have it that the newbies was taking work away from them, an' there wasn't nothing could convince 'em otherwise.

All of which was worth hopin' that Roe got work today.

"You better get movin'," Algaina said. "Early worker 'presses the boss."

Roe nodded at her.

"Zackly what I'm thinkin'. Need a couple rolls to have in m'pocket for lunch," he said. "What was that you wanted me to taste?"

Well, she hadn't wanted Roe tastin' her sparemint, she'd wanted Luzee. Still, she'd said the words and he'd heard 'em–an' it couldn't hurt to have another opinion.

"Here go," she said, holding out the tray. "Take one o'them and let me know what you think. Something new I'm thinking about adding in."

He took a cookie–not quite the biggest–and bit into it, eyes, narrowed.

While he was chewing, she got his two rolls, and wrapped 'em up in paper against the probable condition of the inside of his coat pocket. He took another bite, and was ruminatin' over it, when the bell rang, and a kid scooted in, let the door bang closed behind her–and stopped, big-eyed, and shivering, taking stock.

Algaina considered her: Too young to be out by herself before the sun was up. She was wearing a good warm sweater, pants and boots, but no coat or hat. Her hair was reddish brown and hung in long tangles down below her shoulders.

"Sleet," muttered Roe, not nearly quiet enough for a kid's ears to miss; "it's one a *them*."

Algaina frowned at him, but he was staring at the kid, cold as she was, an' tryin' to decide if she liked where she found herself.

Of a sudden, a big grin lit up her thin face. She rushed up to the counter, dodging under Roe's elbow, and addressed herself at length to Algaina in a high, sweet voice.

Algaina frowned and held up a hand.

"Slow down, now, missy. My ears ain't as young as your tongue."

The girl frowned, reddish brows drawing together 'til there was a crease 'tween 'em, her head tipped to one side. Finally, she raised her right hand palm out, like Algaina had raised hers, and said, "Slow down."

"That's right," Algaina told her with a nod. "Now whyn't you tell me what you just said–slow enough so I can hear it."

"Goomorn," the girl said obediently; "beyou manake–baneken–*cookies*!"

The last word came out as a triumphant shout, like it was the only one she was sure of, thought Algaina. On the other hand, if you only had one word, it was pretty smart to be sure it paid out profits right away.

"That's right," she said. "I bake cookies. You want one?"

"You gonna feed it?" Roe asked, still not botherin' to keep his voice down.

Algaina glared at him.

"Feedin' you, ain't I?"

He opened his mouth, and she shook her finger at him.

"You finish that cookie, Roe Yingling, and get yourself goin' or you'll miss all the good jobs!"

He blinked–and shoved the rest of his cookie into his mouth.

Algaina turned back to the kid. Out from the Wayhouse, sure enough. Looked like somebody at home'd moved their eyes for a half-second, and she decided to go splorin'. Algaina's kid had done the same when he'd been what she guessed was this one's age. Scared her to death, so it had, until she found him wandering the street, or a neighbor brought him back.

Best thing to do, really, was to keep her til whoever was prolly already looking for her came by.

So.

Algaina bent forward some and caught her eye.

"You want a cookie?" she asked again.

The girl blinked.

"Cookie," she asserted.

"Comin' right up," Algaina said, and chose a nice big sparemint from the tray. She held it down across the counter. "You try that and tell me how you like it."

The girl took the cookie from her hand with a solemn little bow, and bit into it, her eyes squinched in concentration.

"Gaina," Roe began, low-voiced.

"Later," Algaina told him.

Roe took a hard breath, an amount of stubborn coming into his face, and who knows what he might've said next, except the bell rang again, and in come a boy wearing an oversized flannel shirt over a high-neck sweater, good tough pants, and worn-in boots, carrying a bright red coat over one arm. He caught the door, and eased it closed, the while his eyes were on the kid.

"Elaytha."

She spun on a heel, and threw up her arms, nibbled cookie still in one hand.

"Donnnee!" she cried, rushing toward him.

He didn't bend down to take her hug, nor even smiled, just stood there with his arms folded, and a frown on his face.

She stopped, arms falling to her sides, cookie still gripped tight.

"Elaytha," he said again, and held out the coat. "It is cold. You wear this when you go out. Also, you frightened your sister."

His voice was level; his accent marked, but understandable.

The response to this was a burst of words as musical as they were unintelligible—which was cut off by a sharp movement of the boy—no, Algaina thought; *not* a boy. A man grown, only a little short and scrawny, like *they* was.

"In Terran, Elaytha," he said, still in that stern, solemn voice. "We speak Terran here."

"Pah," the girl said, comprehensively. She advanced upon her—brother, at a guess, Algaina thought—cookie extended.

"You try that," she said, her inflection and accent Algaina's own, "and tell me how you like it."

"Yes, very well." He took the cookie, and thrust the coat forward. "You will put this coat on," he said sternly. "*Now*, Elaytha."

She sighed from the soles of her boots, but she took the coat and shoved first one arm, then the other into the sleeves.

"Seal it," her brother—Donnie—said in that same tone.

Another sigh, but she bent her head, and began to work on the fastenings.

He watched her for a moment to be sure she was in earnest, then raised his head to meet Algaina's eyes. His were dark brown, like his hair.

"We watch her," he said, in his careful Terran, "but she is very quick."

She grinned at him.

"I remember what it was like, raising my boy," she said. "Yours looks like another handful."

He tipped his head, eyes narrowing, then nodded slightly.

"A handful. Indeed. I am happy that she came no further, and hope you will forgive this disturbance of your peace."

"No disturbing done. Bakery's open for bidness. I'm glad she come inside. It's cold this morning, even for born streeters like us." She nodded at Roe, who hissed lightly, and turned away to pick up the wrapped rolls.

"Thanks, Gaina," he said. "On my ticket, right?"

"Right," she told him, and watched him push past the girl and the man without a nod or a glance, goin' out the door into the lightening day.

"You have a taste of that cookie and lemme know what you think," Algaina said brightly, to take attention away from Roe bein' so rude. "New receipt; just trying it out the first time."

Donnie gave her a particular look, and a nod.

"I am honored," he said, and took a bite, chewing as solemnly as the child.

"Donnnee," Elaytha said.

He held up a hand, and closed his eyes.

After a moment, he opened his eyes.

"The texture," he said slowly. "It wants some–" He frowned, looked down at the kid, and held out what was left of the cookie. She took it and had it gone in two bites.

"It wants–" he said again, and stopped with a sigh.

"Your forgiveness; I have not the word. I will demonstrate. Elaytha, make your bow to the baker."

She turned and did so, smiling sunnily, the red coat meant for a taller, wider child. Like her brother's shirt had been made for somebody Terran sized.

Straightening, she added a rapid sentence, that Gaina guessed was some order of thank you.

"You're welcome," she said. "You come again, anytime you like. But you don't get no cookies unless you're wearing your coat, unnerstan me?"

She pouted, damn if she didn't, but answered, "Unnerstan."

"Good," she said, and turned her head, eye drawn by a movement. Donnie was making his own bow.

"Thank you," he said. "I will demonstrate. For the moment, we are wanted at home." He held out a hand.

"Come, Elaytha."

She took his hand. They turned to the door–and paused, as it opened to admit Luzeal.

"'Morning," she said, giving the two of them a nod and a smile before passing on. "Gaina, I'm starving! Got any mint rolls?"

"When don't I got mint rolls?" she asked, as Donnie and Elaytha exited the shop. "Got something else, too–want you to give it a try."

#

Luzee was carrying a three-ring binder under one arm like she'd taken to doin' ever since the call came out from the Lady and the Perfessor for old records, old letters, old books–all and anything.

Luzeal's family, they'd been in the way of managing the Office of the Boss, 'way back when the Agency was still on-world, and the Boss–the really big Boss, who oversaw it all–was called The Chairman. Even though they'd left her just like they left everybody, Luzeal's great-grandma'd organized a rescue operation, and moved all The Chairman's papers, and files, and memory sticks and, well–everything, down the basement of their own house, so it'd all be safe.

Which, Algaina admitted, it had been, all this time. Safe as houses, like they said. Safer'n most people'd been, includin' Luzee's grandma, who'd got herself retired by standin' in front of The Chairman's front door and tellin' the mob of Low Grades they couldn't come in.

Luzeal headed right for the hot-pot. She drank the first cup down straight, just like every morning, and brought the second over to the little table in the corner, so her and Algaina could talk while one et her breakfast and t'other minded the oven.

Algaina set the roll out on a plate, and ducked into the back to take the next batch out. More rolls, this was; rolls was the best she could do, not havin' a mother-of-bread, like grandpa'd wrote about in his card file. That was all right; her rolls were good an' hot for breakfast, and she was best at making cookies and simple sweets. Sometimes, though . . . she shook her head as she brought the tray out into the shop.

Just as good to wish for flowers in a blizzard, Algaina, she told herself.

Luzee had broken her roll in half, and was busy at breakfast. Algaina slid the fresh tray into the case, then went down to the end of the counter to pour herself a cup of 'toot.

"Was that the Wayhousers, just now leaving?" Luzee asked.

"Couple of 'em, anyhow. Little girl give 'er sister the slip an' gone splorin'. Big brother come lookin' for 'er. Too bad it was Roe Yingling in here when they come."

Luzee frowned.

"He didn't get ugly with a kid?"

"He coulda been less rude, but nothin' past talking too loud."

Luzeal sighed, and picked up her cup.

"He's a neighbor, but *sleet*, I wish that man would learn not to say everything jumps into his head."

"Day that happens, I'll make a cake for the whole street," Algaina said, and nodded at the binder on the table. Most of Luzee's binders had seen work, but this one looked downright *rough*. There were bits o'paper hanging out the edges, including a strip of ragged red cloth, and its edges were banged up like somebody'd thrown it up against a wall–or a head–more times than twice.

"Looks like that one's seen some fun," Algaina said.

"This?" Luzee put her hand on the old binder. "Now, this is the Human Resources manual, all the rules about how the company and the employees was s'posed to act in just about every situation you can think of, an' a couple more you can't. Got lists, pay grades, holidays, memos–I 'spect the Lady's gonna be real glad to get this one–I was up all night reading it and more'n half a mind not to let it go!"

"Agency's long gone," Algaina pointed out. "An' I'm not sure we need a rule book that don't say, right up at Number One: Don't desert your people to die, f'all you ever knew or cared."

There was a small silence while Luzee finished her roll.

"Actually," she said, putting her hands around her mug and meeting Algaina's eye. "It does say that. There's a whole evac procedure. They coulda done it–they *coulda* took everybody offa here, there wasn't no disaster nor any reason they had to make hard decisions. They was *s'posed* to've took everybody."

Algaina stared at her.

"Why?" she asked. "Why'd they leave us? My grandad always said there wasn't room . . ."

"Turns out," Luzee said; "there's room, and then there's *room*."

She took a long swallow from her mug and pushed back from the table, heading for the hot-pot. Algaina picked up one of the sparemint cookies and bit into it, chewing slowly, trying to figure out what Donnie Wayhouse had found missing . . .

"What they did," Luzee said, coming back to put the mug on the table, "was a *cost-benefit analysis*. And it come out that it was more . . . well, *fiscally responsible's* bidness-talk for it. Means they figured it'd be cheaper to leave everybody below Grade Six right here on Surebleak, and declare a loss on the equipment. Woulda put 'em in the red for years, an' given 'em a disadvantage with Corporate, if they'd brung all of us away."

She took a hard breath, and put her hand on the beat-up binder. "It's all in here—the original policies, and notes and the votes from the meetin's that rescinded 'em. Dates, names..."

She shook her head.

"That's what made me decide the Lady needs this more'n I do."

Names and dates. The way Luzeal told it, the Surebleak Historical Search and Archival Liberry din't think there was nothin' better'n names and dates.

"What're those?" Luzee asked, nodding down at the sparemint cookies.

"Hermits. Had the receipt in my granddad's box, but couldn't never get raisins, is what they're called. Always wondered what they'd taste like—the raisins and the cookies. Yesterday, I was at market, and freeze me if there weren't a whole bin o'raisins just come in."

She grinned.

"Couldn't just let 'em set there, could I?"

"Not you!" Luzee said, grinning back. "That what you want me to taste?"

"If you got time. Try one and see what you think."

Luzee chewed thoughtfully.

"'s'good," she said eventually. "Crunchy. You gonna be able to do these reg'lar?"

"I'll talk to the grocer next time I'm in; see what we can and can't do. I got a couple receipts in that box wantin' raisins. I'll look 'em out. In the meanwhile, we'll find does anybody else like 'em."

"Hard to think anybody wouldn't," Luzee said, finishing hers and eyeing the tray.

Algaina handed her another cookie.

"Thank'ee. I tell you what, Gaina—you oughta take that box down to the archive."

"That box is my livelihood! 'sides what's a buncha receipts gonna tell the Lady—or anybody else?"

"Well, this one right here'd tell 'em raisins used to be usual 'nough they got put in cookies–more'n one kind of cookie–and here you never seen 'em your whole life until just now–nor me, neither!"

"Still–giving away my receipts! I don't got 'em all by heart, now do I?"

"See, now, if you tell 'em you're bringing a *working document*, they'll make a copy and give you the original back. You take 'em in a plate o'these cookies and tell 'em how they was last made in your grandad's day, they'll see the importance o'them receipts."

"Anyways, it's what I'm planning on doin' with this book here."

"You want a copy of all the old rules the old bosses voted out when they wasn't convenient? For what?"

"Well, I ain't finished reading it, for one! For t'other, there's maybe things in here we could adapt for the Surebleak Code, like the Lady talks about. It was the *Human Resources* manual, after all, an' far's I know 'bleakers and newbies is all human."

A bell pinged in the back, and Algaina went to bring out the next batch. When she came back out, Luzee'd finished her coffeetoot, an' was pulling her hat down over her ears.

"Gotta get goin'. You wanna take that box to the archive, I'll come with you, whenever you decide."

"I'll think about it," Algaina said, and watched her out the door.

* * *

Kevan had a nightmare again.

Don Eyr woke him, and sat at his bedside, holding his hand until he stopped shaking, and answered the questions that kept *him* awake most nights; answered them to soothe and heal. Not lies; he did not lie to the children, and less so to a comrade. But where there were no facts, *there* a heart might build light and airy palaces of hope.

So, for Kevan, and for himself, he answered–no, there had not yet been word from Serana; not from Ail Den nor Cisco nor Fireyn.

Yes, it was worrisome. But only recall how confused and dangerous it had been in Low Port when Korval's mercenaries arrived.

So four of their house's defenders had gone to show the mercs the alleys and back ways, that they might flank the approaching forces and deny them Low Port.

Don Eyr might have been with them–Jax Ton and Kevan, too. They had the right, and just as much knowledge of the streets as the others. But head of house security–Serana herself–had counted them off; three to go with her to guide the mercs; three to keep the children safe.

Serana had more lives than a cat; she said it herself, and certainly she had survived–they had *both* survived–desperate situations before they had arrived in Low Port, and became the defenders of youth.

Surely, Serana was alive. *Was well*. Don Eyr did not accept a universe in which these things were not facts.

No more than Kevan might come to terms with a universe that lacked the living presence of Ail Den.

And so, in that small space of uncertainty, where the truth was not yet known, they had each built a palace of hope.

Kevan was nodding off, his grip softening; Don Eyr heard a soft step behind and turned his head as Ashti came to his side, holding a cup of tea and a book.

"I'll stay with him," she said, the low light waking sparks of red along her cropped hair.

He slipped his hand free, and stood, flexing his fingers, looking down at the boy.

Ashti put her hand on his arm.

"Sleep, Don Eyr," she murmured. "We need you."

Not for much longer would they two, at least, need him, he thought, though he did not say so to her. She and Kevan were old enough, able enough; the younger ones trusted them. He might leave, and have no fear for any of them–but he would not leave. Not yet; not while there still remained some hope that Serana, and the others, would find them.

He left Kevan in Ashti's care, but he did not seek his own bed.

Instead, he walked through the crowded rooms, checking on each sleeper, straightening merc-issue blankets, picking up fallen pillows, smoothing the hair of those who moved uneasily on their narrow cots; and once stopping to murmur a few words in Liaden.

Their daytime language might now be Terran, but Liaden was the language of home, no matter how little they had been cherished there, and it soothed the fretful back to sleep.

Satisfied that all was well with the children, he descended to the kitchen, where he found the teapot warm and a cup set by. He smiled, recognizing Ashti's hand, and poured himself a cup, which he carried to the window.

The street was a short one, sparsely lit by what a daylight inspection had revealed to be self-adhesive emergency dims. One might wonder who had put them up, and who replaced them, but in that Surebleak was like the Low Port: Someone had taken up the task, for reasons known to themselves, which might or might not have anything to do with the common good.

Halfway down the street, a brighter light flared, and he stepped back against the wall before his laggard brain realized that it was not muzzle-flare, but only the light coming on in the sweet-bakeshop.

He sighed and shook his head. This place . . .

The unit commander charged with seeing them to safety had chosen to interpret her orders liberally, the children having quickly become favorites, and the mercs having no opinion of Low Port. Thus, their eventual arrival at Surebleak, deemed a *damned sight safer'n where we found you. No offense. Sir.* The mercs had seen them generously provisioned, and brought them to the attention of the proper civilian authorities, who took their application and the character reference provided by the unit commander, settled them into transitional housing, and located a 'prenticeship for Jax Ton.

Don Eyr sighed. He was, indeed, grateful to the mercs for their care, which had included putting messages through their internal networks, for Ail Den, Cisco, Fireyn, and Serana.

He closed his eyes, and sipped his tea, deliberately turning his thoughts toward the future.

They would need to find larger quarters within three local months. That was the limit of the local authority's charity, and more generosity than Liad had shown any one of them. He hoped to hear of opportunities, when Jax Ton came to them for his *day off.*

For now, then, they were well-fixed. Locating a more suitable establishment and employment were high on the list of things to be done. The most urgent item on that list, however, was Elaytha.

Elaytha had been theirs from a babe, pulled from a pile of wreckage that had once been an apartment house; the only survivor of the collapse. She had been odd from the first, and remained odd as she grew. Her mind was good; she could read, and cipher, and follow directions. She could speak–Liaden, Terran, and Trade–though she preferred her own tongue, which she shared with no one else they had ever found. She was sweet-natured, and her ability to mime was nothing short of astonishing.

She also had a tendency to wander, heedless of hour or weather, and was afflicted with odd terrors. Lately, she had achieved a horror of food, and would cower away from a bowl of cereal as if from an assassin.

Perhaps worse, she had since arriving in this place, become convinced that there were . . . *shintai,* as it was said in her tongue, which he understood to be akin to ghosts, upon the street, who required her care. The others tried to dismiss it as play, but, if so, it was like no other play in which she had previously indulged.

Ashti suggested that Elaytha was merely framing the strangeness of their new situation in her own terms. For himself, he feared that she was delusional.

Don Eyr left the window to pour himself another cup of tea.

Elaytha needed a Healer, he thought, carefully.

On Liad, that thought would not have been possible. In Low Port, the situation would have been hopeless. The Healers did not administer to the clanless.

He could not have said why he thought the Healers who had come to Surebleak might deal differently, unless it was merely that Surebleak had dealt them a hand, when Liad had refused even to sell them a deck.

He would ask Jax Ton to also find them information regarding the Healers of Surebleak. He sighed. Perhaps, instead, he ought to send one of the elder children to bear Jax Ton company, and to find the answers to all of Don Eyr's questions . . .

He carried his tea back to the window. The sky was brightening; the emergency lights a fading reflection. Down the street, the window of the sweet-bakeshop blazed like a sun, which brought to mind the fact that he had not fulfilled his promise to the baker. One needed to deal fairly with one's neighbors. Neighbors were important, for those who had neither kin nor clan to shield them.

Ashti would scold him for not going back to bed, but, truly, baking was every bit as restful as sleep. Moreso, now that he slept alone.

Turning away from the windows, he set the tea cup aside, and began to assemble his ingredients.

* * *

The bell rang while she was in the back, and Algaina called over her shoulder.

"Make yourself at home; just gotta get this batch in the oven!"

There was no answer, but Luzeal was prolly more'n half-asleep still, at this hour. Algaina glanced at the clock. It was some early for Luzee, but–sleet, it was early for *her*, if it come to that. It'd been one of them nights where bad memories come slipping into your sleep, pretending like they was dreams.

Just as good–better–to be baking, than laying flat in the bed staring up the ceiling, and afraid to close your eyes. So, she'd gotten dressed and come downstairs, started the oven up and pulled a receipt out from the old box without looking at it.

Turned out it was a cake she hadn't made but once before, on account it was so fussy. Well, good. Fussy was just what she needed.

She slid the pans in, closed the oven and set the timer.

Wiping her hands on her apron, she stepped out into the shop.

"You're early for the rolls–" she started to tell Luzeal . . .

'Cept it wasn't Luzeal in the shop at this early hour of the day.

Standin' all solemn right in front of the counter was the little girl from yesterday–Elaytha. Her hair'd been combed and braided, and her red coat was buttoned up against the cold. She was holding a covered plate in two ungloved hands, and smiling to beat the sun.

Just behind her was an older girl, with a good knit cap pulled down over her ears, hands tucked into the pockets of her short jacket–no gloves there, either, Algaina was willing to say. Well, that was easy 'nough to fix. She had the kids' old gloves an' mittens that they'd outgrown. Might as well they got some use. If you didn't look out for your neighbors, who'd look out for you?

"You coulda set that down, got yourselfs a cup of something hot," she said now, looking from one to the other of 'em.

"That's what *make yourself at home* means."

She looked pointedly at the younger girl, who opened her wide eyes even wider.

"We will remember," the older girl said, her voice unexpectedly deep. "We are grateful for the information."

"You're welcome," Algaina said, gruffer than she meant to. She cleared her throat. "Either one of you want a cup of something hot?"

She nodded at the hot pot, steam gently rising from its spout.

"Thank you," the older kid said politely, "but not this time. We are to deliver Don Eyr's cookies. They come with this message."

She gave the younger girl a slight nudge with her foot.

"Try it!" that one said, loudly, holding the plate high, "and tell him what you think!"

"That is correct, Elaytha. Well done."

Algaina took the plate and set it in the center of the counter.

"I'm obliged," she said. "I ain't got anything out yet, but if you–"

"Thank you, no," the older girl said, with a small bow. She held out her hand.

"Come, Elaytha."

"Yes!" said the child, and that quick they were gone, the bell ringing over the closed door.

Algaina shook her head, and lifted the towel from the plate. A warm breath of spice delighted her nose, and she smiled as she picked up one of the dainty little rectangles, and bit into it carefully.

Still warm, and it fair melted in the mouth, soft and sweet, with just a bite of something tangy on the back of the tongue.

She had another bite, analyzing the taste, working out the spices, wondering how he'd gotten it so *soft* . . .

The bell jangled, jerking her out of her reverie. She opened her eyes as Luzeal stepped into the shop, shaking her head from the cold.

"Mornin'," she said, moving over to the hot pot.

"Mornin'," Algaina answered. She pushed the plate down the counter.

"Try one o' those and tell me what you think."

Luzee picked up a cookie and bit into it, eyebrows rising.

"'nother new receipt outta the box?" she asked.

"This," said Algaina, "is what Donnie Wayhouse thinks those cookies I made yesterday oughta be." She took another bite; sighed.

"He had a bite o'one of mine, and I asked him to tell me what he thought–and he *did* think something, but he run outta words. Promised to send a demonstration."

She nodded at the half-cookie still in Luzee's hand.

"That's his demo, right there."

Luzee took another bite, pure satisfaction on her face.

"I tell you what, Gaina," she said. "You know I don't like to meddle in other people's bidness–" That just wasn't so, but let it go; they all meddled in each other's bidness, that's how the street had stayed more or less peaceful, even in the baddest of the bad ol' days.

"I'm thinking you'd do worse'n go partners with that boy, if he don't got other work. Be good for both of you."

"We're thinking along the same lines," Algaina assured her, picking up another of the dark, soft cookies. "I'll return his plate proper after I close up this afternoon. Can't hurt to ask, can it?"

"Not one bit," said Luzee, and reached for another cookie.

#

It was snowing, but only enough to make an old woman wish she'd remembered put on her flap-hat, 'stead of the one that just covered the top of her head.

She knocked on the door of the Wayhouse.

It snowed a little more before the door opened, and she looked down into a pair of bright blue eyes under a shock of bright red hair.

"Yes?" the kid said. "Please say what you want."

Well, that was one way to answer the door, Algaina thought. Right to the point, anyhoot.

"I'd like to see Donnie," she said, and hefted the plate she was carrying covered over with the same cloth. "Wanna return his plate."

L'il Red took a bit to chew that over, then stepped briskly back and raised a hand to wave her in.

She crossed into the tiny hall, and stood to one side so the kid could shut the door and throw a series of bolts.

"This way," was her next instruction, and off the kid went, turning right into the hallway, and Algaina barely able to keep up.

It wasn't a long hall, but they passed four kids, and then a couple, three more on the stairway before the one she was following cut right again, through a swing-door and into a cramped, too-warm kitchen.

There were another two kids at the stove–older kids, Algaina thought, though none of 'em was tall enough to look like anything but a kid to her.

Not even the one standing at the table, working with a spoon in one hand and something else in the other, a plate set before him, and a couple small bowls.

"Donnie, there's a lady," the red-haired mite said, and turned to look up at her.

"Here you are, lady."

And was gone.

Donnie looked 'round from his work, eyebrows lifting slightly on seeing her, his face a study in unsmiling politeness.

"Baker Algaina. It is good to see you. Did the cookies please?"

"The cookies more than pleased, which is something I'd like to talk with you about, when you're less busy. In the meanwhile, I brung your plate back, with a little something to say thank you . . ."

She glanced around. There didn't seem to be any room on the work table. There didn't seem to be any room, anywhere. Every surface was full, and there were kids underfoot, and . . .

"Kevan," Donnie murmured, and one of the kids at the stove turned, gave her a frank smile, and slid the plate out of her hands.

"I'll take care of that," he said, and his Terran was good—not *'bleaker*, but not sounding half-learned, like Donnie's Terran. "Thanks very much, Miz– ?"

"Now, no Miz called for. I'm Algaina from the bakeshop down the street, like your brother here says."

Dark eyes flicked to Donnie, back to her.

"Miz Algaina, then. Thank you; we always appreciate something extra with dinner." He turned back to the stove, uncovering the plate, and showing it to his partner there.

Dinner, she thought. They was cooking dinner, with all these pots 'n pans. Dinner for–

"How many kids you got here?" she asked Donnie, before she had a chance to work out if that was the kind of question he was likely to answer.

Turns out, it wasn't.

His eyelids flickered.

"Some few," he said quietly. "If you do not . . . mind, we may talk now." Another quick glance at her before he said over his shoulder.

"Velix, take Miz Algaina's coat and hat to dry. Cal Dir, bring her a cup of tea. Ashti–"

A stool appeared even as her coat and hat were whisked away to hang on a peg near the stove, and steam that smelled like flowers rising from the mug that was put in her hand.

She took a careful sip, just enough to discover that the tea tasted like the steam. Then, she put both hands around the mug, and watched Donnie make another one of . . . whatever it was it was he was making.

Flowers, birds, leaves . . . all somehow fashioned from one scoop of whatever was in the bowls, and him working with a spoon.

He put the latest creation–a fish–on the plate with the others, and she sighed in mingled pleasure and frustration, which caused her host to look straight at her.

"There is a problem? The tea does not please? We have—"

She held up a hand.

"The tea's wonderful, thank you. It's only—I just watched you make that, and I can't figure out how you did it."

He smiled then—she could tell more by the way the corners of his eyes crinkled up than from his mouth curving, and it come to her then that Donnie wasn't as young as she'd taken him, even on second look. In fact, now she was close, she could see there were some few threads of silver mixed in the dark brown hair, and lines worn in 'round his eyes and mouth.

Still might be the older brother, she thought, at least to some of the kids. An' he wasn't gonna tell her nothin' about 'em at all. Well, she thought, taking a sip of tea, why should he? He didn't know anything 'bout her, and the kids had to come first.

'Course they did.

"Once you have made a few dozen, it comes without thought," he was saying. "These are *chernubia*. Small sweets, to have with mid-morning tea, after the first work of the day is done."

She watched him make two big wings connected at the center; she didn't think it was a bird. Something from his home, prolly. Way she'd heard it, there were a lot of things on his homeworld that never'd quite made it to Surebleak, nor weren't likely to ever arrive.

"I tell you what," she started, and then stopped, turning on her stool to discover the reason for the sudden ruckus out in the hall.

The mob in the kitchen shifted, one kid going out the door with a big bowl held in both hands, calling out what might've been names. She'd scarcely cleared the room when another took her place—older, though younger still than Donnie. This one was wearing a tool-belt and a couple shirts, Surebleak style, heavy over lighter, and a knit cap on his head.

"Jax Ton!" Kevan called from the stove. "I don't think we made enough food!"

"All is well, little brother; I will be satisfied with your dinner, only."

That was greeted with laughter, and a little one came running into the room, arms working, yelling, "Jax Ton! Jax Ton!"

"Kae Nor!" the newcomer called back, and swooped the kid up into his arms, spinning in the tight space like he had the whole street to dance in. The child screamed with laughter; and was still laughing as he was transferred to another pair of arms, to be toted out of the kitchen.

"Jax Ton," Donnie said quietly, and here he was, slipped in close, right between her stool and the table, like it was all the room anybody needed.

"Don Eyr," he said, quietly, and paused, his eye drawn to the plate of fanciful shapes.

"*Chernubia* in cheese and vegetables?" he asked. "I do not think this is one of your better ideas, brother."

"Elaytha has become afraid of her dinner," Donnie—no, Algaina corrected herself, *Don Eyr* said levelly.

Jax Ton looked solemn.

"Badly?"

"Very badly."

"Will this cast work, do you think?"

"It is all that I *can* think," Don Eyr said, sounding suddenly weary. They'd forgotten she was there, Algaina thought, and sat very still while they talked family around her.

"I am happy you came tonight," Don Eyr continued. "She needs a Healer. Can you find if they will they see her at the hall here?"

"They see Terrans at the hall here," Jax Ton said. "They *train* Terrans at the hall here. I will take her with me when I go back to work."

"We cannot leave her alone among strangers . . ."

"Which is why Kevan will accompany us. He will bide with her, and I will join them after the boss is done with me. They will neither be bereft."

Don Eyr took a breath, sighed it out.

"The cost?"

"If the child needs a Healer, that is where we begin. We do not count cost against need." Jax Ton extended a hand and gripped the other's shoulder. "So you yourself taught us."

Don Eyr half-laughed.

"Did I? A poor influence on soft minds, I fear."

"Never that," said Jax Ton.

He removed his hand, and seemed to see her for the first time.

"My apology," he said. "I– "

"Jax Ton, this is Miz Algaina from the sweet bakeshop. Our neighbor."

"Ah!" Jax Ton smiled like he'd been born on Surebleak. "Welcome, neighbor. I am Jax Ton tel'Ofong–or Jack O'Fong, according to my boss."

"Pleasure," Algaina assured him. "You live here, too?"

"I am 'prenticed to Electrician Varn Jilzink, in Boss Torin's territory. It is too far to travel every day, but I come home here for my day off."

"It's good to be with family," she said.

"That is truth," Jax Ton said solemnly, and turned back to his brother, who was holding out a plate full of fanciful shapes.

"Do you think that you might try?"

"Of course, I will try, though it likely means I will have to eat a carrot *chernubia* myself."

"The carrot *chernubia* are very good," Don Eyr told him gravely.

"Everything you bake is very good. Where is she?"

"Upstairs. In the tent."

Jax Ton's smile faded somewhat.

"Ah, is she? Well, as I said—I will try. Miz Algaina, I hope we will meet again soon."

He was gone, bearing the plate, and it came to Algaina that the kitchen was empty now, save for herself and Don Eyr. There were still voices to be heard, but down the hall, in another part of the house.

"Well." Don Eyr turned to her. "Now, at last we may address your topic."

"I don't wanna be keeping you from your supper," she said, "so I'll be quick. I'd like it if you made cookies like you sent down to me this morning, an' some of those *shernoobias*—sweet ones at first, then we'll try and see if the veggies'll sell—"

There was the smile again—easy to see now she knew what to look for.

"I figure the split to be seventy for you, thirty for me. I buy flours and other supplies wholesale, you can buy from me at my cost, if that'll suit. Anything special you need . . ."

She let it run off and waited, taking a sip of her tea, which had gone cold, but was still tasty.

"I will like that," Don Eyr said slowly. "When do you wish the first baking, and how many?"

Algaina smiled, and leaned forward.

"OK," she said. "Now, here's what I'm thinking . . ."

* * *

Don Eyr had gotten up early, to see Jax Ton and Kevan and Elaytha on their way, with two pails packed with food and *chernubia*. Elaytha had been so excited to be going with Jax Ton that she scarcely had time to give him a hug. It pained him to let her go, but that was foolish. Jax Ton and Kevan would keep her safe, both knew her moods and her foibles, and Kevan understood—or seemed to—a good deal of the language she had created for her own use.

He hoped the Healers would see her.

He hoped the Healers would effect wonders.

He hoped . . .

Well.

In the end, it was good that he had the baking to do; it kept him aside of worry, even as he was reminded of other days–better days–when he was up early to bake for the shop in Low Port, and Serana would slip in, cat-foot, to make tea, and sit on a stool to watch him. The early morning had been their time, when they re-affirmed their bond, and their curious orbit, each around the other.

He had expected her to leave, many times over the years.

Serana had a warrior's heart; she had been born a hero, fashioned for feats of valor. Caring for children–for gormless bakers–wasted her.

And yet, she had stayed . . .

. . . until that moment when her skills were at last called for, and she had not hesitated to take the lead.

He took out the first batch of spice bars, and slipped the second into the oven. He had a brief moment of nostalgia for his ovens, then shook his head. What was, was. This oven, this kitchen, was perfectly adequate for the baking of a few batches of sweet things.

At . . . home, he had made loaves, cheese rolls, protein muffins–sweet things–those, too. But it had been the bread that drew customers in, and provided the household income.

He had spoken of bread to Miz Algaina. Her kitchen was also too small to accommodate large baking, nor, she confided, did she have the knack of yeast things.

He had the knack, but his bread-heart was lost in the shambles of Low Port, with his ovens, and the library, and the homey things they had amassed over the years. Algaina had spoken of a larger house at the far end of the street, beyond the gate. It had been part of the former boss's estate. There were ovens, she said, and quarters above that were more spacious than those of the Wayhouse.

They might, so he understood, petition the Council of Bosses Circuit Rider to relocate to this other house. He would have to show that the property would be put to "use and profit," so it was even more important that this venture with Algaina prove successful.

He also understood that the granting of the petition would go easier, if he secured the support of the rest of the neighbors—and here, too, Algaina had offered her aid. All the street came into her shop, and she would talk about the idea. It would also be useful, she said, if he worked the counter a couple hours every day to show the world his face.

This made sense, and was something he could easily accommodate. Without the shop, now that they were settled again, together, he found himself with few duties. The elder children taught and cared for those who were younger, with any disputes brought to Ashti, who now stood as his second. It would be good, to have work, and to meet their new neighbors.

The timer chimed, and he removed the second batch of spice bars from the oven.

While they cooled, he looked in the coldbox where the *chernubia* prettily adorned their plates. He glanced at the clock and did a quick calculation. Yes, he did have time to make a batch of quick cheese rolls—not real bread, but satisfying enough. Perhaps Algaina's customers—his new neighbors—would find them pleasant.

* * *

Well, that might not've been the best decision she'd ever made in her life, Algaina thought, but it'd sure do for now.

She waved day's done to Don Eyr and Velix, and locked the door behind them. He'd taken to bringing one of the kids with him on-shift, so the neighbors would get to know all of them.

Don Eyr taught her his way with the hermits—spice cookies, according to him—so that baking came back into her shop, while he continued to provide *chernubia*, and day-rolls. She'd shown him the receipt for flaky pastries, and the sorry result of her efforts. He took it away and brought back a plate of buttery crescents so light she feared they'd float out the door and into the sky.

An' more than his baking improved the shop. He'd brought in two more hot-pots, each with a different kind of tea—one fruity and light, and the other grey and energizing. Her pride was piqued at that, and she ordered in a better grade of coffeetoot, for them that had the preference.

Luzee saw that people wanted to linger over their sweet and their cup, so her and Binni Bodyne went together to get some old tables from down the cellars up into the street, then wheeled a hand o'kids, including one of the Wayhousers, to scrub 'em clean.

Erb Fliar come down to see what all the commotion was about, went back inside his place, an' a half-hour later reappeared, holding a bolt of red-and-white checkerboard cloth.

Well, Pan Jonderitz knew just what to do with that, din't he just? An' while he was doin' that, Luzee organized *another* hand o'kids to clean the windows and wash the walls, and by the time it was all done . . . din't it just look fine?

Better'n the place lookin' fine, and bidness bein' up, Don Eyr was making a good impression on the neighbors, and the kids were, too.

The best sign she saw, though, was the afternoon she walked to the door to close up for the day, and there was a confusion of kids running 'round the street, armed with snowballs—street kids, Wayhouse kids—all of 'em shouting with laughter.

The only oil on the ice was Roe Yingling.

If he came into the shop while Don Eyr was on counter, he turned on his heel and left. He quizzed her on each roll, cookie, and cupcake to find which'd been made by *them* and flatly refused to try any of it—even when a sample was offered for free, which was just unheard of.

Worse, he didn't see any reason why *they* should move into the old catering house. If *they* needed more space, *they* could find some other street to live on. Sleet, they oughta buy their own damn place up on a hill somewhere; everybody knew the newbies was rich. Look at the Road Boss, bringing his own damn *house* with him, on account of nothing on Surebleak was good enough!

Well, fine, *they* could do what *they* wanted–somewhere else. Chairman Court hadn't asked for 'em, Chairman Court didn't need 'em, Chairman Court was better off without 'em–and *that*, by sleet, was exactly what he was gonna tell the council's circuit rider, next time she was by.

Algaina shook her head.

Roe was only one voice, after all, she told herself. There was still the whole rest of the street who liked Don Eyr and his kids just fine. All they had to do was say so.

Everything would be fine.

* * *

The house was noisy when he and Velix entered, having done their shift at Algaina's shop. Not merely noisy, thought Don Eyr, stopping with his hand on the lock, head tipped to one side–jubilant.

He stood, listening, Velix at his side, until one voice rose above all the others. Velix was off, running down the hall toward the gather-room, shouting, "Fireyn!"

Hope flared in his breast, so fiercely he could scarcely breathe, yet somehow his feet were moving, not quite Velix's headlong flight, but quickly enough that he was in the room before his heart had settled; sweeping in, gripping an arm, wringing a hand, taking in the familiar faces of his kindred-in-arms, those who guarded the children with him–

"Ail Den," he murmured, "Cisco. Fireyn–"

He stopped, searching faces gone suddenly still. It was Fireyn who gripped his hand, and Ail Den who caught him 'round the shoulders, even as he whispered–

"Serana?"

"No," Cisco said, voice rough, his face thinner, worn, and wet. "Old friend, no. We were separated. We searched, we checked; the mercs counted out their wounded, and the dead . . . Serana . . ."

"We lost her," Fireyn finished. "We had hoped . . . she was already with you . . ."

He took a hard breath, ears roaring; an edge of darkness to his vision. All three of them closed 'round him in a comrade's embrace, while he gasped, trembling, and saw . . .

. . . the bright palace of his hopes crumble beneath the weight of truth. Crumble, flicker, and die.

* * *

"So, that inflatable tent we found in the cellar when we went down to get the tables?" Binder cuddled against her chest, Luzee was talking to the crowd pushed in as tight at they could be, some sitting at tables, some standing 'round the walls.

"Well, that tent was special made for the year-end block party. I got all the information right here!" She raised the binder over her head and shook it like a bell.

"Happens that The Chairman threw a party for all the Grade Six an' belows, at the end of the fiscal year. It was s'posed to increase morale and team-buildin'. I showed this to the Lady and to the Perfessor, and they both said that one of the things that pulls people together is a shared holiday. They was wonderin' if us here on Chairman Court wouldn't like to follow the directions in this Human Relations manual, and throw a block party. The Bosses'll be invited, to see how it works out, and might be next year, Surebleak entire'll have a block party, and . . ."

Algaina went into the back and pulled out a tray of cookies. Spice cookies, they were. She'd made an extra batch for the meetin', which was good, because there wasn't nobody, always exceptin' Roe Yingling, who didn't like the spice cookies.

But it was also a bad thing, because they reminded her of Don Eyr . . . who hadn't been in to the shop for more'n a week, which was bad enough. Worse was the notion that he wasn't baking, neither.

"Don Eyr is . . . ill," Ashti had told her. "He will come again when he is able. In the meanwhile, two of us will come to you every day, to give you rest, as we have been doing. We do not wish to stint a neighbor."

Stint a neighbor? Algaina thought, and–

"How sick is he? Can he bake?"

"He . . ." Ashti had closed her eyes and taken a deep breath. "I regret, not at the moment. None of us has his touch with *chernubia* or the other small sweets. We may continue to provide rolls; several of us are proficient."

"Rolls, yes; that would be good–people like the cheese rolls. But–I don't want to meddle–should he see a medic? Or I could come and take a look– "

"Our medic has rejoined us," Ashti said. "She is watching Don Eyr very closely."

She'd managed a smile then, shaky, but true.

"He is dear to all of us, as to you. We will not lose him."

* * *

He ought to stand, he thought, for the dozen dozenth time that day. He ought to leave this room, and be sure that all, and everyone, was well. The children needed–but no.

Ail Den, and Cisco, and Fireyn were home. The children had no further need of him. He was free to leave, to strike out again alone, as he had wished so often to do, when they had first come into Low Port, on a day-job.

Day-job. What use was he on a day-job? But, there, his delm had called him home, the least of the clan's children, to fulfill a debt owed to Clan Abra. The terms of settlement required an agent of Clan Serat to hold himself ready at all times to fulfill those tasks Abra required of him.

Serana had come with him; his bodyguard, as she explained herself, which Abra found to be a very fine joke, and so it had been the two of them, sent down to clear a newly-inherited parcel in the Low Port.

Clear it of *debris*.

They had not understood the nature of the *debris* until they arrived at the corner they were to clear.

Eight children and one barely past halfling; their leader, who had promised them safety, and, judging by his grip on the piece of pipe he had chosen for a weapon, was prepared to die for his word.

Together, the three of them cleared the area. He and Serana, they had thought they would establish the children safely, give their protector advice, and such small funds as they held between them–a few days spent, only that.

They had been fools.

Over time, they had gathered to themselves, to their service, other fools, and so the children were kept safe.

Serana had died, to ensure their safety, and he–

He heard the door open; raised his head, and took a breath. It was Ashti, perhaps, come to tempt his appetite, or–

"Donnee?" came a high, sweet voice, followed by Elaytha herself, unruly hair braided; cheeks plump; eyes wide and bright.

"Ah, *shintai*. Donnee *zabastra kai*."

"Elaytha," he murmured. "Welcome home, child."

"Welcome home," she repeated in a tired, flat voice, and climbed into his lap, putting her arms around his neck, and leaning her forehead against his.

"Donnee is filled with light," she said, in a voice he did not recognize. "*Shintai goventa.*"

#

Jax Ton was in the kitchen, eating soup. Velix, at the stove, immediately filled another bowl, brought it to the table with a mug of tea, and slipped away, leaving them alone.

"Ail Den told me," Jax Ton said softly, rising. "*Al'bresh venat'i,* brother."

They embraced, cheek to damp cheek.

"The child is a Healer?" Don Eyr asked, when they sat again to the soup.

"The child *will be* a Healer," Jax Ton corrected him. "She shows some early ability, which, while unusual, is no cause for alarm. She has received instruction in controlling her gift, and also in its best use."

He cocked his head.

"I would say that, so far, her training has been adequate."

"Indeed. However–trained in best use, young as she is?"

"As I understand it, once a gift has manifested, it cannot be denied. So, yes. As young as she is."

He spooned soup; looked up.

"The Healers will want her back with them for a full evaluation and training on her twelfth name day. In the meanwhile, they have Healed her of most, if not all, of her terrors. My challenge lately has been to feed her *enough.*"

Don Eyr smiled.

"They did not Heal her of talking nonsense."

Jax Ton moved his shoulders.

"It is, according to the Healers, not an affliction; it causes her no distress; and creates no impediments for her in daily life."

"Ah," said Don Eyr, and pushed his empty bowl aside.

"What other news do you bring me?"

"Boss Jilzink's associate has taken Kevan to 'prentice. He will learn the art of resource reclamation from Esser Kane, who has several teams working for him, and sees in Kevan a future leader of a new team. Master Kane is well and favorably known to the Employment Office. Kevan will tell you all, when he comes home on his day off."

"Soon, we will be scattered all over Surebleak," Don Eyr said, not without dismay.

"Children grow up," Jax Ton said, and reached to catch his shoulder in an affectionate embrace. "This is what you set yourself to do, brother, and I will tell you that there is not a morning that I wake in which I do not thank the gods, should they exist, that it was you and Serana who came that day. I had promised to keep them safe, but you–you kept my honor for me."

"You do me too much– "

"That is not possible," Jax Ton said firmly, letting him go.

"I have one more piece of news, which may not be so delightful as I had hoped, as Ashti informs me that you have given over baking."

Don Eyr looked at him.

"Perhaps I shall begin again, if the news is of interest."

"Well, then, I bring it forward at once! There is a baker in Boss Conrad's territory, with an established shop, who is interested in adding Liaden delicacies to her offerings. I may have shared one or two of your *chernubia* with her. If you would be willing to provide these to her, non-exclusively, she will pay you a percentage of the profit, and will seal the contract with a portion of her mother-of-bread."

* * *

The block party hadn't been much of a 'spense to The Chairman, Algaina thought grumpily. Management provided the tent, and some prizes, and–all right, bought the beer and the desserts. Most everything else, though, was made and brought by the guests. Eating each other's food and trading receipts was s'posed to be good for morale and team-building.

There were games set out in Luzeal's binder, and a timeline of how things were s'posed to go. F'rinstance, there was a space o'time put aside where everybody said what their best accomplishment had been in the last year. An' another space o'time when the year's just-borns were called by name.

An' a space o'time right at the beginning of the party where everybody stood in a circle, and said outloud the names of those who'd died during the year.

Algaina'd made a batch of almost everything in grandpa's receipt book, and had the neighbor kids moving them out of the shop the second the tables went up inside the tent. For drinks, Erb Fliar'd promised to put out tea, 'toot, juice, an' beer–*light* beer, he'd added. No sense anybody getting stupid.

Algaina was pulling on her bright green sweater, which was too good to wear in the bakeshop, when the bell over the door rang.

She turned around, and there was Ashti, and Elaytha, and Jax Ton, and Velix, all carrying a tray of *chernubia*, each one looking different.

She looked at Jax Ton.

"He's better?"

"Better, yes." Jax Ton smiled and nodded at Elaytha. "He said to tell you that the *chernubia* on that tray are made from carrot, and kale, and cheese."

She laughed, in equal parts relief and fun.

"Well, that's just fine. You come with me and we'll get them set up in the tent." She looked at each of them, sharply, in turn.

"You're all comin' to the party, now?"

"Yes," Ashti said. "All of us are coming to the party. We are sent ahead with the trays."

"Good," said Algaina, and added, believing it for the first time since Luzeal had decided on having a block party, "it's gonna be fun."

* * *

Don Eyr closed the sack, and crossed the kitchen for his coat. The others had gone ahead, leaving him to pack his contribution to the shared meal alone.

His offering–his personal offering–to the goodwill of their neighbors was bread–a small loaf for each. He had also made a loaf–one loaf only– of Serana's favorite: a crusty, chewy round, with a dense, nutty crumb.

Coat on, he shouldered the sack and left the Wayhouse. It was snowing, densely, diffusing the tent's glow into an iridescent fog.

The street was filled with the sound of voices, and laughter, and for a moment, he stood, frozen in the snow, every nerve in his body marking Serana's absence.

A deep breath; a memory of the light Elaytha had given him. Serana was here, because he was here; her memory, as her life, a benediction.

Centered, he walked the short distance down the street, then out of the snow, into the bright warmth of the tent.

"I ain't sitting here with *them*!"

Roe Yingling's voice soared over the pleased chatter of those gathered.

"They invaded our planet! Took our jobs! They ain't really *people*! Sure, they want a party, let 'em have their own party, and let us real 'bleakers alone!"

Carefully, Don Eyr put the sack on the table by the door, and moved across the room, toward the man confronting Jax Ton, with Ail Den and Cisco flanking him, and the others spread behind.

"Roe," that was Luzeal, moving between the angry man and the children. "These are our neighbors. They don't stint the street, an' nor do you, nor anybody here! We're neighbors, we depend on each other."

The man threw his hand out, pointing at Elaytha, who had stepped out from behind Jax Ton.

"It ain't bad enough that they don't belong here, but they're broken, too! That one can't even talk!"

That brought a hush, shortly broken by a quiet voice.

"I can talk," Elaytha told him, evading Jax Ton's hand, and walking forward until she stood before the man in all his anger. She glanced at Don Eyr as he arrived, near enough to kick the man's legs out from under him, if he dared try to–

Elaytha smiled and looked up at Roe Yingling.

"You can be more happy," she said. "You don't need to be angry. You don't need to always want to be mad."

"Why you–" Roe Yingling began–and stopped, a perplexed look on his face.

"What do you know about what I want?" he said, at a somewhat lesser volume. "Newbie can't know what I want. Strangers can't . . . How can I tell you what I want?"

"Don't you want to be more happy? You came to the party to be more happy. Have a *chernubia*, or a cookie. What do you want? Which?"

The crowd closed, listening. Elaytha leaned toward him, hands in a gentle gesture of request, eyes locked on his.

"What I want is . . ."

It seemed to Don Eyr as if he swayed.

"Roe?"

A woman came out of the crowd, glanced at Elaytha, and took the man's hand.

"I'm sorry, missy," she began; "he's a good man, but sometimes he don't think before–"

"What I want is," he tried again, his face losing tension, "is a *reason* to be happy. Can you understand that?"

Ashti stepped around Jax Ton, bearing a tray of *chernubia*. She paused at Elaytha's side.

"A reason, yes," Elaytha said. "Please, take a sweet. Be happy with the day. Be happy with your neighbors. You will feel better– "

Don Eyr, felt that last strike hard against his chest; the child was performing a Healing, here and now? He held his breath as she plucked a flower from the tray, and offered it to the man on upraised palm.

"This is very good, made by my brother. Please, take it. Be pleased with it. Do not be mad at everything, and you will not hurt so much! Look, we have a party. The neighbors have a party. Better is now. For your friends, be happy."

He stared down into her face, then, like a man in a dream, he took the *chernubia* from her hand, and ate it. A long sigh escaped him; there was no other sound in the room.

"Roe?" his wife asked, putting her hand on his arm. She looked down at Elaytha, eyes wide, and Don Eyr tensed, even as Luzeal stepped up, taking each by an elbow, and turning them toward a table at the side of the room, where two children were watching, eyes wide.

"She's right, Marie," Roe Yingling said suddenly. He stopped and looked around the tent as if he had just woken to the realization of the gathering.

"She's right," he said, more loudly. "I don't *hurt . . .*"

"Well, who *could* hurt," Luzeal said practically, "with one of them good sweet things inside you? Now, you just come on over here and have a sit-down, Roe Yingling..."

In the back corner of the tent, someone said something, and someone else laughed. Don Eyr felt a small hand slide into his, and looked down into Elaytha's smile.

"Will that last?" he asked her.

She frowned slightly.

"Maybe?" she said, and moved her shoulders. "*Kai zabastra, kai?*"

A sound, then, of quiet engines, and someone near the entrance called out that the Bosses were here.

Most people moved further into the tent, finding chairs and tables. Luzeal and Algaina were heading for the entrance–the hosts, Don Eyr understood, coming to greet the Bosses.

He stepped back to let them pass, and Algaina reached out to catch his free hand.

"You, too!" she said; so he and Elaytha joined the reception line, just as a dark haired man–Boss Conrad himself, he heard someone whisper, loudly–stepped into the tent, shaking the snow from his hat. He paused, turning back to the entrance, one hand extended to the woman who followed, leaning heavily on a crutch, snow dusting her cropped red hair like sugar.

She paused, just short of the Boss's hand, and threw out the arm unencumbered by the crutch, but Don Eyr was already moving.

He caught her in an embrace perhaps too fierce. She was thin, so thin, and the crutch...

"I said I would come back to you," she whispered roughly into his ear.

"Even a cat comes to her last life," he answered. "Cisco, Fireyn, Ail Den–they lost you in the fighting; the mercs had no records."

"All true. But not dead. Quite."

"I'm a fool," he answered, and, even softer, "What happened?"

"I will tell you everything, my small. But, for tonight–you must introduce me to our neighbors."

Our Lady of Benevolence

Beyavi voz'Laathi, Our Lady of Benevolence, as she was widely known, stood in the window and surveyed the street below.

It was a fine street. Unlike other streets she had overseen, here there were light poles spotted at intervals, and at the corners. The buildings this kindly illumination revealed were unmistakably of the Low Port: cramped, crooked, and not quite clean, yet there was something about them, some quality not found in similar buildings on other streets.

She frowned, seeking after this quality, and in a moment, let go a sharp breath–surprise, perhaps, or laughter. For as poor and unbeautiful as they surely were, the shops and dwellings below her were not *mean*.

There were some few signs that all was not–or had not been–peaceful here: the charred remains of what might have been a shed, or a dwelling; a boarded-up window, glass glittering on the crete; a pole light dark; cracks in the surface of the street.

The building from which she conducted her survey had itself taken some damage. The door she had passed through had been bent, as if it had buckled under multiple attempts to ram it. The locks had held, and it had required the not inconsiderable skills of one of her oathbound to open them in good order. The gate to the courtyard off the back alley had fallen, and some pots from the tiered rows were smashed, but that might have been the result of the temblors that had followed the strike against the homeworld.

The interior of the house was a little disordered. Not, she thought, from the world's quaking, but from the hasty departure of its former occupants. It surprised her, that they had left their base, hard-won and hard-held as it had been. Still, when word came to her ears that, once the Scouts and the soldiers had withdrawn, the bakery was proved empty–well, what could she do, but annex it for herself?

Even Low Port has its legends, as she knew, being one herself. The bakery had been of a different order: it taught, it protected, it healed, and most astonishing of all, it had engendered hope. Improbable even as one beheld it, rich as it must surely have been, the bakery had been a target, many times. It *ought* to have fallen a dozen times over, yet it stood, four-square, decent and brave.

Then came the fall of fire from the skies, opening a wound in the planet, birthing earthquakes, sparking riots in Mid Port and murder in Low Port. In the wake of this, came Scouts and Terran mercenaries, intent on imposing order, healing the wounded, burying the dead, and rebuilding those things–those very many things–that had fallen down.

The bakery, formerly a barracks, had served as a base for these rescuers, which was scarcely surprising.

The surprise had come when the soldiers withdrew, leaving the building utterly empty, as if the retreating troops had absorbed the occupants into their ranks, and taken them away not only from Low Port but from Liad altogether.

A step sounded behind her, a throat was cleared.

"My lady?" murmured Gly Sin, senior of her Guns, who had been with her from the first.

She turned from the window, and inclined her head.

"It will do," she said, in calculated understatement. "Make certain of the locks, and arrange for interior guards. For the moment, leave all as it is. We will do a proper inventory on the morrow."

"My lady," Gly Sin bowed. "There is a room half a floor above this. Defensible. It is cluttered, but if I might suggest–"

"You might," she told him. "Show me to this cluttered chamber."

* * *

The youngest Healer paused in the garden, to say her good-byes to the flowers. She and Dyoli had planted a small bed together in the year Aazali had come to the Hall. The bulbs had come from Dyoli's aunt, a gardener of note, with a detailed list of how best to care for them. Every second year–the instructions were firm on this point–the bed was to be dug up, the bulbs divided, and replanted. This they had done, she and Dyoli together in the first years, and after Dyoli had . . . gone . . . by Aazali alone. The small hill at the back of the garden was now awash in flowers, bell-shaped and brilliant. It gave her a pang to leave them, and for a moment, she trembled on the edge of reversing her decision, only–

Only, she had completed her training, and been reassigned. The Hall Master had been very pleased to tell her that the Guild had placed her in higher Mid Port, quite close to the markets. It was, the Hall Master said, an acknowledgment of her skill, remarkable in one still so young.

It was also, Aazali thought, because her talent operated on both the physical and the emotional planes. The Hall nearest the markets received a high percentage of broken arms, and bruised heads, due to its very proximity to the markets, and physical healing sapped a Healer's strength. Most physical Healers were young; the talent burning out in only a few years.

And in any case, it made no matter. She would not be going to the Hall by the markets.

She was going–home.

Abruptly, she turned away from the hill, and walked back to the gardening shed, returning with a small bucket and a spade. Quickly, she transferred a clump of cream, yellow, and pink blooms into the bucket, and carried the spade back to the shed. Serana would like to have the flowers, she told herself.

Her heart plummeted to the bottom of her boots to find Elder Grasy standing by the bucket, head tipped to one side, as she considered the hole among the rioting hillside.

Aazali took a breath, centering herself.

"Good day, Elder," she said. "Is there aught I might do for you?"

"I only wonder–but of course, you will wish to have your flowers at your new location," the elder Healer said softly. She turned her eyes upon Aazali. "Mid Market Hall is your assignment, is it not?"

Aazali sighed. It was possible to lie to a Healer, but she had no intention of trying. Especially not to Healer Grasy, who had been her favorite teacher.

"I was assigned to Mid Market Hall," she admitted, "but I have refused the posting."

Grasy's grey eyebrows rose.

"Will you try for a spot at one of the Halls in Solcintra City?"

Positions in the city Halls were so much sought after that there was a grand joint interviewing twice a year for hopeful Healers.

Aazali shook her head.

"I am for Low Port," she said.

Healer Grasy frowned.

"There is no Hall in Low Port."

"That is correct," Aazali said, tartly. "There is, however, need."

"The Guild will not grant a charter to open a Hall in Low Port."

"Where is the Healer," Aazali quoted, from one of Elder Grasy's own lessons, "there is the Hall."

"Hah." Dark eyes gleamed. "You *were* listening."

Aazali laughed. "You needn't sound surprised!"

"Merely for effect," the older woman told her, with a smile.

Aazali felt her merriment fade. She picked up her pack and shrugged it on.

"Refresh my aged memory," Elder Grasy murmured. "Your home is in Low Port, is it not?"

The Elder needed no refreshing on that point, as Aazali well knew. The Elder's memory, in fact, was most excellent, as anyone who had trained with her knew.

"Yes, Elder. At the corner of Crakle and Toom. There is a school, a medic's station, and a bakery. They took me in after my mother died. When it was seen that I would be a Healer, they arranged for me to be brought to this Hall, for training. Now that I am trained—"

She stopped there, words drying in her mouth. Serana had said that she might go back, after she was trained. Well, she *was* trained, and older, too. She was not dangerous unless she chose to be, which Dyoli had taught her was the proper order of life, and she wanted so very much to *go home*, to be certain that they were safe, to *help* however she might, for her training made her useful to the house, and to those–

"You would walk alone, into Low Port?" asked Elder Grasy, interrupting these thoughts.

It was no small risk, Aazali knew that–few better. And yet . . .

"I was born in Low Port, Elder."

"Yes, of course."

She glanced aside once more, at the hole in the garden, and the bucket.

"When do you go?" she asked.

Aazali bit her lip, but again she told the truth.

"Now. While it is still light."

"I understand. I wonder if you may tarry six minutes more."

Aazali blinked.

"For what purpose?"

"So that I may return to my rooms and pick up my bag. My intention is to accompany you. You make your point eloquently–Low Port has too long been denied the care of a Healer. Perhaps two will not be too many."

* * *

Had she been . . . less harried, she would have taken possession of the bakery in the bright light of day, making a display of her arrival, and sending to have the Gossip and the street boss brought to her.

However, the aftermath of the strike had created more than one sort of convulsion, and it had been incumbent upon her to move, quickly.

So she had arrived in the deep middle of the night surrounded by those remaining to her, waiting in the shadows while the door was opened and the building secured.

It had lacked but moments til dawn by the time she had lain herself on the wide bed in the small space behind the cluttered balcony room.

She was wakened not many hours later by a shout, a crash, a scream—and the the sounds of a child crying.

She swept down stairs, Gly Sin at her shoulder, and strode toward the racket, which now included a barrage of abuse in a woman's voice, underlain by soft murmuring, and the child's diminished sobbing.

Down a small hallway, and through an open doorway, into a large kitchen, where stood Tezi, gun out, covering the scolding woman and a youth holding a sobbing child in his arms. The boy was swaying slightly, murmuring into the child's ear.

The woman was pointing at the counter, where sat a large sealed crock. One of several stools pushed against the counter had fallen over.

". . . think I'm a thief?" the woman was yelling. "I saw lights, and thought they was back! Knew he'd want his heart of bread, soon's he got the ovens going! If I'd known there were stupids in the house—"

"What," said Lady voz'Laathi, her voice cutting through the scolding like a saber through hot butter, "is the meaning of this disturbance?"

The scolding woman turned to stare at her, mouth suddenly pressed tight. Tezi did not take her eyes from her targets, even as she made answer.

"These, my lady, broke into the house through that door over there."

She used her chin to point at the portal in question.

"Broke in!" sniffed the woman. "Got a key, don't I?"

"Do you?" asked Lady voz'Laathi with interest.

"'course I do. I was on early morning prep and baking. We all of us have keys. It's

only– "

"How many," Lady voz'Laathi interrupted once more, "is *all*?"

This question had an unexpected effect. The woman turned her face away, shoulders stiff. It was the boy holding the baby who answered.

"Four 'prentices and two bakers lived outside the house," he said, his voice peculiarly calming. "Two 'prentices were delivering down Verkil Mews when the skyblaze fell and the Beehive collapsed."

Lady voz'Laathi knew of the Beehive. Everyone in Low Port knew of it, and an unlikely number had lived there at one time or another. A massive, ramshackle rooming house of cracked crete and timbers, held together with wire, rope, and ignorance, by rights it ought to have fallen down decades ago. She had not heard of its collapse, but had no difficulty believing the boy's report, or in doing the sum in her head.

The two 'prentices had been crushed, and the contents of their pockets with them. The number of wild keys that opened her kitchen door was now four.

"Bry Tin suggested himself to the Scouts as a guide, and was killed in ambush." The boy's voice was absolutely flat; the woman's shoulders heaved once, and she drew a hard breath, before she raised her head and met Lady voz'Laathi's gaze.

"His key came back to us with his body," she said. "I hold it and my own."

Lady voz'Laathi waited. When neither one spoke further, she nodded at the woman. "You hold two keys, and two 'prentices hold two more. Is this correct?"

The baby made a small, cranky sound. The boy shifted her softly, and she put her head on his shoulder with a sigh.

"I have my key," he said, "and Cleyn's. She took up with a soldier, signed on as a recruit, and left when they did."

"I see. There are in fact four keys, and the two of you hold them all. That is convenient. Please return them to me."

"Is Don Eyr dead, then?" asked the woman, her eyes not . . . quite sane. "Serana gone? Fireyn, Ail Den, Cisco?"

It was Lady voz'Laathi's opinion that this was exactly the case, and also that the wild-eyed woman knew it to be so. However, one did not become the protector of six blocks of the worst territory in Low Port by being either gentle or giving.

"The subject is the keys to that door. I will have them from you."

"Who'll make the bread?" asked the woman. "Who'll deliver it to those who're left?"

"We have," the boy said, "a list of those who want to receive bread. We've been doing what we can, in our own kitchens, but we're not bakeries. Don Eyr–the ovens here are needed to fulfill demand."

Lady voz'Laathi stared at the two of them, mad as they were. They stared back, as if they had no idea who she was.

"Why," she asked, "did you not use your keys and make yourselves free? Why, indeed, have you not taken this place for your own?"

The woman and boy exchanged glances.

"It wouldn't have been right," the woman said at last. "This is *the bakery*. It's not ours to *take over*. Only to keep it safe until–until we go on, or go forward."

"They are not coming back, and *I* have taken over," Lady voz'Laathi said flatly. "Put the keys on the counter and go. I will let you live if you do so, now."

It was the boy who stepped forward, the baby raising her head to stare into Lady voz'Laathi's face.

"Our meeting has been awkward," he said. "I am Ray Ven, here is Cazyopea, and our mother Florenta. May we know who you are?"

Tezi was heard to gasp.

Lady voz'Laathi inclined her head. Indeed, they should learn who she was.

"I am Beyavi voz'Laathi, Protector of the Six Blocks."

"I've heard of you," Florenta said surprisingly. "Our Lady of Benevolence."

Lady voz'Laathi narrowed her eyes. "That is correct. Be certain that I am no easy lord. I keep my bargains—*all* of my bargains. Cross me at your peril. Accept my word as your law, and we both profit."

Silence in the wake of this. That was well; let them reflect upon the nearness of doom.

"We're something far from gayn'Urlez Hell," Florenta said. "Expanding your territory?"

That—was an astute question. It was true enough that her whim had been fact across the Six Blocks. Then, the skyblaze fell, petty bosses and wolf packs rising in the confused aftermath much more quickly than she could contain them. The Six Blocks were no longer hers.

"No," she said to Florenta. "I am acquiring a new territory."

"We're well-met, then," said Ray Ven. "We are in need of someone like you. We have contracts dating from before the skyblaze; we have new orders, as we have said. We—" he waved between himself and his mother— "and the others, know the baking side. What we require is someone to organize and protect, so that business can go forth."

She stared at him. He met her eyes.

"If you will engage to do that, then I at least will engage to do what I know to do, as best I can," he said in a tone of calm reason.

"I will likewise engage," said Florenta.

As oaths of fealty, they were not particularly fervent, but nor were they born of either fear or mortal need. The need for an administrator did not give rise to passion, it seemed. Well, and she had no need of passion, merely that they stood at their words, and if they did not—they would stand as an example to others.

In the meanwhile, if she wished to secure this new territory and stronghold, she had best begin.

"I accept you," she said, and looked to Florenta. "In one hour, bring the Gossip to me by the front door."

"Yes."

"Yes, Lady," she coached, and Florenta gave her a considering look, before moving her shoulders, and repeating, "Yes, Lady," as if she were indulging a child with a treat.

Lady voz'Laathi inclined her head, and turned to the boy.

"Your first task is to bring others here so that I may accept their oaths. I will see them one at a time, starting in the half-hour after the Gossip comes to me." She moved her hand, showing the young Gun, who had slipped her weapon away, though she yet stood alert.

"You may have Tezi with you, as protection."

Ray Ven blinked, then nodded, with a bright look at Tezi, and bounced the baby on his hip.

"Yes, come with me, do. We should introduce you to the neighbors."

* * *

tal'Qechee's Corner claimed a Mid Port address for itself, a conceit that might have been more believable if it were not well-known that Mr. tal'Qechee owned three Hells and parts of several other unsavory enterprises in Low Port.

Aazali paused on the broken curb, remembering the last time she had passed this way, holding Mar Tyn's hand as they crossed the pitted crete road, and up onto a walkway that was not very much of an improvement over the one they had left. There was a light on a pole at the corner, and another, a block away, and in the early morning, both had cast brave cones of illumination onto the ragged walk.

"We are now," Mar Tyn had told her, "in Mid Port."

She had turned then, he with her, to gaze back the way they had come.

"It does not seem . . . much different," she had observed, and Mar Tyn had laughed his quiet laugh.

"Let us go on a little further," he answered, bringing them 'round again to walk away from all and everyone she knew and loved; into the unknown.

"Healer?" Elder Grasy murmured at her side. "Is something amiss?"

"No, Elder," Aazali said, looking into the old woman's face. "I was only recalling the day I came to our Hall, and the friend who had brought me there."

"I recall Dyoli speaking of him," said Elder Grasy. "A Luck, I believe?"

"A friend," Aazali corrected, perhaps too sharply. "A brave friend, who risked his liberty if not his life, to bring me to the Hall so that I might be properly trained."

"Yes," Elder Grasy spoke softly. "So also did Dyoli represent him. May I know his name?"

"Mar Tyn," Aazali whispered, her voice gone rough. "Mar Tyn eys'Ornstahl."

"I hope to meet him, that I may thank him for his care of one of our more extraordinary students."

Aazali felt her cheeks heat.

"I hope to see him again, too," she said. "I hope he has done – that they all have done well."

"Indeed; we wish our friends to prosper," said Elder Grasy. "Do we go on, Healer?"

"Yes," Aazali said, drawing in a deep breath and bringing herself to center. She stepped off the curb.

"We go on."

* * *

Vasha the Gossip was young, where most Gossips were old. She was missing an arm, which would be, thought Lady voz'Laathi, an acceptable substitution for age. Indeed, it was a surprise to see one maimed and not merely alive, but in what appeared to be very good health. In Low Port, the weak and the wounded died quickly.

"My lady?" she said, when Gly Sin brought her to the bookroom.

Lady voz'Laathi inclined her head. Possibly, Florenta had schooled her in the proper forms.

"Gossip," she replied. "What is the Word on the Street?"

Vasha tipped her head, dark eyes speculative.

"Word on the Street is that Our Lady of Benevolence has been rousted from her stronghold. Nor Ish the Wolf has announced himself Protector of the Six Blocks." She paused, mouth pursed, as if in distaste, or amusement.

"Nor Ish succeeds Skale vin'Ard, who stood up in the place left empty when gayn'Urlez cut Torn the Butcher's throat."

Lady voz'Laathi took a careful breath. Rini gayn'Urlez had been a stalwart ally.

"Word on the Street," Vasha Gossip said again, her voice gone somber. "gayn'Urlez has left this life, with the Hell burning around her."

That—was a blow. It might even have been a blow to the heart, had she one. She kept her face bland under the Gossip's sharp eyes. Some words were best kept off the street.

"Does the street lay odds on the Wolf's survival?"

A hand flipped; palm up, palm down.

"Longer than Torn the Butcher, says the street, but not so long as Skale, who left Guns and allies behind her."

Yes; Skale had the spark, as Lady voz'Laathi had, in her youth. Those who had placed themselves under her protection; those who had sworn themselves to her service . . . some had loved her, and would not allow her to go unavenged. Had Lady voz'Laathi been minded to name a successor, it would have been Skale, who had been one of her Guns, whom she had assisted in securing three streets adjacent to her six, an ally and a buffer.

"Does the street whisper aught of the previous protectors of this area?"

"The street has a long memory. The bakery and the blocks around it served as a base for the mercenaries, and a team of Scouts. As well, many of us served as guides lower in—the house soldiers, as well. The call to remove came while the house soldiers were yet absent, and the mercenary captain would not leave the children scant of protectors. They were to be removed to a "safe place," is what the captain told the street, and Don Eyr confirmed it. We thought—and Don Eyr, also, *I* think, my lady—that they were only to be removed to Mid Port, and would return when their soldiers did."

She paused, and looked briefly aside.

"I have now come to believe that they were taken further than Mid Port, and will not—can not—return. The street hopes on."

"And the house soldiers?"

"They did not return. Which my lady knows how to understand as well as I do."

The soldiers were dead, then; she had nothing to fear from their return.

Lady voz'Laathi inclined her head.

"I think we understand each other. The street requires a protector."

Vasha Gossip's smile was a thing of dazzling brilliance.

"Why, *yes*, my lady. It does." She paused, and lifted her hand in inquiry.

"Shall I whisper to the streets that Our Lady of Benevolence has spread her hand over us?"

"Not yet," Lady voz'Laathi said, and narrowed her eyes. "You understand me, I think, Vasha Gossip?"

"Very well, my lady," the Gossip said with a bow. "Will you have my pledge? Our previous protectors did not require it."

"I hold with tradition," Lady voz'Laathi told her. Vasha the Gossip bowed once more, and pledged fealty to Beyavi voz'Laathi, Protector of Bakery Square.

#

"Einar will be up and awake," Ray Ven said, nodding at a small dwelling beside a burned building. "Here, hold Cazyopea."

He thrust the baby at Tezi, already turning away, and she had either to accept or see the small body drop to the street and break. Tezi had frankly seen enough of bodies bleeding out on crete. She snatched the child to her breast.

Cazyopea grabbed her hair, and she raised a hand to disentangle small busy fingers, while watching Ray Ven approach the door, and rap against it–three fast, two slow, four fast–and move backward a rapid six steps.

The door slammed open, and a large person swung out into the street. He held the short, thick length of metal in one hand as if he knew how to use—as if, Tezi corrected herself, he *had* used it, often, given the pipe's numerous scars and dark stains.

"Good-day, neighbor Einar," Ray Ven called cheerily, open hands held before him, chest-high, palms out.

"Oh, it's you, boy." The pipe vanished into a long holster sewn down the outside of his left pant leg. "Who has need?"

His voice was rough, and he spoke the Low Port pidgin with an accent that pitched the words oddly against the ear. Tezi finished working the baby's fingers loose, and set her firmly against a hip. Einar caught the motion, and looked at her, a frown on his pale, rumpled face.

"Who?" he snapped.

She pulled herself up, aware of her vulnerability; her stupidity. What her ladyship would say, when she found Tezi had allowed herself to be made helpless by a mere boy . . .

"That is exactly what I came here to tell you!" Ray Ven said, sounding positively cheerful. He waved a negligent hand in her direction.

"This is Tezi, who serves as Gun to the street's new protector, Lady voz'Laathi."

Einar's brows pulled together, and he gave Tezi one more hard look before turning to Ray Ven.

"Protector," he repeated. "Is that so?"

"She has agreed to take the lists in hand and put the business of the house in order."

Phrased thus, in that sunny voice, this outrageous claim sounded—perfectly possible. Tezi had been in the kitchen, and, yes, her ladyship *had* agreed to put the business of the house in order. In return for fealty, and obedience, and those other things that Lady voz'Laathi dealt in.

"Don Eyr sent her to us?"

Ray Ven's face darkened.

"No. There's been no word of Don Eyr, Serana, nor any of the others. Lady voz'Laathi is our going forward. She wants each and all of us 'round the square to go to her, tell her our worth, and swear to serve–with honor."

And that, Tezi thought, was nothing that her ladyship had agreed to. *Honor* was for people who had enough of everything they desired.

"Fireyn's not sent word?" Einar asked.

Ray Ven sighed. "She has not. If we are to go forward–"

"Yes," the man said heavily. "I step into her place. Forward. Let me get my kit."

#

It was Tor Hei on the door. Ray Ven having taken his sister back into his care, Tezi stepped forward with Einar at her side.

"This is Einar of the street," she told her colleague. "Her ladyship has called for a show of fealty, and he is the first come to her. Ray Ven of the street and I will rouse the rest, and send them to you. Her ladyship is wishful of having the matter settled soon rather than late."

Tor Hei gave a sharp nod to show he understood, and Einar stepped forward, wearing his kit, so-called, slung over one shoulder.

"Einar Berg, medic," he said, his voice crisp and cool. "Come to take my place in the house."

Tor Hei stared, then looked to Tezi, eyebrows up.

"To give his fealty to her ladyship," she confirmed. Tor Hei lifted one shoulder in a half-shrug, and reached behind to rap on the door, which was opened from the inside. He stepped aside, jerking his head to indicate that Einar was to enter, and took up his position again once the door had closed.

Behind her, she heard Ray Ven take a deep breath, as if it were his first in some time. She turned, he smiled, and stepped back into the street.

"We'll send Danel to her ladyship next," he told Tezi, leading the way down a narrow passage between two houses. "She'll be wanting the back garden set to rights as quickly as can, I think. Then, we'll go to Nanti."

Danel was found in a lot between two houses. There must, Tezi thought, have been a third house at one point, though there was no rubble or rubbish to support this theory. Indeed, there were rows of neat plas boxes filling the space, many with plants growing in them, some in the the process, perhaps, of being planted, or just harvested. There was a figure bent over a box on the far side of the lot, a barrow and tools hard by.

"Danel!" Ray Ven called, and the bent figure looked up, straightened carefully, and came toward them.

Much as he had to Einar, Ray Ven explained Lady voz'Laathi's presence, her intention to stand as protector, and the need for the back garden to be tended. Unlike Einar, Danel did not ask after Don Eyr, Serana, Fireyn, or any other. Merely, they inclined their head, and murmured, "So, we step forward."

"Will you go to her ladyship?" Ray Ven asked. "It will have to be now."

"I'll go, boy, but if it's now, I'll want a runner later, to bring what things I find needful."

"If there's no one else by then, I'll serve you myself."

"Well enough; to her ladyship go I."

#

Nanti came to the door with a child braced on her hip, and another pressed tight against her knee. Her face lit when she beheld them.

"Cazyopea! I wondered, when your mother didn't come at the usual time."

"We were detained," Ray Ven said, and waved at Tezi. "This is Tezi Gun. We would all be improved by some tea and a roll, and I'm sure Cazyopea would like a word or two with Pyan."

Nanti laughed.

"If not, Pyan has a word or two for her. Come in, come in."

That quickly they were swept into a large room cluttered with chairs and tables. At some of the tables, children were eating, while other children wiped empty tables clean. Nanti swept Cazyopea away from Ray Ven and deposited her in the arms of a tall girl with a patch over one eye.

"Delif, take Cazyopea to the the smalls room, and see she gets something to eat."

"Yes, Nanti." The girl vanished, and Nanti shooed them toward a newly cleaned table. "Tea and a roll for each, I think I heard. I will bring it, and jam, and you will eat and tell me the details of this delay."

The tea was good, the rolls better, and the jam beyond Tezi's experience of foodstuffs. Nanti sat with them, sipped tea, and refused to hear a word until they had eaten.

At last Ray Ven sat back in his chair with a sigh and a smile.

"I have a task for the runners," he said, "and information for you."

Nanti put her cup on the table.

"Information first, if you please, Master Ray Ven."

"Lady voz'Laathi of the Six Blocks has come to the bakery and claims it for her own," Ray Ven said, more seriously, and, in Tezi's opinion, more accurately than he had framed the facts for the others.

Nanti inclined her head, and waited.

"She agrees to put the house in order, and extend her protection over us, in exchange for oaths and promises."

"Yes," Nanti said quietly, "of course she does."

"Yes." To Tezi's surprise, Ray Ven did not produce a bright smile or breezy assurance for Nanti. Indeed, he looked rather somber; older, and more worn.

"Her ladyship wishes to meet the street and accept the oaths from all who agree to her protection. She had Vasha Gossip to her first. I sent Einar, and Danel."

"And you want the runners to rouse everyone else."

"Yes, but not too noisily. I think my lady did not leave the Six Blocks willingly."

"Oh." Nanti frowned. "Yes, I see."

"My lady," Tezi said, at last finding a point on which she could be firm, "will wish to consolidate quickly. A challenge is sure to come from those who think that the fall of The Six Blocks means she is weak."

Nanti turned to look at her.

"She is not weak," she said, firmly. "We have her back."

Tezi blinked, unsure of what to say to this piece of audacity, but Ray Ven was speaking again.

"Every half hour is the schedule," he said.

"And we don't wish to attract attention from unfriendly watchers. We'll use the evac routes," Nanti said. "It will be a good drill."

Ray Ven smiled. "I knew you would see how to make it work."

"Flatterer. What else?"

Ray Ven leaned forward, his arms on the table and looked directly into Nanti's eyes.

"It's time to step forward."

"Into the future." She sighed, looked down at her hands, shoulders slumped, then sat up, and met Ray Ven's eyes with a smile. "Of course it is. Past time, really. Don Eyr would not have chided us for our hopes, but he would have said that one might hope and stand up at the same time."

She smiled, and stood.

"I'll start the runners before I go to my lady. The sooner the school is back in place, the better."

* * *

The bakery was four blocks from tal'Qechee's Corner, each more crowded and decrepit than the last. The streets around the bakery were an oasis of civilization, as Aazali now knew. When she had arrived there as a child she had only known that it was like nothing she had ever experienced before. Five blocks further along from the bakery, in the heart of the Six Blocks, that was where she had lived with her mother, Ahteya the Luck, until the night one of Ahteya's clients had raped, robbed, and killed her before taking her daughter away in the belief that the child would make him lucky.

It was his misfortune that the child had been not been a Luck, but a nascent Healer, and no use to him at all.

Aazali sighed, stopped, put the bucket down, and adjusted the shoulder straps on her pack.

"The next three blocks," she told Elder Grasy, "are . . . unregulated, and more dangerous than those we have traveled thus far. Once we gain Crakle Street, we will be safer, again."

"Not safe?" the Elder inquired as she adjusted the straps of her own pack.

"Nothing in Low Port is safe," Aazali said. "Only some places are safer, and a taunt to those who value danger."

"I see. But I wonder if anyone truly *values* danger."

"Perhaps they do not. But they seek to destroy that which they do not have."

"Ah. That is a very different thing."

"But no less dangerous." Aazali turned to face the old woman. "I mean no insult, Elder, but I suggest that it would not be wise for you to come further. I will happily escort you to tal'Qechee's Corner."

"And put off your reunion with your home? That is kindness, indeed. However, I am quite determined to go on."

"There is no need," Aazali said carefully, "to escort me, Healer. I will be quite safe."

"So you have said, and so you believe," Grasy said comfortably. "However, your point regarding the lack of Healers in the Low Port carries weight with me. You are determined to stand in service to those in need. That determination honors your training, and your teachers. I likewise wish to honor my training and the memory of my teachers by serving those in need."

"There is need in Mid Port," Aazali said quietly.

"So there is, and more than two Healers to answer it. Do we go on?"

There was, Aazali realized, nothing she could say that would prevail upon the elder to embrace prudence, and the longer they stood in one place, the longer they flirted with danger.

"Yes," she said, picking up the bucket. "We go on."

#

Trouble lunged at them from out of the shadows clogging a passway between a burned-out storefront and a careless pile of packing crates. Leading with the knife, her target was obviously the elder.

Aazali swung the bucket out, striking the woman's knee. She went down with a cry. Healer Grasy dropped beside her onto the broken crete, and Aazali bent to retrieve the fallen blade.

It was, she saw before slipping it away into a pocket, quite a good knife, clean, and well-honed.

The woman who had attacked them was in no such good repair—desperately thin, the cheek that Aazali could see was scored deep, as if by claws. She considered that more closely, using all of her senses, and found the taint of infection throughout the woman's body where she was curled in on herself on the walkway, sobbing weakly.

"Healer . . ." Aazali murmured to Grasy, who had her hand on their attacker's head. Aazali could See the lines she was extending–peace, comfort, calmness–all sorely needed. The downed woman's emotions were a maelstrom; a black vacuum of pain, despair, and grief that shredded Healer Grasy's learned, elegant lines.

"There is need," Grasy answered, as she began again, the lifeline she offered now more like to steel cable than silk.

Aazali could scarcely argue that; the little she could glimpse of the woman's pattern beyond the storm of her anguish was a horrifying landscape of ruin, incomplete–though surely *that* could not be. Howeverso, it was a bad case; one that wanted a team of Healers experienced in extreme trauma, working inside the studied ambiance of a Hall. One elder Healer, no matter how experienced, and one junior Healer, no matter how strong, here and now, on the broken crete, with shadowy fingerings of violence beginning to intrude upon her senses–

"Healer," Aazali said again. "We have drawn notice."

"So what if we–" Healer Grasy began sharply, and bit off her words. "Ah. I understand. And here we have this little one in mortal need. What will you, Healer?"

"You have the knife," the wounded woman gasped suddenly. "Kill me now, quickly."

"That solves nothing," Aazali said, and threw herself open as wide as she might, reading those who thought them easy meat, feeling a tingle against her senses that she hadn't felt for years, so thin that she might have thought she imagined it. She *did* think she imagined it, but no thread was too scant to grasp in this moment.

"You are a Luck," she said to the woman on the ground.

"*Was* a Luck," the woman gasped.

"Born a Luck, die a Luck," Aazali said, which her mother had used to say. "Stand."

She extended her will, ceding the fallen Luck strength enough to rise. Grasy rose, too, her hand under the other woman's arm, lending support.

"You know where the bakery is," she said, not a question.

"All of Low Port knows where the bakery is," the woman agreed, her voice firm with borrowed strength.

"Guide the elder there," Aazali said, and it was a command.

"Aazali," Grasy began.

"*Now*," Aazali said sharply. "I will catch you up as soon as I might. Here." She thrust the bucket of flowers into Grasy's hand. "Go."

One more hard look from the Healer's knowing eyes before she turned to her client, the ill and broken Luck.

"Come, let us see you to safety."

Aazali watched them gain the corner before turning to show danger her face.

Healing is accomplished by first establishing a rapport with the one in need. The Healer initiates the connection and controls it. Typically, the first connection conveys hope, calm, and comfort. As the client relaxes into these feelings, they open more fully to the Healer, who is then able to survey the pattern of the personality, and understand such injuries and misalignments as may be causing distress or denying the client the fullness of joy. Once these matters are understood, the Healer regrows, repairs, and aligns as necessary. In all cases, the Healer acts upon the client. The client's state is quiescent; they cannot reach back along the connection to influence the Healer.

Training emphasizes the benefit to the client, and embraces the wisdom that *less is more*. Often the best Healing is merely to align the tapestry of the spirit, so that the client experiences more contentment. The Hall Masters and the Guild emphasize the benevolence of Healers, and of Healing. They never mention, and it seemed to occur to no one independently, that a person who is able to secure emotional access to another person, might also be able to use that ability for–

Self-defense.

The patterns that opened before her Inner Eye were undergrown; stunted, as the body might become stunted from having known want. Three of them stood revealed before her Sight, two grim and grimy, stitched rigid with the glaring orange of anger, and the thick crimson of blood-lust. The third was likewise grimy, but somewhat less grim, with a flexibility that suggested youth. Of anger, there was a little, but the desire for mayhem and death was entirely absent, replaced in part by the sharp green of curiosity.

Dyoli had told her that, for less nuanced work, such as crowd control, a practiced Healer might hold as many as two dozen lines open at once. Aazali did not make the error of thinking she was practiced. She was, however, quick, and her message was very simple.

She established one connection, and a second, stretched, thrust fear into the center of their patterns–

And closed the connections.

Screams and pellet fire from the alleyway opposite; more screams, and the sounds of footsteps, pounding away.

Aazali sighed and considered the third pattern, still in place, still curious, though somewhat distressed.

"You may come out and speak with me or you may leave," she said. "If you wish, you may walk with me."

She Saw a ripple of surprised alarm before a shadow detached itself from a doorway three buildings to her right. It had a shock of red hair, and wore a flowered tunic over a pair of dark pants with one knee out. A wide strap crossed one shoulder to the opposite hip, supporting a travel flask. The boots were good and well-cared-for, like the knife Aazali had put in her pocket.

"You're for the bakery?" The voice was husky.

"Yes," Aazali said. "Will you come?"

A flicker of hesitation across the pointed face, a gleam of resignation along that pleasingly flexible pattern.

"Haven't a choice. I've got Dorin's drink, that the medic said she needed. Doesn't do her any good unless she drinks it."

A medic, thought Aazali. She thought of Fireyn, but Fireyn would not have let a woman so ill as the knife-wielding Luck–Dorin?–out of her care until the infection was gone.

The child came closer, and she felt that familiar tingle once more.

"You're a Luck," she said.

The child stopped, wariness apparent. She understood that, all too well.

"My mother was a Luck," Aazali offered, and saw the faint relaxation in the child's stance.

"So's mine. What House?"

There were three Houses into which Lucks on Low Port might buy, if they earned enough to pay the dues, and thus claim some small amount of safety. Ahteya hadn't been able to afford even the least of them.

"My mother is dead," Aazali said, beginning to walk. The child kept pace.

"*You're* not a Luck, though. Never saw a Luck could do what you did to those two Roughers."

"No," she said, "I'm a Healer."

A frown showed on the thin face.

"What's a Healer?"

"Like a medic," she said, "only for the heart. What's your name?"

"Mish."

"I am Aazali."

"Why're you going to the bakery?"

"To offer my service as a Healer."

"Why?"

"I was born in Low Port. There were no Healers here to teach me, so I was sent to Mid Port. Serana told me–" *Serana promised me!*– "that I could return, after my training was done."

They walked on, Aazali scanning ahead with all her senses. They crossed the street, turned left and walked on.

"Bakery's empty," Mish said, as one reluctant to impart bad news. It was a blow to the heart.

Aazali took a sharp breath against the sudden pain. *You knew this was possible*, she told herself. *You prepared yourself, to find it empty, even–gone.*

But she had *hoped* differently.

"Still going?" Mish asked.

"Yes," she said. She took another breath. "If the bakery is empty, we must fill it again, and go forward."

* * *

Lady voz'Laathi closed her eyes. *I am*, she thought, *getting old.* It was not a new thought, nor was she the first to have noted it. Indeed, it was her age as much as the disturbances caused by the skyblaze that had prompted Torn the Butcher to wrest the Six Blocks from her hands.

Of course, she had a back-up plan. Juntavas Boss Toonapple had trained her team leaders rigorously in the necessity of back-up plans, and back-ups to the back-up plans. Beyavi voz'Laathi had carried that training with her into Low Port after Herself left Liad and the next three sent in to replace her proved to be short-lived idiots.

When the Butcher made his move, she invoked the back-up plan. But there had been a spy in her organization. She lost people, lost streets, lost, in the end, an old and valued friend, before those who had survived found each other, hid for a time, and then came away.

And now, she thought, feeling the weariness in her bones, here I stand, an old woman with six Guns holding to their oaths, and four streets to make her own.

The taking of oaths had been surprisingly quick. No one challenged her authority to stand as protector of their streets. No one balked at offering fealty. All were forthcoming with names, and greeted the information that my lady's Guns would be by to inspect their conditions with equanimity.

Still, it had been a long day following a short night, after weeks of uncertainty and, yes, fear.

Lady voz'Laathi was tired. And for the first time since the skyblaze had fallen, she was in a place of relative safety.

"I believe," she said to Gly Sin, "that I will repair to the overfull rooms and rest."

"Yes, my lady," Gly Sin said. "There are sandwiches in the kitchen, my lady, and tea. The Guns have tested them, and they are safe. Will you eat? I can bring a tray."

She considered him, the oldest of her Guns.

"Are you a servant now?"

"I serve you, my lady, as ever I have done," he responded, and considered her as he would a raw recruit.

"You must eat, and you must rest. For the good of us all, my lady."

He was right. She inclined her head.

"Very well, if you will have it so, bring a tray. There was a table, I think, by a window."

"Yes, my lady."

He bowed and left her.

After a moment, she rose and sought the stairway to the half-floor above.

* * *

"Why did you come back?" Mish asked.

"I was born here," Aazali answered. "My friends are here."

"If it was me who got sent up Mid Port to be taught," Mish said frankly, "I'd never come back. I b'lieve Dorin would murder me if I tried it."

"Dorin is your mother?"

"Right you are. Dorin pai'Fortana."

The House of Fortune was the first of the three Houses of Luck in Low Port. Dorin had being doing well, as Low Port measured such things.

"A friend had hoped to sponsor himself into Fortune," she said slowly, hesitant to receive another blow so soon after the first. "Perhaps he did and you know him. Mar Tyn eys'Ornstahl, he was."

"Mar Tyn," Mish said, in a changed tone. "Yes, we knew him–a Luck's Luck, Dorin said. He was one of the Taken."

Aazali felt her breath go; forced herself to keep walking. Forced herself to keep scanning.

"Taken?" she asked, her voice thin. "Taken where?"

"That we never knew," Mish said. "We said *taken*, you know, not *dead*, because there were never no bodies found. People just–vanished. Just like, the Hall Master said, somebody was making a collection of Lucks. We thought there was someone daft enough to believe, if they had all the Lucks, than no one would be so lucky as them."

"It doesn't work that way," Aazali said, reflexively.

"No, it don't, but that doesn't keep people from thinking stupid things. Anywise, we thought that 'til Dorin was almost Taken, and then we knew better, much good it did us. Fortune won't have us back, not with Dorin like she is, even though they're gone now–*they're* dead, certain enough, but they say Dorin's Luck is broke, and aside that, the collector touched her . . ."

"Touched her how?" Aazali asked, remembering the sense that the woman's pattern had been shredded; that sections were *missing*.

"Long tale told short," Mish said, after a minute, "there was somebody collecting Lucks, all right. After the first went missing, House Fortune sent out teams, to try and find *who*, but the teams didn't come back. That's how Mar Tyn disappeared. After that, the House started hiring Guns, and paired them with a Luck. I wasn't supposed to go when it was Dorin's turn to search, but–I was worried."

Mish took a hard breath.

"I saw her–the collector–take Dorin. I was near but not with her. I saw it happen. Saw her go blank, and turn just like the collector was the sun and Dorin a flower. It was right then the Gun took notice and shot the collector in the head.

"Dorin screamed, and I–it was stupid, but I didn't think. I ran to grab her and hold her up. I *felt* her heart stop, I swear, and then–it started again. I don't know why."

"You *do* know why," Aazali said. "You are a Luck. There was a chance."

Mish wiped a sleeve across a dirty face.

"You're right. And I did wrong. The Hall won't have us back, and she's broken in the head. Got into that fight–you saw her face. The medic says maybe she'll recover from that, if she drinks his medicine and doesn't get hurt again, but–she's never going to be . . . herself. Coming at the both of you with a knife–she's not *like*–well. *Now*, she's like that, and I suppose she will be, going forward."

"Perhaps not," Aazali said. "Healer Grasy has her in hand, now."

Mish considered that for the space of a dozen steps.

"That's a good thing, is it?"

"Yes," Aazali said, "it is."

Only one more block separated her from the bakery. She quickened her pace, noted a lack, and turned.

Mish was behind her, apparently rooted to the walk, face twisted with a particular anguish.

"I—my feet are going this way." She nodded to the alley mouth at her right. "Mar Tyn said, never fight your feet."

"I remember," Aazali said, returning. The child pulled the strap over her head and held out the canteen.

"Take this to Dorin. I'll—when my feet allow, I'll come to the bakery."

"I'll come with you," Aazali said.

"No, you don't know—"

"Nor do you. Let us find out together. Here." She unslung her pack and stowed the canteen, then shrugged the pack back on.

"Now," she said, with a lightness she was far from feeling, "let us see where your feet would take us."

* * *

The sandwich was fish paste between thin slices of what Lady voz'Laathi supposed must be the famous bread for which there were so many orders. It was, she thought, very good bread, far above the usual Low Port fare, which gave one to wonder after flours, contacts, deliveries, and other matters, that were more of a challenge then they might be even at the line to Mid Port. Such details had been her specialty, when she'd worked for Boss Toonapple, and it was surprisingly easy to think in such terms, even after years.

Don Eyr and Serana had contacts, obviously, but it appeared that they had also had money, which was an even rarer commodity than the truly excellent tea Gly Sin had brought up with her meal.

Lady voz'Laathi knew very well how she had gotten *her* funds, but there had been no whisper of piracy attached to the bakery. They must, she told herself, walking to the window with her second cup of tea in hand—they *must* have charged those in their care a fee for protection. Interesting that they had seen this amount of success with that scheme. In Lady voz'Laathi's experience, collecting fees from those under her protection, while necessary, did not provide one with *wealth*, not even as Low Port counted wealth.

The window overlooked the back courtyard, and its array of tiered shelves. Pleased, she saw that someone had tended to the broken gate, and swept the broken pots up.

In fact, there was someone at the tiers, putting new pots up, and–it was not one of her people.

Lady voz'Laathi put the teacup on the table on her way to the stairs.

\#

"Gly Sin, with me!" she snapped as she hit the the main hall and kept on, stride unbroken. She swept 'round the corner, into the hall that led to the back entranceway–

And stopped.

The hall was awash in children, each carrying books, saving those who carried a chair. Each child wore a backpack, and they were notably quiet as they stood in line before a door Lady voz'Laathi had noted, but not yet opened.

Gly Sin stepped around her, arms crossed over his chest.

"What're you kids doing in the lady's house?"

Heads swiveled in their direction. No one spoke, then a dark-haired figment holding three books that looked to weigh more than he did, grinned, and said.

"We're bringing the school back, Lady!"

"The school," Lady voz'Laathi repeated.

"Indeed, yes, your ladyship!" A tall, dark-haired woman with slanting blue eyes, and dark brown skin slipped out of the room into the hallway. She bowed.

"Your ladyship will perhaps recall me? Nanti oyl'Erin. I know that you will recall that I promised to open school properly on the morrow." She swept her hand out, showing Lady voz'Laathi the children. "In order to do that, we must bring in our tools and equipment, which had been moved elsewhere to make room for the soldiers. Very nearly, we have everything back where it belongs, your ladyship, and I do swear to you that lessons will begin on time tomorrow, with all students and teachers present."

"Do you?" said Lady voz'Laathi, staring at the mass of young things cluttering the hall, all of them staring at her, or perhaps at Gly Sin. There was no fear in their eyes; no anxiety in their faces. Really, it was extraordinary.

"I warn you that I may arrive to test the strength of your oath," she said to Nanti oyl'Erin, who was also remarkably calm, though perhaps not as guileless as those she had in charge.

"By all means, my lady! We welcome you at any time. And, perhaps, some day, when you are not so busy, you might consent to talk to the students about how you came to us, and your plans, going forward."

Lady voz'Laathi stared at Nanti oyl'Erin, who did not look away.

"We will discuss that, later," she said.

"Certainly, my lady. Now, if you will allow, there is still some work to do so that all will be ready for tomorrow."

"I allow. And I ask that a way be made for me. I am wanted in the courtyard."

"Of course, my lady." Nanti oyl'Erin turned to the children, who were already moving to one side of the hall.

Gly Sin went first, she perforce following down the hall and out the door, into the courtyard.

A tall, spare figure in mud-stained trousers and shoes, a cap crammed down so tightly that grey hair stood out like an aurora around the head, was filling a new pot with dirt from a wagon that had been drawn up next to the tiers. Three more pots sat to the left, each showing plants. Two more empty pots sat to the right.

Lady voz'Laathi asked, stern, but not sharp. "What do you here?"

The figure turned, a beaked nose and a pointed chin visible, the rest of the facial features shadowed by the brim of the cap.

"Afternoon, your ladyship. Danel, the gardener, as came by this morning." They touched the rim of their cap briefly. "Putting all this right again, so the kitchen's got its fresh vegetables."

They turned toward the pots, turned back.

"Good thing you came by, as it happens. You'll be wanting flowers? Real fond of his flowers, was Don Eyr–and Serana, too. Got some night bloomers I can pot up and set around, like they used to was. Got jazmin, cozmo, lissum–pretty flowers, good scents."

Flowers. Lady voz'Laathi tried to remember a time in her life when she had been asked about *flowers*.

"I depend upon your expertise," she heard herself say. "You are, after all, the gardener, and I have no opinion of flowers."

Danel nodded, apparently unperturbed by this.

"I'll get it set up t'way it was. Can always make changes once you grow an opinion. That gate'll want some work done to it. Me an' Ray Ven got it up as best we could, but it'll only come down again. Meantime, I'm waiting for the rest of my tools and such to–well, here they are, now."

The gate swung unsteadily back on hinges that screamed, pushed by none other than Tezi Gun. Following her, pulling another wagon piled high with items Lady voz'Laathi didn't even try to categorize, was Ray Ven, absent his infant sister.

"Tezi," Gly Sin said.

The girl looked up.

"One moment, Top Gun," she said, holding the gate until the barrow had cleared, then pushing it closed and setting the latch.

"Ray Ven, duty!" she called, and he looked up, then to Gly Sin, and past.

"Your ladyship," he said, bowing lightly. "Gun Gly Sin. Tezi has been a great assistance in the tasks her ladyship set me. I thank you for pairing her with me."

Lady voz'Laathi felt Gly Sin's eyes on her, even as she continued to study Ray Ven. He met her eyes without a flinch.

Well, and the lad had done everything she had asked, witness the fact that she had been taking oaths all day. She was not yet so diminished that she would strike out at one who had served her as she had bidden.

Nor did she mean to have him think that he might make his way around her whenever he wished it.

So.

"You are of course welcome," she said with heavy irony. "Is there anything else that you require of my Youngest Gun, Master Ray Ven, or may I reclaim her to proper duty?"

Ray Ven settled the barrow and stepped forward. He was sweaty with exertion, and his face was grimy, but his eyes were steady.

"Your ladyship, if I overstepped your intention, that is my remedy to make."

"Is it? Tezi Gun, how did you interpret your orders?"

"That I was to guard Ray Ven from harm while he fulfilled the task you gave him, my lady."

"And it is your belief that this included pushing wheelbarrows and opening gates?"

Tezi turned her hands up.

"It became apparent that the order was simple, but the execution was not," she said, and Lady voz'Laathi heard Gly Sin make a sound rather like a sneeze. "But it is true, your ladyship, that I ought to have checked in with Top Gun."

"So you ought. I leave you to him, then." She turned aside. "Danel, is there anything else you require of me?"

"Not right at the minute, my lady," the gardener said, without turning around. "I'll be by every day or few to see to the plants and talk with you about necessities."

Oh, indeed?

Lady voz'Laathi did not close her eyes, though the temptation was strong. Instead, she exchanged a glance with Gly Sin, turned and walked back into the house.

There was an . . . aroma in the air as she came out of the now-empty back hall and into the main. A rather delicious aroma. She followed her nose to the kitchen, to find a halfling at the stove, and two others of about the same age washing down counter tops and sweeping the floor.

"What's to do, now?" Lady voz'Laathi said, mild with recurring astonishment.

The boy at the stove turned, smiling.

"Making supper, your ladyship. Only soup this evening, but we'll do better tomorrow. Well, it stands to reason–there'll be a baking tomorrow, Florenta swears it, so that's fresh bread, which makes everything else taste that much better!"

He turned back to his pot, gave another stir and looked at her over his shoulder.

"Something I can get for you now, your ladyship? We've nut butter, cheese, and plenty of crackers. Tea right there in the pot." He used his chin to point at the hot-pot on the sideboard. "Cups next to it."

"Thank you, no. I wonder, though–from whence come these supplies?"

"From our usuals," the halfling said brightly, turning back to his pot. "Not all of 'em survived the skyblaze, o'course, but a good many did. The records are in Don Eyr's desk; you'll be wanting those, I s'pose."

"I suppose I shall," she said. She turned toward the door, and stepped back as it swung open to admit a man.

"Kaz Dee, is that my supper I smell?" he called.

"It will be. If you're hungry now, there's snacks on the counter."

"Just tea, thanks."

He turned toward the hotpot, and paused, turning to face her again.

"I'm all settled in, my lady, and seen my first patient. She's resting with me, but her friend's waiting in the parlor for you."

"Indeed. And you are?"

He raised his eyebrows.

"You'll have met a lot of people today," he said after a moment. "Doubtless we're all a blur. I'm Einar, the medic, attached to the clinic here in the house. I have my own quarters there, and I take my meals here in the kitchen. Hasn't this scamp Kaz Dee given you a full tour, yet?"

"I was doing deliveries!" Kaz Dee cried from the stove. "Only got here an hour ago and with supper to find so her ladyship don't think less of us."

"Perhaps tomorrow," Lady voz'Laathi said, and inclined her head, both in acknowledgment of his information and honor for his duty. It was no ill thing, after all, to have a medic in the house. "Medic Einar, you will send to me immediately, if the clinic requires aught."

"I'll do that, my lady," he said, and turned back toward the hotpot.

Lady voz'Laathi left the kitchen, pleased to meet no one else on her way to the parlor.

* * *

Slender though they were, the alley was too thin to allow them to go side-by-side. Mish's feet providing the imperative, she led, with Aazali coming after, probing ahead with senses wide open, flashlight in hand, its beam on low, and pointed down, happily illuminating nothing more than cobblestones sticky with mud.

So intent was she on her scans, that she bumped into Mish when the girl stopped, and went back a step, blinking.

"Here," said Mish.

Aazali tightened her scan, frowning.

"I don't–" she began, but Mish had fallen to her knees in the muck that lined the stones, breathing, "*Here*–"

Carefully, Aazali stooped beside her, and brought the light forward.

Green fire blazed back at her from a crevice in the crete wall, and she felt defiance, sharp as a pinprick, and sharper still, the bite of loneliness.

"A cat?" Mish said. "My feet brought me here for a *cat*?"

"Possibly, your feet are fond of cats," Aazali said. "Are you compelled to go on?"

"No-o," Mish said. "My feet are at rest."

"Can you leave?"

The girl stood, shifted away–one step, two–and returned.

"A cat," she said, and came back down to the alley floor with a sigh. "Now what?"

"Now," Aazali said, feeling curiosity wake, and defiance dim. "We have her out. Hold the light. I have gloves in my pack."

* * *

In the parlor, she discovered a woman of about her own age in deep conversation with Tor Hei Gun. No mean feat, as Tor Hei was mute. There was nothing wrong with his ears, and he was fluent in Old Trade. However, he found few enough to converse with him in that elegant language of hand-signs. It appeared that her visitor was one of those few.

Both turned when she entered, Tor Hei bowing, his companion merely inclining slightly from the waist.

"And who," Lady voz'Laathi asked, very calmly, "are *you*?"

"Grasy bel'Dona. I am a Healer, and brought a client chance-met on the street to your medic. It was suggested that I present myself to *her ladyship*." She cocked her head, amusement on her face. "Are you *her ladyship*?"

"I am Beyavi voz'Laathi. My street name for many years has been Lady Benevolence."

"I see. You are not, then, Serana of whom I have heard so much?"

"I am not."

Grasy bel'Dona looked grave. "I wonder if you have news of Don Eyr, or Mar Tyn?"

"To the best of my knowledge, the former occupants of the bakery are gone, and will not be returning. I am told that this place was a base for the soldiers and Scouts, after the skyfall. When they drew back, they left the building empty."

"That will be a blow." Grasy bel'Dona indicated a bucket on the floor by the tea-table. It was full of dirt and flowers.

"I came ahead with my chance-met client, but I expect the head of this expedition to arrive very shortly. She was born in Low Port, her mother murdered and herself abused as a very young child. The folk of the bakery took her in, cared for her, and determined that she was a Healer born. They sent her to Fountaincourt Hall in Mid Port to be trained, doubtless thinking she would remain. However, they did–your pardon, *Serana* did–promise that, when training was done, my young friend could, if she wished, return. It has been her long-held determination to return. Today, she acted."

Another nod at the bucket. "Those were intended for Serana, who I am told very much liked flowers."

"So I have been told as well."

Lady voz'Laathi looked to Tor Hei, who raised his eyebrows. She gave him his orders in a crisp succession of signs.

Take the bucket to the courtyard and give it to the gardener.

Tor Hei bowed–to herself, and to Grasy bel'Dona–picked up the bucket and departed.

"An interesting man. Has he served you long?"

"Many years." After his family had been murdered, he had came to her at gayn'Urlez Hell, a gun nearly as long as he was strapped to his waist, half-mad, and ready to swear anything, did she find the murderers and give them to him.

She looked at her visitor.

"What is your intention, I wonder?" It was something she had asked often, in her role as protector of the Six Blocks.

"My intention is to join this enterprise, perhaps as part of the clinic. Medic Einar and I have spoken briefly of this."

"You are a medic?"

"No, madam, I am also a Healer. I am informed–indeed, I know for myself, that there are no Healers in Low Port, which is an error that has been too long allowed to stand."

"And you have determined to correct this error."

"Not, I, my lady. Aazali sen'Pero, the companion I spoke of, identified the need, and determined that it was hers to solve. I was so struck by her dedication to her service that I came with her, for surely, if one Healer is a benefit, two Healers can only be moreso."

She paused. "Also, the Guild has given me leave to retire. My time and my life are my own to spend."

"I . . . see. And this chance-met client now in Medic Einar's care?"

"A badly damaged woman, bearing wounds of body and soul. Medic Einr is confident that he can defeat the infection. When that victory is won, she and I will sit together and see what may be done for the lacerations of her soul. In the meanwhile, I have done the merest patch job, so that she may regain her strength in peace."

"A word in your ear, Healer. This is no place of peace. Even under the previous protectors it was seen as a challenge, and many times attacked. I cannot believe that it will go differently now that the challenge is occupied by one who had been powerful and is now made low. Seek peace elsewhere."

Knowing eyes met hers.

"I will beg your patience, for I must stay at least until my companion arrives. We had left it that she would find me here."

"And when she has done so, you will leave," my lady said, annoyed to hear her voice not so stern as she had intended.

Healer Grasy lifted a thin eyebrow, but what she might have said to that was lost in the opening of the door. Tezi Gun bowed on the threshold.

"My lady, there are two at the front door. One calls herself Aazali sen'Pero and states that she is a Healer. The other represents herself as Mish the Luck, and says we have her mother here."

Beyavi voz'Laathi sighed.

"Bring the Healer and the Luck in, Tezi," she said, and pretended not to see Healer Grasy smile.

#

It was a bedraggled twosome who arrived in Tezi's wake. The younger was red-haired and meager. The elder was scarcely more substantial, though better cared-for; Her hair was pale and sleek, her eyes equally pale. Both were ragged, the pale one holding what one assumed was her jacket bundled in arms that showed angry scratches.

"Healer Aazali," said Healer Grasy. "Her ladyship and I were just discussing our worth to the house."

Pale brows rose, as the elder of the two newcomers looked to Beyavi.

"A Healer in the house is no ill thing," she said, and her voice was larger than she was, shivering along nerves Beyavi voz'Laathi thought long ago burned to ash.

"I can afford no more dependents," she said blandly, "and I am mistress here. My name is Beyavi' voz'Laathi. Make yourself known to me."

She bowed slightly, tender of the bundle in her arms.

"Aazali sen'Pero, Healer. This place is my home. I understand that those who promised that I might return here after I was trained have themselves gone away. However, my value to the House and to the mission of the House remains. I am a two-plane Healer, able to repair physical injury, as well as emotional. It is true that I am young in my craft, but I have completed all my training. I say again—a Healer in the house is no ill thing."

Beyavi stared at her. She stared back. The jacket in her arms let forth a yowl.

"Healer Aazali," the other Healer began, before Beyavi could speak—and was interrupted by the younger member of the party.

"It's a cat—a kitten, really. I—my feet took me to her, and wouldn't move 'til we had her out and brought her with us." She turned to face Beyavi, and produced a modeless Low Port bow.

"I'm Mish pai'Fortana. The elder Healer had my mother in charge. I have her drink from the Scout medic on Birn Street, and she'll need it soon, if—"

"I will take you to her," Healer Grasy said, stepping forward and beckoning the child to her. "She is with the house medic, who has already begun treatment."

Beyavi drew a breath. Healer Grasy paused with her hand on the door and turned back.

"Healer Aazali, will you come? Those scratches should be seen by the medic, and your client, also."

"The Healer will follow you directly," Lady voz'Laathi said. "After she and I have come to know each other a little better."

Elder Grasy inclined her head. Aazali sen'Pero stepped toward the door and gave the bundled kitten over to Mish pai'Fortana.

"Have the medic examine her," she said. "There had used to be other cats serving the house, as well."

"Yes," said the girl, and she and the Healer exited.

* * *

Aazali sen'Pero turned to regard the new protector of the house.

She was an elder, and at first glance nothing like to Serana, who had been lean and tall and quick. At second glance, however, there were the eyes–sharp and knowing, and a gleaming strength of purpose that beguiled the Inner Eyes.

Lady voz'Laathi's pattern was dark where Serana's had been lit by an apparently unlimited capacity to love, yet there were similar stains upon both–blood, Aazali thought, for Serana had been a warrior.

As was this lady.

"So, Healer, you have come to change Low Port," the lady's voice was sardonic, her face without expression. Her pattern showed the very faintest flicker of humor.

In fact, thought Aazali, she must be a ridiculous figure–dozens of years this lady's junior, her arms ribboned with scratches, and her face doubtless dirty. Serana would not have laughed at her, but this lady was not–had never been nor would become–Serana.

Serana, Aazali reminded herself, was no longer mistress here; Beyavi voz'Laathi now stood as protector of the bakery and the streets, and it was to that person that she must demonstrate her worth.

"I am here to comfort and Heal those in need," she said. "It is what Healers do."

"Yes, but very rarely here. Low Port is full of evil people, who live only to do their worst."

"Possibly that is so. If it is, then they are little different from those who applied to the Hall where I was trained."

Lady voz'Laathi's eyebrows rose.

"How old are you, Healer?"

"Fifteen Standards, my lady."

"And you were guaranteed a place here, by the previous protectors, once your training was done?"

"No, my lady. I was told that I might come home, when my training was through, if I wished to do so."

"I wonder why you wished to do so."

"Because this is my home, and I am a Healer. I would pursue my rightful work, in the place where I was born. It may be that I can change some few things, and for the better. Serana and Don Eyr made a difference here. Fireyn told me they had come to Low Port intending to change—to *improve*—what they found."

"Fireyn?"

"One of the house guards, and the medic. Even as a child, I could see her pain, but I could do nothing, then, to assuage it."

Lady voz'Laathi paused, the weight of her consideration cold and hard. Aazali folded her hands and waited.

After a moment, the lady spoke again.

"There is a spy in my household, Healer. How do you counsel me to proceed, when they reveal themselves?"

Aazali blinked, and bowed, for this question *did* fall within her honor as a Healer.

"Find their reasons, my lady, and consider if you believe them. It may be that reparations can be made."

"Shall I not make an example, to instill fear in those who might take the same path?"

"We are taught that fear is an uncertain tool, which may itself produce betrayal."

There was a small pause before Lady voz'Laathi inclined her head.

"You may seek the medic, Healer," she said. "I grant you one night, while I weigh what is best for the House, and myself."

Aazali bowed.

"Thank you, my lady," she said, and turned away, the door closing quietly behind her.

Beyavi voz'Laathi stared at the door. She should, she knew, have them all rousted out into the street to fend for themselves.

"Allow them even one night," she said to the empty room, "and you will never be rid of them."

And while that was undoubtedly true, she did not call for her Guns to clear the house of unwanted Healers and Lucks.

"After all," she murmured. "A Healer in the house is no ill thing."

* * *

They were gathered in the clinic's intake room. The kitten was asleep on Healer Grasy's lap. Aazali, scratches treated, had pulled an overshirt from her pack and put it on. Mish had satisfied herself that Dorin was asleep, and accepted Medic Einar's decision not to wake her for the Scout medic's elixir.

"Dosed her up, myself," he said, reclining in the chair behind his desk. "No sense giving her too much of a good thing. Though, here's what you can do for me, young Mish. Take a note from me tomorrow morning to this Scout medic. I'll want a consult, or at least the formula for this drink."

"I can do that," Mish said.

"Good. Best to stay the night. Plenty room right here– 'less they'll miss you at Fortune House?"

Mish shook her head. "Fortune says Dorin's Luck broke, and I can't pay dues."

Einar sighed.

"Right, then. You're here 'til we get Dorin on her feet. You'll be expected to work as you're needed, and we'll feed you and keep you safe."

Mish bowed.

Einar nodded toward the hallway. "There's a fresher down the hall. Clothes in the closet by the door. Get cleaned up. The kitchen'll send the meal down soon."

Another bow and Mish was gone. Einar turned his head and considered Aazali.

"Healer Grasy told me your intentions, Healer. You'll've seen things've changed since you were last with us."

"Yes," Aazali said, and swallowed. "My intention remains fixed, as the heart of the bakery remains."

Einar nodded.

"You'll need to talk with the section heads."

"Section heads?" Healer Grasy murmured, and Einar gave her a brief grin.

"You're thinking that her ladyship doesn't know about the section heads?"

"My impression is that her ladyship considers herself the first and only authority."

Einar's grin grew wider.

"She'll learn," he said, as a clatter came in the hallway.

"That'll be supper," Einar said, coming out of his chair. "Come meet Kaz Dee."

* * *

Aazali had spoken to the section heads, one of them a boy no older than she was, with the glow of . . . *some*thing about him. Not a

Healer, of that she was certain, nor yet a Luck. Possibly he bore a new gift. Gifts evolved, after all. Even the gift of a particular Healer might change, over time.

Well, that was a mystery for later. For now, it seemed that the section heads were inclined to allow her and Elder Grasy to establish themselves at the bakery under the guidance of the medic. This arrangement would be reviewed, after a time. To Aazali, it seemed equitable, and much like Serana and Don Eyr would have put into place.

Aazali had settled herself at last into the room she had been given in the infirmary, after she had bidden sweet dreams to Elder Grasy and Medic Einar. She had looked in at Mish, finding the girl curled into a nest of blankets, sound asleep, the kitten under her chin.

It had been a full day, and Aazali was asleep bare moments after lying down in her own bed.

She woke abruptly some time later with the conviction that she was needed. She rose, slipped on the clothes she had left lying on the end of her bed, and left her room.

* * *

Beyavi voz'Laathi woke all at once in the crowded room between floors. Someone was moving in her house.

She lay still a moment, considering that certainty. She had been closely aligned with her previous base—so closely that she could without question know when someone was moving who should, perhaps be abed.

It seemed unlikely that she would be thus aligned with *this* house—and certainly not so soon.

And, yet – there! Again! Someone *else* was moving.

She swung her legs out of the bed, finding her boots and shoving into them. Rising, she– *reached* for the house, gaining the impression that the back door had opened–and closed.

Gly Sin, the house whispered, and there was sense to that, after all. Gly Sin was First Gun; doubtless he was doing a perimeter check.

Another door opened, and that was the little Healer.

Lady voz'Laathi took a deep breath, suddenly seeing it–the back-up plan in the hands of her enemy, herself separated from her Guns and her oathsworn for days–the means, but not yet the motive.

Lady voz'Laathi made certain of the weapon on her belt, and left the cluttered chamber, moving with quick silence down the stairs, to the hall, and the door at the end of it.

* * *

The halls were quiet, lit by night dims. No one roused as Aazali opened the door, and slipped out into the back garden.

The pole lamp outside the fence threw more shadows than light into the enclosed space, yet she did not have to strain her eyes to see the dark figure standing by the gate, as if debating the wisdom of going through.

Aazali paused in the shadow by the infirmary door, opening herself, allowing her gift to sample such things as were available to her.

Grief slapped her in the face; regret sanded her throat. Her instinct was to shield herself; instead, she stood, quietly accepting what came to her.

Across the yard, the door to the main house opened, throwing down a bright pathway. Lady voz'Laathi walked to the end of it. She sighed; Aazali felt her sorrow and the weight of the gun at her waist.

"Gly Sin," she said, her voice soft with power.

"My lady," said the man at the gate. "I am leaving your service."

"Ah," she said, and sighed again. "But you did that some time back, did you not? When you sold the Butcher the back-up plan? I've wondered what it cost him."

The man by the gate turned, raised his hands and let them fall.

"Your ladyship will recall my sister."

"I do—one of Elberra's seconds. Dead in the skyfall, you told me."

"Yes, my lady, but not before I had paid the Butcher her life-price."

"I see. And where do you go, now, I wonder? The Butcher is dead. Do you mean to offer your service to Nor Ish the Wolf?"

"Not my—service, no," Gly Sin's pattern was bleak; his tears sprang to Aazali's eyes. "This place—I thought the tales were only that, but I see now that it was true. I would lay my last service at its feet, my lady, and destroy the Wolf before he comes here."

"The Wolf goes down, and another rises in his place," Lady voz'Laathi said. "We have seen it many times. And you would leave me less an experienced Gun, when the next one comes against us."

Silence.

The lady's sorrow lightened somewhat; she took her attention from the weapon on her belt, and went one more step forward, standing between the shadow and the light.

"Why not remain?" she asked, against the continuing silence, and again— "Why *not* remain?"

"You cannot trust me," Gly Sin said, though Aazali felt the rising of his hope.

"Can I not? The Butcher is dead, your sister likewise. I am determined to hold this place, these streets. We will go forward, Gly Sin." She paused, and her next words were nearly a whisper. "Will you sell these streets?"

"No!" the man said sharply. His sincerity made Aazali's head ring.

"It seems to me that there is nothing left to say, in that wise," said Lady voz'Laathi. "Come in, Gly Sin, and go to bed. We will speak again tomorrow."

The man hesitated, then turned his back on the gate and walked toward the light. When he reached it, he bowed.

"My lady," he said. "I offer you my gun."

"I accept it and you," she said formally, and stepped aside. "Go and rest yourself, Gly Sin."

"Yes." He passed on, down the rectangle of light and into the house.

Lady voz'Laathi raised her head somewhat, as if she were looking to the sky.

"Well, Healer, what say you? Is he my man?"

"Yes," Aazali said. "He is sincere."

"And I?" the lady said then. "How do you read me?"

"As a most determined protector," Aazali said, "who holds what is hers, who has the capacity to forgive, and to change."

The lady huffed a laugh.

"Change, is it? If you have your way, little Healer, you *will* change all Low Port. Is that how I am to understand you?"

Aazali pulled herself up in her shadow, chin high.

"Yes, my lady," she said, projecting truth and the sense of determination into the dark peace of Serana's garden.

"Good. We go forward together, Healer of my House. Give you good even."

"Give you good even, Lady Benevolence," Aazali answered, and watched her enter the bakery and close the door.

She waited another moment, breathing in the scent of the flowers, and examining the light in her heart.

"We go forward," she murmured, and bowed as one honoring the past, before she turned and walked into her future.

About the Authors

Co-authors Sharon Lee and Steve Miller have been working in the fertile fields of genre fiction for more than thirty years, pioneering today's sub-genre of science fiction romance–stories that contain all the action, adventure and sense of wonder of traditional space opera, with the addition of romantic relationships.

Over the course of their partnership, Lee and Miller have written thirty-three novels, twenty-four in their long-running, original space opera setting, the Liaden Universe®, where honor, wit, and true love are potent weapons against deceit and treachery.

There are more than 300,000 Liaden Universe® novels in print. Liaden titles regularly place in the top ten bestsellers in *Locus Magazine*, the trade paper of the speculative fiction genres. Twelve Lee and Miller titles have been national bestsellers.

Liaden Universe® novels have twice won the Prism Award for Best Futuristic Romance, reader and editor choice awards from *Romantic Times*, as well as the Hal Clement Award for Best YA Science Fiction Novel, proving the appeal of the series to a wide range of readers.

Lee and Miller's work in the field has not been limited to writing fiction.

Sharon Lee served three years as the first full-time executive director of the Science Fiction and Fantasy Writers of America, and went on to be elected vice-president, and president of that organization. She has been a Nebula Award jurist.

Steve Miller was the founding curator of the University of Maryland's Science Fiction Research Collection. He has been a jurist for the Philip K. Dick Award.

Lee and Miller have together appeared at science fiction conventions around the country, as writer guests of honor and principal speakers. They have been panelists, participated in writing workshops, and given talks on subjects as diverse as proper curating of a cat whisker collection, techniques for creating believable characters, and world-building alien societies.

In 2012, Lee and Miller were jointly awarded the E.E. "Doc" Smith Memorial Award for Imaginative Fiction (a.k.a. the "Skylark" Award), given annually by the New England Science Fiction Association to someone who has contributed significantly to science fiction, both through work in the field and by exemplifying the personal qualities which made the late "Doc" Smith well-loved by those who knew him. Previous recipients include George R.R. Martin, Anne McCaffrey, and Sir Terry Pratchett.

Sharon Lee and Steve Miller met in a college writing course in 1978; they married in 1980. In 1988, they moved from their native Maryland to Maine, where they may still be found, in a sun-filled house in a small Central Maine town. Their household currently includes three Maine coon cats.

Steve and Sharon maintain a web presence at korval.com

Novels by Sharon Lee & Steve Miller

The Liaden Universe®: *Agent of Change * Conflict of Honors * Carpe Diem * Plan B * Local Custom * Scout's Progress * I Dare * Balance of Trade * Crystal Soldier * Crystal Dragon * Fledgling * Saltation * Mouse and Dragon * Ghost Ship * Dragon Ship * Necessity's Child * Trade Secret * Dragon in Exile * Alliance of Equals * The Gathering Edge * Neogenesis * Accepting the Lance * Trader's Leap * Fair Trade*

Omnibus Editions: *The Dragon Variation * The Agent Gambit * Korval's Game * The Crystal Variation*

Story Collections: *A Liaden Universe Constellation: Volume 1 * A Liaden Universe Constellation: Volume 2 * A Liaden Universe Constellation: Volume 3 * A Liaden Universe Constellation: Volume 4 * A Liaden Universe Constellation: Volume 5*

The Fey Duology: *Duainfey * Longeye*

Gem ser'Edreth: *The Tomorrow Log*

257

Novels by Sharon Lee

The Carousel Trilogy: *Carousel Tides * Carousel Sun * Carousel Seas*
Jennifer Pierce Maine Mysteries: *Barnburner * Gunshy*

Pinbeam Books Publications

Sharon Lee and Steve Miller's indie publishing arm

Adventures in the Liaden Universe®: *Two Tales of Korval * Fellow Travelers * Duty Bound * Certain Symmetry * Trading in Futures * Changeling * Loose Cannon * Shadows and Shades * Quiet Knives * With Stars Underfoot * Necessary Evils * Allies * Dragon Tide * Eidolon * Misfits * Halfling Moon *Skyblaze * Courier Run * Legacy Systems * Moon's Honor * Technical Details * Sleeping with the Enemy * Change Management * Due Diligence * Cultivar * Heirs to Trouble * Degrees of Separation * Fortune's Favor * Shout of Honor * The Gate that Locks the Tree * Ambient Conditions * Change State * Bad Actors * Bread Alone *

    Splinter Universe Presents: *Splinter Universe Presents: Volume One * The Wrong Lance*

    By Sharon Lee: *Variations Three * Endeavors of Will * The Day they Brought the Bears to Belfast * Surfside * The Gift of Magic * Spell Bound *Writing Neep*

    By Steve Miller: *Chariot to the Stars * TimeRags II*

    By Sharon Lee and Steve Miller: *Calamity's Child * The Cat's Job * Master Walk * Quiet Magic * The Naming of Kinzel * Reflections on Tinsori Light*

THANK YOU

Thank you for your support of our work.
Sharon Lee and Steve Miller